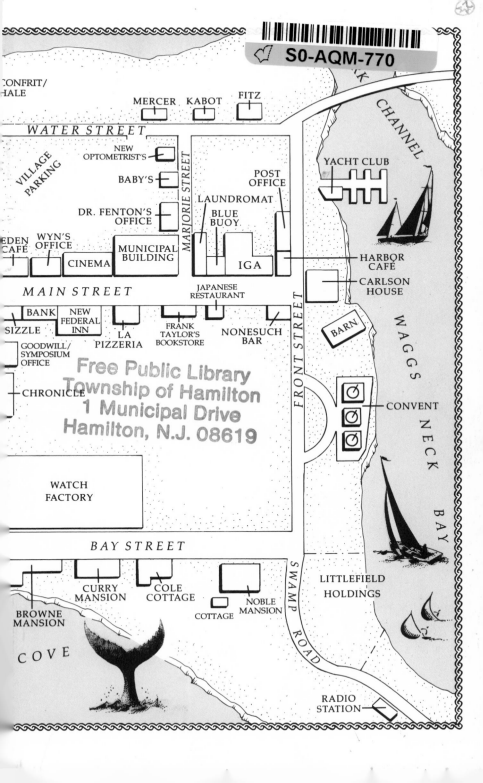

CONFRIT/
HALE

MERCER KABOT FITZ

WATER STREET

VILLAGE
PARKING

NEW
OPTOMETRIST'S

MARJORIE STREET

BABY'S

POST
OFFICE

YACHT CLUB

LAUNDROMAT

DR. FENTON'S
OFFICE

BLUE
BUOY

EDEN
CAFÉ

WYN'S
OFFICE

MUNICIPAL
BUILDING

CINEMA

IGA

HARBOR
CAFÉ

CARLSON
HOUSE

MAIN STREET

JAPANESE
RESTAURANT

FRONT STREET

WAGGS

BANK

NEW
FEDERAL
INN

LA
PIZZERIA

FRANK
TAYLOR'S
BOOKSTORE

NONESUCH
BAR

BARN

SIZZLE

GOODWILL/
SYMPOSIUM
OFFICE

CONVENT

CHRONICLE

NECK

BAY

WATCH
FACTORY

BAY STREET

CURRY
MANSION

COLE
COTTAGE

NOBLE
MANSION

LITTLEFIELD
HOLDINGS

BROWNE
MANSION

COTTAGE

SWAMP ROAD

COVE

RADIO
STATION

CHANNEL

The Winter Women Murders

Also by David A. Kaufelt

Six Months with an Older Woman
The Bradley Beach Rumba
Spare Parts
Jade (*under the name Lynn Devon*)
Late Bloomer
Midnight Movies
The Wine and the Music
Silver Rose
Souvenir
The Best Table (*under the name Richard Devon*)
American Tropic*
The Fat Boy Murders*

* Published by POCKET BOOKS

The Winter Women Murders

A Wyn Lewis Mystery

David A. Kaufelt

POCKET BOOKS

New York   London   Toronto   Sydney   Tokyo   Singapore

This book is a work of fiction. Names, characters, places, and incidents are products of the author's imagination or are used fictitiously. Any resemblance to actual events or locales or persons, living or dead, is entirely coincidental.

POCKET BOOKS, a division of Simon & Schuster Inc.
1230 Avenue of the Americas, New York, NY 10020

Copyright © 1994 by David Kaufelt

Kaufelt, David A.
    The winter women murders : a Wyn Lewis mystery / David A. Kaufelt.
        p.   cm.
    ISBN 0-671-76094-7
    1. Women real estate agents—New York (State)—Long Island—
Fiction. 2. Women detectives—New York (State)—Long Island—
Fiction. 3. Long Island (N.Y.)—Fiction.   I. Title.
PS3561.A79W55   1994
813'.54—dc20   93–47454
                                                       CIP

First Pocket Books hardcover printing July 1994

10 9 8 7 6 5 4 3 2 1

For Dick Briglia

Author's Note

After the publication of the first mystery in the Wyn Lewis series, *The Fat Boy Murders,* a number of knowing readers (especially those who didn't bother with the Author's Note) swore that the village known as Waggs Neck Harbor was, in reality, Sag Harbor, Long Island. They were perfectly right, with the proviso that all of the characters and events, as well as the establishments and much of the geography, were pure invention. Ditto for *The Winter Women Murders.*

I'd like to thank the redoubtable Joan Carlson, who continues to provide me with the tidbits of village gossip and fact that so inspire me; Molly Allen, an editor with a sure touch and a fine sense of madness; Diane Cleaver, that rarity, an editorially hip agent; Bill Grose, whose kindred spirit for lo these many years has provided inspiration and illumination; and the Mystery Writers of America and Sisters in Crime, two of the most supportive writers' organizations one could hope for.

D.A.K.
Key West, Florida

PART ONE

November
1992

Chapter

I

Sophie Comfort Noble, eighty-two and solely concerned with her own shrinking needs, was propped up by three oversized needlepoint pillows in the gigantic twig chaise longue that was beginning to feel like a cot in a prison ward. Or a crib in an Adirondack nursery. It was no secret that Sophie, once a big playful girl of a woman, was getting smaller each year, daily infusions of calcium notwithstanding. One of the unkinder local wits (Dickie ffrench) invariably referred to her as the Incredible Shrinking Woman. But Sophie was finally on the mend from a painful hip replacement and the doctor's prognosis was encouraging.

"I'm really beginning to feel myself again," she had admitted in a small burst of optimism to the nurse on the previous afternoon while that admirable woman was making her goodbyes. Hoping that the customary farewell present would be cash rather than scented soap, Nurse McBride departed with some speed when she realized she was going to receive neither. Sophie was, to put it charitably, a touch tight with the Noble fortune.

Her optimism having worn thin by this morning, Sophie was feeling isolated, bored, and sorry for herself. She was reminded of that old song about the lonely rich woman pining in her penthouse while the janitor's wife had a perfectly good love life. Not that Sophie wanted a love life; one husband and one lover had been sufficient, thank you very much. And not that she was in a penthouse in Manhattan, singing the blues. She was in the commodious second-floor sitting room in her Bay Street mansion in the eastern Long Island village of Waggs Neck Harbor, and all she desired, at the moment, was diversion. Cheating at solitaire had lost its charm.

Rhodesia, Sophie's daughter, wouldn't have been any help in the diversion department even if she had been in attendance, which she wasn't (though she certainly should have been). Rhodesia had been named for the country in which she had been conceived during Sophie's 1934 honeymoon with her now long-dead husband. Rhodie was, dollars to doughnuts, down at the Literary Symposium office, scheming with the executive director, Jane Littlefield. Rhodie had insisted upon hiring Jane despite the really fierce objections Sophie had made from her sickbed.

In the almost fifty years in which Sophie had been founder and chair of Waggs Neck Harbor's Annual Literary Arts Symposium (ALAS), there had never once been the need for paid help. Sophie had begun the Symposium as a distraction for the winter women of the day, and they had been damned glad to volunteer for even the most menial jobs.

The winter women, Sophie thought, had been very different then from now. In those days, in the beginning of the war, they had been young brides, escaping the uncertainties of the city, waiting out the war for their husbands in the quiet comfort of the village. Of course they had knitted and juggled their ration books and made silver foil balls and put in their time with the Red Cross ... but they had needed cultural enrichment as well. Sophie had provided it with the Literary Symposium, held on the first weekend of every February,

4

drawing on local writers, real and imagined, to discuss their art and craft.

After World War II, Waggs Neck developed a vague literary reputation (Sophie credited it to the Symposium) and genuine published writers began to move into the village. Some even took part in the Symposium. The new breed of winter women were thrilled, but then they had learned the hard way to be easily pleased.

Widows and divorcées and spinsters and discarded mothers of a certain age, they were women alone in the world, a bit soured on life, finally aware that whatever goals they had once aspired to were not to be. They were, by and large, discouraged and disappointed, but still they hoped to find comfort in the village of Waggs Neck Harbor, where, if they were careful, they just might make ends meet.

Sophie was always having the winter women to her house, especially during those harsh months when the Waggs Neck Harbor Cinema closed and they had nothing to do but freeze in their ill-heated cottages. The locals had families and church groups and bingo night and the Women of the Moose to keep them busy from November through April, when the summer people and the weekenders and life would return to Waggs Neck Harbor. The winter women had Sophie and the Symposium.

Now, Sophie reflected, there were more winter women than ever. A hundred or so out of the village population of twenty-five hundred and nearly all members in good standing of the Friends of the Annual Literary Arts Symposium (FALAS). Upper-middle-class, upper-middle-aged educated women making do, characterized by bitterness, light irony, and a mild sort of spunkiness. Escapees from retail and publishing and dubious public relations careers that hadn't panned out. Refugees from marriage, living in their former weekend houses. The younger ones, those with children—usually one frail and difficult teenager—were forced to take advantage of the Waggs Neck Harbor school system now that private education was out of the question.

5

More than one winter woman wondered what on earth she would do during the off-season without the teas and the ad hoc committee meetings and the fund-raising drinks parties arranged by and for the Friends of the Symposium.

But Rhodie, of all people, had threatened to freeze the winter women out of the Symposium. She had begun undermining "the Symposium bricks and mortar" when Sophie had fallen and her left hip had been painfully and not all that successfully replaced, some four months before.

Rhodie, knowing her duty, had taken what she hoped would be a brief sabbatical from her well-to-do single woman's socially responsible life in Manhattan. Having reluctantly asked for and received leave from her unpaid but rewarding position as the fiscal officer of a Lower East Side settlement house, she had resignedly closed the family's big Fifth Avenue apartment. She would be back, she said, in a few weeks.

When three weeks in Waggs Neck turned into six, Rhodie had become desperate for something, anything, to occupy herself. "I'm not the sort of female," she told her mother in a not subtle rebuke, "who can sit around and read mystery novels and worry about her nails." For want of a larger sphere, she had assumed her ailing mother's chairmanship of the Symposium.

It proved surprisingly gratifying. Rhodie had been agreeably astonished at how delicious the role of ultimate decision-maker could be. Her settlement house position had invariably involved a certain amount of wheedling and compromise with other volunteers and, worse, the professional social workers. Sitting at the head of the battered ALAS boardroom table in the shabby office atop the Goodwill Shop on Washington Street, lecturing the executive committee on how to run a successful program, Rhodesia was queen.

Ignoring her bedridden mother's protests, she had immediately announced plans to turn the Symposium into "a world-class" event. After a brief search for an executive director, Rhodie had engaged dotty Lucy Littlefield's niece and keeper—Jane Littlefield—despite Sophie's increasingly strident objections. Sophie had felt so helpless, kept instantly abreast of all developments by the loyal members of the Friends.

Sophie had watched (well, listened) as the two of them—Jane and Rhodie—with the tacit approval of the traitorous quislings on the executive committee, had gone about destroying the heart and soul of the Symposium to which Sophie had devoted a good deal of her last half century. Now, with the new hip finally "taking" and her general health improved, Sophie was ready to face them head-on.

The Symposium would stay true to its roots. It would remain small and pure and strictly a volunteer organization. Rhodie and Lucy Littlefield's niece would turn it into a "world-class" event over her dead body. Sophie was still officially chair and she now felt quite up to waging battle for the soul of the Symposium.

She was very, very careful. She was going to listen to the doctors and take her time recovering. She had already been downstairs once in the early morning, using the wide, ambassadorial front staircase her father hadn't let her use—except on special occasions—when she was a child.

The house had been built in the mid-nineteenth century by a whaling millionaire named LeBow and bought, soon after, by Sophie's grandmother Comfort. But such was the force of Sophie's personality, it had become known as the Noble mansion after Sophie had decided, as a war widow, to live in the house permanently.

She was reminiscing about the days when General Noble was alive as Annie Kitchen helped her down the marble steps, one baby step at a time. Annie had suggested the back stairs because they led to the kitchen but Sophie hadn't used the servants' staircase since she was a child playing hide-and-seek and she wasn't about to do so now. Nor was she about to take her breakfast in the kitchen.

She had it in the privacy of the library where the one telephone she permitted in the house was located. Feeling remarkably peppy, Sophie joyously engaged in a polite, bitter telephone exchange with Jane Littlefield while chomping on a heavily buttered English muffin and slurping oversweetened Sanka. Sophie was firm in the belief that basic manners didn't apply to the stratum of society in which she ranked herself.

She told Jane that her services were no longer needed, that the rightful chair was back in the saddle and she didn't give a tinker's damn who had hired her, she was firing her. Sophie hung up while Jane was in midsentence.

Licking her lips, sighing with exhaustion and pleasure, Sophie decided she'd had enough and instructed Annie Kitchen to help her walk—very, very carefully—back up the marble stairway to the bed in which she now disconsolately lay.

The morning's euphoria had passed with her long nap. She had awoken to an ineffably gray November Monday afternoon but she refused to give in to depression. That very grayness combined with Sophie's view of the bay waters—roiling and white-capped and relentless as misery—strengthened her resolve. She decided to make one more foray to the telephone with the help of Annie Kitchen. She had to alert her allies for the coming brouhaha.

Annie Kitchen, who resembled a middle-aged Orphan Annie, was downstairs in the big pantry, polishing silver, fixated on the soap opera being vividly and loudly broadcast over the color television console Annie had held out for before she had agreed to work for Sophie. Offsetting a deserved reputation for cantankerousness and an often convenient loss of hearing, Annie possessed the great virtue of an invaluable service person; she always turned up. In addition, Annie was a dedicated cleaner and not a bad cook along chicken sandwich, tomato soup lines. There had been a good deal of ill-natured vying for her services when her last employer died. Sophie—whose former housekeeper had decamped for a rich up-island orthopedic surgeon's family—had been forced to dangle the color TV and an exorbitant salary before she had taken the prize.

Not surprisingly, Annie did not hear the old-fashioned electric summons that rang weakly in the adjoining kitchen. The soap opera's tale of incestuous rape and priestly paternity was all-engrossing, especially with the volume set at fever pitch. Upstairs, Sophie, increasingly impatient, jabbed away with her arthritic index finger at the black button in the brass device next to the bed.

She thought she could probably get downstairs to her trusty rotary telephone in the library by herself but she wasn't taking any chances. Feeling renewed piss and vinegar flowing in her thin veins, Sophie was in a hurry to line up her ducks. It's been a long time coming, she said to herself, sliding one delicate, varicose-lined leg over the side of the bed, following it with the other. After all, she told herself, if it weren't for Sophie, there wouldn't be a Symposium.

The thought helped her stand up, despite shooting pains from the new hip. With some difficulty, she got into her tan cashmere robe and slipped on the black velvet slippers with the embroidered gold fox heads. En route, she glanced into the gilt-framed mirror that took up one wall of the oversized sitting room and wondered what the hell that forbidding old lady was doing in her house.

It was hard to believe it was herself. Sophie, who had once been quite nice-looking, stared at her image for a few moments, not liking what she saw: bifocals, dual and sometimes dueling hearing aids, a metal hip, and an expression that could curdle milk. Mrs. Frankenstein, she thought, making her way on steady feet out of her suite and into the large, wainscoted hallway.

Sophie paused at the head of the servants' stairs and listened for sounds of Annie Kitchen. All she could hear was the rumbling hysteria of the TV. Supporting herself on a thick, carved banister, she stood on the small, precious, tattered Gorovan and shouted at the top of her lungs for assistance. She thought she might as well wring whatever pleasure she could from Annie's inattention.

"And I'm still an invalid," she said aloud, getting into it. She was about to put everything she had into one more shout when the wispy white hairs on the back of her wrinkled neck stood up. Someone was standing behind her.

Pivoting with the new hip was a skill she hadn't as yet mastered. She managed to twist her neck to the far left and let out a small, stifled scream at what she saw. All that passionate hate. Then a pair of strong hands placed themselves squarely on her rounded, calcium-deficient back and pushed.

Sophie Comfort Noble got out a humiliating yelp as she careened down the steep servants' stairs like an out-of-control bowling ball, winding up in a heap of crushed bones in the drafty rear hallway that led to the kitchen.

Sophie's assailant quickly walked down the steps and realized that Sophie was still breathing. Taking Sophie's fragile head, the murderer struck it several times against the thick floor molding. There was a satisfactory cracking noise and Sophie stopped breathing.

A commercial selling a personal injury attorney's suspect skills had come on the TV so Annie decided she might as well see what all the racket was about. She emerged into the rear hall as her employer's assassin walked across the once-opulent and still impressive main foyer, leaving the house unobserved through the massive black tombstone-shaped double front doors.

Several people in her acquaintance thought it ironic that Sophie Comfort Noble had left this world via the servants' stairs she had so eschewed. But no one doubted that a slippery hall rug combined with overmedication and a new hip had caused Sophie's demise.

PART TWO

January–
February
1994

Chapter

2

WYN, PRETENDING SLEEP, INDULGED IN ONE OF HER FAVORITE SECRET PAS-times: watching Tommy Handwerk *potchke* (a Yiddish word inherited from her ex-husband, Nick Meyer, meaning to engage in idle and pointless housekeeping) around the bedroom.

Probity, Wyn's nearly white Labrador, followed Tommy as if she knew what he was about. Probity adored everyone indiscriminately but she had a grand, enduring passion for Tommy Handwerk, master carpenter by trade, that enabled her to sit at his feet for hours while he labored away at some intricate piece of woodwork.

A number of females—and one or two men—in the village shared Probity's ardor. Wyn allowed that she, too, had a grand passion for Tommy Handwerk, but she wondered how enduring it would prove to be. After all, she had had a grand passion for Nick and now the thought of him induced acute embarrassment.

She watched Tommy, graceful as Baryshnikov, pick up his red plaid boxer shorts with his toe and flip them into his

13

hands. (Wyn had bought the shorts at a down-island shopping mall she had been trying to sell for over a year now. She regretted taking the listing, down-island malls not exactly hot stuff in the current market.) Tommy sniffed the shorts cautiously and, dissatisfied, used them to perform a hoop shot into the wicker hamper.

Tommy, Wyn reflected, and not for the first time, was nothing like Nick. Nick had been a classic spoiled prince, allowing soiled clothes and marzipan cookie crumbs and primo marijuana ashes to fall where they might. Tommy bordered on the compulsively neat, even on Sunday morning, when Wyn believed sloppiness was mandatory.

Nor did Tommy resemble Nick physically. Nick was all blue-white skin, devil-black hair, and thick, sports-related muscle. Tommy was tall and broad-shouldered and yellow blond and Gary Cooper lean and he had a thin line of golden hair that began at his chest and moved south, pointing the way. Nick had looked like Satan incarnate and worked at it; Tommy was a made-in-U.S.A. angel, his heavily lashed American-flag-blue eyes habitually wide open in awe at the wonder of it all. Even, and maybe especially, when he made love to her.

Last night, one of their sacrosanct Saturday nights at home, he had kissed her from head to toe as if she were a giant lollipop. The memory of what Tommy called his "lick job" and the sight of the fading tan lines—his butt white and dimpled and irresistible—made Wyn, a dedicated nonsquirmer, wriggle under the quilt, alerting Tommy, who had been waiting for the moment, to the fact that she was awake.

He gently but firmly escorted Probity out into the large hall and, shutting the door on that disappointed but ever-hopeful animal, returned to join Wyn in bed. He lay on top of her and put his tongue in her mouth. He was the only man in the world, Wyn suspected, who could wake up after a night of beer, pizza, and heavy lovemaking and still possess the kind of sweet breath the mouthwash people were always promising and never delivering.

"Want to make love?" Wyn whispered, moving her body against his, feeling his hands reach behind and work their way down.

"What do you think?" he asked, demonstrating that he was more than ready and able. Tommy was endearingly proud of what he called, thanks to his mother, who once had been a school nurse, his private member. The first time Wyn had seen him unclothed, she had commented on its size and beauty. Tommy had turned bashful, saying formally, "Thank you, Wyn," which made her laugh.

She wasn't laughing now as Tommy, the object of his pride engaging her full attention, said, "I love you so much, Wyn."

Tommy continued his one-sided conversation after they had both reached a joyous climax, holding her tight with his muscled, tattooed (a snake) right arm, his left arm behind his angelic head. "I don't want to marry just to marry, Wyn. I want to have a kid with you. Can you imagine what kind of kid we'd have?"

"A Nazi genetic dream come true," Wyn said, turning to answer the bedside phone. She had said she didn't want to marry Tommy so often she believed it. However—tick-tock, tick-tock went the biological clock—she wasn't so certain about not having a child. "This may amaze you, Handwerk," Wyn said, picking up the receiver, "but you can have one without the other."

She talked briefly and hung up, Tommy idly wanting to know who the hell would call at nine A.M. on a Sunday morning.

"Our very own cultural czarina, Rhodesia Comfort Noble. I've been summoned for tomorrow morning in my Realtor capacity. Rhodie wants to talk real estate, my kind of language."

"You sure you don't want to talk marriage?"

"Absolutely."

"What about baby talk?"

"Ditto," Wyn said after a moment. Tommy, who was not

15

nearly as simple as he appeared, heard what he hoped was the opening note in a hesitation waltz.

"I'm going to have a baby with someone," he unwisely said, not as adept as Wyn at leaving well enough alone.

"Be mine guest," Wyn said, again using a phrase of her ex-husband's, a bad sign. She got out of bed, put on the old T-shirt dress she sometimes slept in, and allowed Probity back into the room.

"What do you want to do today?" Tommy asked, conciliatory, reaching for her long, soft hand with his wide, calloused one, looking up at her with those patriotic eyes.

"A long bike ride, coffee with your mother—and let's hope she made her cookies . . ."

". . . you know she did . . ."

". . . Chinese takeout and an old movie, preferably starring Katharine Hepburn." She kissed his bow lips, refusing to think about marriage and/or babies, wondering what Rhodesia Noble had in mind.

Chapter

3

Wyn's question was answered early the following morning, a gloomy Monday. "I want to view half a dozen or so modest village properties in the adorable, restorable cottage line, suitable for Symposium offices."

As she said this, Rhodesia Comfort Noble's exophthalmic Bette Davis eyes—newly contact-lensed—were staring out through the French doors at the mean January day. The turquoise eyeballs were startling enough but what was most incredible to Wyn was that Rhodie appeared if not actually happy, at least somewhat content.

The drawl was also disconcerting. Rhodie had always drawled in an off-putting, upper-crust Anglo, way. But the old drawl had been as dry as dust and now it was as dry as gin. On the whole, Wyn decided, an improvement.

"It has to be commodious enough to provide living space for the Symposium executive director."

One of Wynsome Lewis's great assets in real estate negotiations was that she could appear simultaneously poker- and sweet-faced, despite grave misgivings. She used this facility now. Her friend, the ALAS executive director, Jane Littlefield, lived nicely with her wacky aunt Lucy in the old Littlefield house and didn't need new quarters. Wyn said as much.

Rhodie, back in village residence after a year's absence following her mother's death, had lost no time in reestablishing herself as the chair of the Symposium. Once Jane Littlefield's staunchest champion—she had hired Jane against her mother's wishes—Rhodie had returned from California with not only a new persona, but new sympathies.

Jane, she said, was a capable administrator but Jane did not understand the finer points of the Symposium's literary mandate, and it was time to go the extra step with a new director who did. What's more, Jane had made a major blunder in choosing a feminist theme—New Directions in Women's Literature—for the upcoming Symposium.

"I am not against the women's movement per se and I don't suppose, Wynsome, you are either. After all, we both were victims of predatory males, we shed them early, and have learned to live autonomous lives. You're an attorney and a Realtor and I'm, for my sins, a rich woman with a cultural mission. What we don't do is run amok bragging about how sexually liberated we are. I find it especially distasteful that a sensationalist like Keny Blue has been invited to speak. If the Symposium weren't only three weeks away, I'd ask the executive committee to scrap the program and start anew."

Though Wyn had been warned—the village hot line was taut with talk of the transformation—this new Rhodie was a revelation. She was brisk and determined and wearing a pink-beige silk dress that certainly hadn't been purchased in Waggs Neck Harbor. The last time Wyn had seen Rhodie, she had been wrapped in a ton of brown wool overcoat and self-pity, heading for the airport in East Hampton en route to California. She had seemed as brisk as a water-deprived goldfish.

Her mother's death was the popular cause of Rhodie's much discussed breakdown. Turning her back on her mother (and Waggs Neck) for most of her adult life, Rhodie had reluctantly returned nearly eighteen months ago to nurse Sophie through what had been billed as a brief convalescence from a hip replacement.

But there were complications, the convalescence lengthened from a few weeks to a few months, and instead of being a comfort, Rhodie had become what Sophie called her nemesis. She took over Sophie's Symposium in a bloodless coup d'état, making it plain, especially to Sophie, that the senior Noble was hors de combat forever.

But when Sophie died, Rhodie freaked. From guilt, pure and simple, the village armchair psychoanalysts opined. She had treated her mother—the Sophie apologists declared—abominably, casting her aside like an overly used foundation garment.

John Fenton, the village doctor, thought Rhodie was suffering from old-fashioned grief. He had prescribed Prozac and change. Rhodie embraced both, dumbfounding the village several times over, never more than when she returned after that year's absence accompanied by her ex- (and long dead) husband's extremely presentable—or extremely déclassé, depending upon your point of view—nephew with the, well, *odd* name: Peter Robalinski.

Wyn, facing this new, improved Rhodie, wondered what changes she herself might experience when her own not especially beloved mother died and then put that thought away, too complicated to contemplate.

"When may I look at property?" Rhodie lit a mentholated cigarette without a do-you-mind. "The Symposium's executive committee is going to have to approve the acquisition, even though I'm donating it. I looked it up in the charter and there it is, so we're all going to have to trudge around together. What is today? Monday? How's Wednesday morning? Ten A.M. I'll have the committee meet here and you can lead the caravan. No need to knock yourself out, Wynsome. I don't want to be shown every unsalable dilapidation in the village."

Wyn did not appreciate Rhodie's madam-to-servant tone. Deciding, however, that it would be unprofessional, not to mention counterproductive, to tell Rhodie to go fuck herself, she said Wednesday would be fine. She asked a few questions about locale, condition, and price, and when the newly installed high-tech telephone chimed and took up Rhodie's attention, Wyn indicated she would make her own way out.

As she was exiting the old library, which had once been a model of tattered clutter and was now a minimalist showplace, Rhodie's California nephew was entering. Wyn greeted him without enthusiasm, agreeing with Ruth Cole (the village opinion maker) that he looked like all icing, no cake.

"You didn't bring your Jag," he said, ready for conversation.

There didn't seem to be any witty answer to this so Wyn, who didn't like the look she was getting from Rhodie, still engaged in telephone conversation at her snazzy new desk, agreed.

"Whenever I see you in that Jag," he told her, "I go all gooey inside."

This Wyn could understand. Her car was a ravishing vintage convertible and often, when she drove it, she got all gooey inside, too. The lively green Miata Rhodie had given Peter paled in comparison.

"You going to let me drive it someday?" He made the mistake of making this sound like a sexual proposition.

Wyn said it was a possibility and moved on. The people she allowed to drive her car made up a small, extremely exclusive club and she didn't think Peter Robalinski was going to be able to join it.

Wyn found herself thinking about the California nephew as she crossed Bay Street and walked down Washington, passing the *Chronicle* and the Symposium/Goodwill offices, housed in narrow early nineteenth-century wood-frame buildings that had escaped the great fire of 1892. She was making her way toward a windswept Main Street and the coffee shop masquerading as a restaurant, named the Eden in honor of the loquacious, neon-pink-hair-roller-addicted woman who owned it.

It was well known that Sophie had sympathetic cousins in

California and that she often resorted to their sequestered San Marino estate when a soothing atmosphere was required. Rhodie had followed suit when her mother had died. What had come as a surprise to the village chroniclers was this California nephew.

In a short time he had cut a swath among the largely man-less Friends of the Annual Literary Arts Symposium. Peter Robalinksi had unruly chocolate-brown hair, a football-player torso, and a sensuous lower lip often displayed to its best advantage in what many members of FALAS considered "a smile to die for." A chipped front tooth, reportedly suffered in his teen years during a lacrosse match, came as a pleasant surprise, a naughty but welcome imperfection.

It was only when one got close that the laugh lines around his greedy puppy-dog eyes gave away the fact that he was on the other side of forty.

He subscribed to the left-out-on-the-terrace-to-weather tweed jacket, unbuttoned button-down shirt, tasseled-loafer style of casual dressing. He usually looked, Wyn thought, as if he had recently graduated from the University of Ralph Lauren. That he was a Californian, born and bred, was beyond doubt: his mellow voice held not a trace of regional accent, his skin was eternally tan with only a hint of orange (Wyn suspected sunless tanning cream), and he was relentlessly good-humored.

Like many men who spent most of their time among women, he had a charming boy's need for universal approval. Why does this guy give me the creeps? Wyn asked herself as she negotiated Main Street. She knew the answer, of course. She found him sexy and didn't like the fact that she did. He reminded her of a California-ized version of her ex-husband. She guessed that he reserved his real passion for cars.

"He's the kind of soft-living lifelong charmer who leaves destruction in his wake," Wyn maintained to Jane Littlefield, who had been waiting for her in the Eden's powder blue Naugahyde-upholstered back booth.

"Please," Jane had said, giving her closed-mouth smile,

21

pushing her oversized pink-tinted glasses up on her long, thin Yankee nose. " 'Destruction in his wake' indeed."

Despite the fact that Peter Robalinski was usurping her job, one that admirably suited bookish, straight-arrow Jane, Wyn had the feeling that Jane was one of Peter Robalinski's admirers. This was confirmed by her next statement.

"He has beautiful hands," Jane said, examining her own unadorned fingers, which seemed less bony than usual. In fact, Jane's entire being seemed less bony than usual. "Strong, yet sensitive hands."

Uh-oh, Wyn thought to herself. In her experience, women who gushed about a man's hands were, for better or worse, in them.

Jane was seeing a lot of Peter, Wyn thought. Perhaps in the literal senses to judge from the unnatural pink blush that was now suffusing Jane's usually parchment-pale cheeks. Rhodie had Peter spending his days at the current Washington Street Symposium office, apprenticed to Jane, learning, as she put it, "the Symposium tricks." It suddenly seemed likely that Peter was teaching the heretofore virginal Jane a trick or two himself.

Wyn had missed the previous afternoon's ALAS executive committee meeting due to a house closing that had threatened to fall apart over a one-inch property line discrepancy. Neither the buyers nor the sellers wanted to solve the problem until late in the day, when they finally realized the truth of Wyn Lewis's statement that if the deal fell through, no one would get what they wanted. The buyers graciously decided that one inch wasn't a problem and the sellers decided, what the hell, to throw in the pool table and the vintage jukebox.

It was at the end of that missed meeting that Rhodie had dropped her bombshell: Peter was going to take over as executive director immediately after the detested feminist Symposium.

When Dolly Carlson had the temerity to ask what Peter's credentials were, Rhodie answered that he had taught literature at a well-known college in the San Fernando Valley. "And if that's not sufficient, Dolly, you might take into consideration that I pay the executive director's salary. That should do it, don't you think?"

Dolly and any other potential doubters had been put in their place, for the moment, but an acidic strain of resentment wasn't to be denied. In Dolly Carlson's scenario, Rhodie intended to freeze out all FALAS volunteers, and then Dolly asked, as if she cared, what were the winter women to do from October through February?

Wyn, dunking a doughnut in a cup of chemical-based hot chocolate, asked Jane if she weren't just a wee bit pissed.

"At what?" Jane asked.

"At Rhodie for hiring you in the first place, disappearing, giving you carte blanche for fifteen months, and now reappearing and firing you on insubstantial, nepotistic grounds." Wyn, furious at what she perceived as great injustice, dunked her doughnut vehemently.

Jane, who believed dunking doughnuts was down there in the social canon with picking greens from one's teeth with one's fingernail, looked away and then permitted herself a small satisfied smile. "It's nice of you to be concerned, Wyn, but I honestly believe it's all going to work out to everyone's satisfaction."

"Even Rhodesia's?"

"Well, maybe not Rhodesia's."

"Are you sleeping with Peter Robalinski?"

"To be strictly accurate, Wyn, we don't 'sleep' together." Jane said this in her sere fashion, looking, for the moment, nearly attractive in a Barbara Pym-ish way. She *was* putting on some poundage. Not that Pym heroines could ever be thought to be anything but slender. And then Wyn looked away, staring at Selma Eden's curler-bedizened head without seeing it, saying no to herself in horror.

"She could make it in Hollywood." Peter Robalinski was referring to Wyn as he lounged in the new sculpted red leather Italian chair (twenty-eight hundred dollars through your decorator) facing Rhodie's new green-marble-topped desk (a Tommy Handwerk confection) in Sophie's former study. The room had been extensively redone since Rhodie had inherited the house.

Dickie ffrench, the token male Symposium executive committee member and a sometime interior designer, had been engaged prior to Rhodie's return by telephone to "bring the old girl into the twentieth century, room by hideous room." Peter, who usually didn't pay much attention to decor, thought that Dickie, now marbleizing his way through the "public rooms," was doing a super job.

"I doubt Wynsome Lewis could 'make it' in Hollywood, as you so nicely put it, Peter," Rhodie said, finding herself especially irritated this morning by his penchant for proposing alternative lives for people he barely knew. "I don't believe the motion picture people are any longer interested in women with Prince Valiant–cut nearly white-blond hair and butter-wouldn't-melt expressions. Not that all that innocence should fool you. She is as tough, smart, and savvy as any New York attorney, and when she's talking, it pays to listen. Luckily, she has inherited her father's looks and her mother's self-containment."

Peter said that if Wynsome Lewis couldn't make it in Hollywood, her car sure could.

"You *are* obsessed."

"Married?" Peter went on, finding a certain satisfaction in baiting Rhodie.

"She was married straight out of university—Brown, I believe—to a parvenu attorney who summarily shed her after a couple of years to marry his boss's daughter."

Rhodie, never loath to participate in the village's principal preoccupation (i.e., idle gossip), went on to fill Peter in on Wyn's background. Her divorce had been, it was rumored, devastating but one wouldn't know it from Wyn, who had wisely used her settlement to put herself through law school. When she graduated, she returned to the village to reestablish her late father's realty office and to practice real estate law.

At the same time Wyn's mother, the irreproachable Linda Lewis, Waggs Neck's dread former high school principal, had wrangled herself a position with City College in Manhattan. It had all been serendipitous, Linda swapping the not very distinguished Waggs Neck family house on Madison for Wyn's not very luxurious Manhattan co-op on West 73rd.

Wyn, Rhodie went on, had been quite successful. She had arrived just at the time when the old families were cashing in, selling their gingerbreaded workers' cottages to weekenders from Manhattan for what to them were enormous amounts of money. They in turn had bought into the radar-range-equipped town-house developments springing up in the sparse pine woods on the western edge of the village. And they trusted Wyn. She was homegrown and she was Hap Lewis's girl.

"Boyfriend?" Peter wanted to know.

"Tommy Handwerk, the gifted carpenter responsible for my new desk. Dickie ffrench has convinced Tommy to call himself a cabinetmaker, an odious pretension, typical of Dickie. Just before I went to California, Tommy left his mother's house and moved in with Wyn. Very egalitarian, our Wynsome. She's thirty-six years old . . ."

". . . doesn't look it . . ."

". . . and that charming, innocent visage masks a razor-sharp mind and a tongue to match, which she nearly always manages to have under control. She helps maintain a home for unwed teenage mothers over in West Sea, keeps a Lab in her garden (weather permitting) and Tommy Handwerk in her bedroom. Are you compiling a dossier, Peter?"

Part of Peter's enduring charm depended upon his knowing when to stop and he did so now, switching the subject to one Rhodie was interested in—the new home for the Symposium offices.

For a number of private reasons, he was amused at how determined she was to get hold of the old cottage next door. He knew she didn't have a prayer but he had a keen sense of self-preservation and wasn't telling her that.

He gave her his chipped-tooth smile, appearing to be hanging on her every word. He wasn't. He was thinking of an article he had read in the *Los Angeles Times* about a scientist who believed he had identified an accident-prone gene, passed on from mother to daughter. Reaching across the desk, lighting Rhodie's third cigarette in a half hour for her, he wondered how long a woman like Rhodie—neurotic, a chain smoker, accident-prone like her ma—might be expected to live.

Chapter
4

"THAT PARTICULAR SHADE OF BROOKE ASTOR CHAMPAGNE RED DOESN'T come free," Lettitia Browne was saying, referring to Rhodie's new hair color.

The oft-retired Broadway star and village hotel owner was taking Wednesday lunch with her fellow FALAS executive committee members at the tearoom known as Baby's. They were cranky and tired, having spent the morning following Rhodie and Wyn up and down and through half a dozen shabby and mildewed potential new Symposium headquarters.

The weather had started out mild but had taken a sudden dip. Only Rhodie had been prepared for the cold, wearing her mother's old sable coat with its huge shawl collar and commodious pockets in which Sophie, and now Rhodie, kept all manners of odds and ends. The pockets allowed both women to dispense with handbags and lent them an undeserved insouciance.

Ruth Cole, who would have done without her eyeteeth rather than her green clutch purse, had taken advantage of seniority and bulk and chosen the best seat, her back to the wainscot wall, her Eleanor Roosevelt-ish face directed toward the main dining room. Fanning around her, clockwise, were: her younger sister, Camellia, billed as "the pretty one" for well over half a century; Dolly Carlson, owner-manager of the recently launched Carlson House B&B and the major survivor of the illustrious Carlson clan; Lettitia Browne; Dickie ffrench, "editorial consultant and decorative adviser to the stars"; and next to him, and to Ruth's immediate right, Wyn Lewis.

Wyn was a great favorite of Ruth's and vice versa. Ruth had viewed Wyn's father, Hapworth Lewis, as a model of village integrity. Wyn had Hap's same ingenuous expression and sea-foam-colored eyes; and though she was eons more sophisticated than her father, Ruth believed, Wyn had inherited his singular honesty. The two women, a number of decades apart, quietly admired one another's undemonstrative, controlled way of being and had grown closer since the village had experienced a series of devastating murders two years before. "She's sensible, responsible, and above all, trustworthy," Ruth would say about Wyn when her detractors started in. "Her sexual life is none of your beeswax." Wyn said the same about Ruth.

Each member of the executive committee shared a long village heritage, but only Dickie and Dolly, both in their forties and not about to admit it, had actually grown up with the person Camellia Cole insisted on referring to as "the bone of contention" . . . Ms. Keny Blue. Dickie and Keny had been, for reasons having to do with their own eccentricities, unpopular freshmen at Waggs Neck High. Dolly, then a senior, had sat at the still—even in the late sixties—poodle-skirted social center of the school.

"She's dropped at least thirty pounds." Lettie was going on about Rhodie. "And for once her clothes don't look as if they came from the Deceased Old Ladies' Room at Goodwill. She's had a lift. And I bet a tummy tuck while she was at it. Whoever did it knew what he was about and must have charged accordingly. Imagine Rhodesia Comfort Noble spending money like the proverbial drunken sailor and turning glamorous, in the bargain, at sixty. Sophie must be whirling like a dervish in the family mausoleum."

It had begun to rain and the chill of mid-January was in the air, as was the stench of the proprietors' wet dog, an elderly, distressed spaniel called Baby, for whom the tearoom was named.

They were sitting in the rear room, which had been a kitchen when Baby's was a modest Johns Manville-sided village home. It still possessed signs of old-time domesticity: yellow-painted wooden kitchen chairs; a blue-and-white decal frieze running around the ceiling featuring heavily bonneted Dutch girls carrying milk to and from some mythic dairy. A dulled and patchy Oriental linoleum covered the floor.

In the front room—the former living room, now Baby's principal dining area—the rickety gateleg table with the view of the back side of Main Street shops was occupied by one of Waggs Neck's most discussed couples: Sondra Mercy Confrit and her husband, the serious novelist, Rupert (a.k.a. Ginger) Hale. They both looked especially debauched, not to mention disenchanted—with the village, one another, life.

"Who would you rather have sex with," Dickie ffrench whispered to Wyn while the others were trying to decide whether to go for it and have lunch or try to get by with a lower-calorie and lower-priced pick-me-up. "Sondra or Ginger?"

"Dickie . . ." Wyn began, laying aside the menu that she had long ago memorized, "I don't . . ."

"You have to answer."

"Dickie . . ."

"Dear God, Wyn, it's only a game. Loosen up. Now come on: Sondra? Or Ginger?"

Wyn knew Dickie wouldn't stop until she answered so she said, "All right. Sondra."

Dickie smiled. "I always knew you had a thing for Sondra."

"It's only that she prefers masculine lovers," Lettie ob-

David A. Kaufelt

served pointedly as Wyn decided on the trusty tuna–tomato surprise.

Sondra Confrit's canary yellow mane seemed especially frazzled. "Like a zillion escaped lunatic nerve endings, reaching for the light," Lettie observed. Tall and thin to the point of emaciation, it was said that Sondra had lived for years on cocktail party tidbits. Discounting everyone who hadn't jumped on her sexual liberation bandwagon in the late 1960s, she had antagonized a number of village denizens with her deliberate meanness. Several of her less than enthusiastic acquaintances were sitting at Baby's other occupied table.

Sondra ignored them and was, as usual, talking at her husband.

She had wed Rupert four years before, despite her well-established opposition to the institution of marriage. Her enemies, in letters to various newspapers and magazines, had a good time with this late-life union, accusing Sondra of betrayal and opportunism, questioning her very commitment to the Feminist Free Sex Movement.

But Sondra was then experiencing a *crise,* feeling—with justification—that she had been left in the dust by newer and more vibrant voices; that marriage would be an important statement illustrating just how *genuinely* liberal she had become; that the tides of free sex were turning to include old mores. What was left unsaid by Sondra—but no one else—was her hope that having an "important" writer as a spouse might help get her back in the swim.

Rupert Hale, known for dense, literary novels and for being wrong about almost every step he had taken in his private life, had married for peace and comfort. He was possessed of a thin fringe of fading reddish hair, which gave him his enduring nickname. That Ginger Hale sounded like a popular soft drink had tickled the fancies of a number of people over the years.

Rupert ignored Wyn's table, too, just as he managed to ignore his wife while she jabbered on about real and imagined insults. His melancholy Hibernian eyes gazed absently

30

through the yellowing lacelike curtains at the abandoned supermarket carts in the puddle-filled village parking lot.

Sondra, long a weekend and summer village resident, had only that year retired full-time to Waggs Neck Harbor to devote herself to writing and to being as rude to as many people as she could. Though the hot young bloods in the feminist sexual freedom camp thought of her as a back number, Sondra still had her devotees. They considered her the "midwife of the new sexuality." Sondra took this historic role seriously. Scheduled to be one of the three principal speakers at the upcoming Symposium, Sondra had noisily retired when she learned Keny Blue was the star turn.

She had "knocked their socks off" at the most recent Friends of the Annual Literary Arts Symposium meeting after Jane Littlefield had read Keny Blue's acceptance fax. "You can take your stupid, sexist Symposium and shove it up your collective flabby asshole," she had said as she stomped out in her Adidas cross trainers. "Include me out."

Keny Blue, who portrayed herself as the Charlotte Brontë of the Feminist Free Sex Movement (more Barbara Cartwright, some critics opined), had once, long ago, badly bested Sondra on a national morning television program. Sondra Confrit liked to say that she sometimes forgave but never forgot. In the end, after her FALAS loyalists begged and pleaded and otherwise demeaned themselves, Sondra deigned to speak at the Symposium, if only to refute Keny Blue and "her pornographic interpretation of the sexual revolution in those unreadable, trashy novels her ghostwriter—*a man!*—churns out."

"Sondra looks like a sour pickle left too long in the brine," Lettie was saying, sotto voce, as she polished off a slice of heavily buttered French bread. "The woman has chronic diarrhea of the mouth. Ginger will never finish his magnum opus with her going on at him night and day. Not that that would be such a tragedy. If one person at this table can admit to reading past page six in a Ginger Hale novel, I'll give them a nice fat apple."

"Too generous, Lettie," Dickie ffrench said, yawning wide,

revealing small, artfully capped teeth and healthy pink tonsils.

"Didn't Rhodie look splendid?" Camellia Cole asked no one in particular, sipping at her hot chocolate dreamily, aboard her own train of thought, as was so often the case.

Lettie and Dolly, usually not mutually sympathetic, shared a look of tired understanding. Camellia was about to launch into one of her time-warp reminiscences and they had learned the hard way (e.g., Camellia's big eyes filling up and running over with heart-shaped tears) that it was easier to let her toot along for a while than attempt to derail her.

"I remember when she and Sophie came to live at the Noble mansion after Sophie's husband went to war," Camellia was going on, true to her fashion, while the others—who had heard these stories before—pursued their own thoughts.

The Cole sisters still lived in the large four-story turn-of-the-century cedar-shingled "cottage" on Bay Street in which they had been born, not far from the Noble mansion. Ruth had, early on, given up any hope of romance. Teaching math at the no longer existent Mary Immaculate Star of the Sea Academy had satisfied her intellectual needs, but her emotions, always tightly packaged, had few outlets. Her stargazing hobby, born of sleepless nights, had remained one of the great village secrets for five decades: from her aerie on the attic floor of the Coles' cottage, Ruth's high-power telescope— inherited from her father—was often focused on more down-to-earth sights than the stars. She was a woman who enjoyed having her worst suspicions confirmed; there was nothing like the goings-on in the parking lots and lanes of Waggs Neck Harbor to afford this particular delight.

Camellia, conversely, lived in a daydream world filled with "nice" people, run by a benevolent god who greatly resembled her deceased father. She had still been in her hopeful, girlish twenties when Sophie and Rhodesia moved into the Noble mansion on a year-round basis in 1942. Camellia had attempted to draw out the eight-year-old Rhodie but the child hadn't trusted Camellia's jollity. Rather, she had preferred the more serious Ruth, who only paid attention to her when she asked for it. Which wasn't often.

On one or two occasions, however, she had confided in the older Cole sister that she couldn't wait for the war to end, her father to come home, and the family's return to Manhattan. She adored her father and thought her mother fatuous. She hated Waggs Neck Harbor and kept as aloof as she could, refusing to acknowledge other children. She was, she said, offhandedly using an adult expression, "marking time until my father comes home."

Her mother, on the other hand, had plunged into village cultural life, such as it was, pulling together string quartets and starting the Symposium. Sophie was having the time of her life playing Lady Bountiful to the war brides and the families of the men at war and most especially to the winter women who had just then begun moving into Waggs Neck Harbor.

The winter women were Sophie's natural constituency and knew it. She invited them to tea and Sunday dinner and Thursday evening poetry readings. And they came, even to the musicales. After all, winter in Waggs Neck wasn't exactly a never-ending swirl of glamour and Sophie was generous. Camellia supposed she liked the blatant flattery and the dependency: the winter women a flock of blind, orphaned lambs, Sophie their shepherdess.

Rhodie, who liked no one—save her father and possibly Ruth—especially disliked the winter women. Camellia guessed she had been jealous of the attention her mother paid them.

Nearly a decade later, long after her father had been killed in the war and Sophie had moved permanently to the village, an eighteen-year-old Rhodie had returned from boarding school for an uncharacteristic Christmas visit. Sophie had used her presence as an excuse for a dinner party, inviting the most favored of the winter women and some of the more presentable locals in an attempt to involve them in the politics of her cultural pursuits. (She was just then hard at work persuading the shortsighted mayor—a bricklayer by trade—to proclaim an annual Village Cultural Arts Week.) Rhodie had been placed between Camellia and Ruth at dinner; not unexpectedly all three found conversation uphill work.

It wasn't until after dessert—baked Alaska and utterly delicious—that Camellia wondered aloud if the girl might not be ill. Rhodie's complexion was linen white and there were unattractive beads of sweat lodged in the unfortunate fringe of mouse-colored hair hiding her forehead. Rhodie glanced at her mother, laughing with one of the more sycophantic of her followers, and then pushed herself away from the table.

"I'm not ill," Rhodesia had told Ruth rather than Camellia. "I'm frightened. Frightened that I'm going to turn into one of those," she said, looking with terrible disdain at the women who made up her mother's court. She left the beautifully set table—Camellia remembered acres of Waterford—and the overheated room as if she were escaping from Alcatraz.

Not long after, Rhodie had her mandatory coming-out in Manhattan—not brilliant, it was said—and soon married one of the unknown young men who somehow managed to be present at those late postwar debutante balls. He was said to be a Middle European war hero with, almost certainly, a title.

After their hasty elopement, the unlikely couple settled in Los Angeles—a very un-Rhodesia sort of place—where the groom had prospects, he said, of a film career. Sophie, who after all had other interests, decided to make the best of it. "Imagine Rhodie a Slavic princess," she said when the subject was brought up.

That spring Sophie made an unscheduled, hasty trip to Los Angeles. "Trouble in Paradise," was all she allowed herself to say. Upon her return to the village she announced that the marriage had been a disastrous mistake, that Rhodie was divorced, had resumed her maiden name, and was living in the family apartment in Manhattan. "She's interesting herself in social work," Sophie said when pressed. "Oh, Rhodie's resilient. She'll bounce right back."

Even Sophie had seemed concerned; after all, everyone

knew Rhodie must have been in dire straits if she had had to resort to calling in her mother. But over the years Rhodie managed to make a life for herself, becoming a Manhattan humanitarian board sitter who took her responsibilities seriously. Every so often there would be a bit in the second section of the *Times* mentioning that Rhodesia Comfort Noble had been appointed to a commission looking into some inner-city affliction.

It was only when Sophie had broken her hip after that first calamitous fall that a diffident Rhodie had come back to Waggs Neck Harbor. A payback, Lettie and Dolly decided, for the time Sophie had gone to California to extricate her from that marriage.

And then, months later, with the hip replaced, Sophie—who was always tripping or missing a step—had her final tumble down those treacherous back steps. When a greatly upset Rhodie had left for California, of all places, no one expected her to ever return to Waggs Neck. And yet she had, absolutely dedicated to transforming the Symposium into a national treasure, planning to live in the village permanently.

"And though it's not funny," Camellia summed up, "one does have to smile just a little at the irony of it all, because here Rhodie is now, Queen of the Winter Women. Life is peculiar . . ."

"Darling Camellia," Lettie said, when she could, as she put it, get an edge in wordwise, "you're being a teensy weensy bit verbose. Now what do you think of the spurious search for new Symposium headquarters, Dolly?"

Dolly said it was a sheer waste of time, that Rhodie already knew what she wanted and was just "putting us through the paces because she likes to pretend the Symposium is run on democratic lines." Dolly, as everyone at the table knew, was unhappy because she had been acting chair while Rhodie was away and had her own agenda: moving Symposium headquarters from above the Goodwill on Washington Street to the ground floor of her recently opened B&B. This would have the triple advantage of attracting publicity and new guests and the year-round rent set aside in the Symposium budget. "The Nobles are," she concluded, "after all is said and done, summer people."

"Dolly, dear, they've lived in that magnificent example of whaling industry affluence on Bay Street since aught one," Dickie ffrench said, looking askance at the raspberry jam he had gotten on the sleeve of his elegant blazer with the working buttonholes and the Tiffany buttons. "Sophie's forebears gave us the library and the pond, unfortunate as both those improvements are, and Sophie has lived here full-time since her husband, the renowned one-star general, went to his reward in World War Two. I know we're all members of the founding families but Dolly, kitty cat, let's give the Nobles the benefit of longevity and stop calling them summer people."

Knowing neither Dolly nor she intended to do any such thing, Lettie asked, "What did you think of the properties we saw today, Dickie?"

"I rather liked the tiny cottage joining the far end of the Noble property. It's a falling-down mess but it does have possibilities . . ."

"You like it because Rhodie likes it," Dolly said. "We don't even know if it's for sale. Do we, Wyn?"

Wyn, always half entertained, half appalled by these get-togethers, said she'd have to check. "Certainly no one has been actively trying to sell it."

"Keny Blue lived there with her mother when she attended Waggs Neck High," Ruth Cole put in.

"Oh, Lord, there's that name again." Dickie ffrench, who had recently retired his horn-rimmed glasses, rolled his contact-lens-assisted baby blue eyes. With the coming of the new avant-garde optometrist in the village, Wyn wondered if everyone she knew had decided to change the color of their eyes and then thought, why not, if it made them happy.

"She's your pal," Dolly, wisely content with her own limpid Nile green Carlson eyes, announced, folding her napkin, which had started life as a colorful dish towel. "It was you who suggested her the second you heard Jane's idea for a seminar on feminist writings."

"She's not my pal," Dickie said, pouring another spoonful of sugar into his double decaf. "She's one of my employers. I'm not proud that I've written all four of her best-selling feminist gothics, masturbation fodder for the millions of women who buy them, but I wouldn't care for anyone to think we're friends. Even when we were outcasts in high school together, we were not friends. Nobody is friends with Keny. She makes you and me look like rank amateurs in the opportunistic sweepstakes, Dolly, dear." He sipped at his coffee and gave his dying boy's smile.

Lettie made that ironic trill that, for thousands of theatergoers, signified sophisticated amusement. (Female impersonators, when "doing" Lettie Browne, made great use of it.) Dickie wanted to know what was so hilarious. "I can't wait until Rhodesia comes face-to-face with Keny," Lettie answered. "It's going to be the all-girl version of *King Kong Meets Godzilla*."

"How did that film end?" Camellia Cole wanted to know, and Dickie said dryly, "With massive destruction and tons of corpses. Best close your eyes."

Chapter

5

⊰✴⊱

A NUMBER OF DISPARATE WAGGS NECK HARBORITES, SEVERAL OF WHOM had been present at Baby's midday meal, would have been surprised (though not consoled) to learn they were entertaining similar sour thoughts for the rest of the afternoon. All these cerebrations and ruminations were concerned with the imminent arrival of Keny Blue.

Dickie ffrench sat at his square nineteenth-century pine dining room table, pleased with its lack of symmetry (one leg needed a matchbook to give it balance), congratulating himself on having the wit and taste to buy American. English pine was so *ordinaire.*

The table, doubling as his drafting desk, took up most of the narrow dining room in his cedar-shingled School House Lane cottage. He had bought the house five years before after a series of unfortunate events: Mildred Griffiths Venue, the Manhattan society interior decorator, had axed him after he had broken the rules by going into her office during lunch hour to filch a cigarette. Instead of finding a Balkan Sobraine—

his and Mildred's brand—he had come upon Mildred being sandwich fucked by a pair of heavyset deliverymen.

"I'm not merely letting you go, Dickie," she had said, after she had gotten herself out of what she termed "dishabille" and cornered him in his cubicle. "Nor am I cutting back for economic reasons. I want to make this very, very clear, Dickie; for you, for our profession, and for the gum-cracking lowlifes at the unemployment office. I am firing you for poor judgment. You blundered into the wrong door and got the tiger instead of the princess. *Quel dommage.*"

At that particular moment in Manhattan, everyone in the profession was groveling at Mildred's crocodile-shod feet. This was because she had climbed, slept, and ingratiated her way into responsibility for choosing the short list of decorators who were to participate in the prestigious Turtle Bay Boys Club Show House charity fete. No one would think of hiring Dickie, much less take a lunch with him.

To make matters worse, soon after he was fired, the rent-controlled Manhattan apartment house he was living in was slated for demolition. Following on the heels of that announcement, an East Broadway mugger relieved Dickie of his beloved twenty-two-karat gold identification bracelet, not to mention eighty-five dollars and the seventeenth-century signet ring his former roommate but one had bestowed upon him.

He decided it was time to return home. Using what was left of his inheritance, he purchased from his last surviving relative—his mother's estranged sister-in-law, Aunt Rebecca—the old family cottage, which had appeared rock solid when he first moved in. "Needs nothing," he told friends, "but paint and the fabled 'A Few Good Pieces.'" The cottage quickly turned into the kind of financial sinkhole (it needed a new roof, a new oil burner, new eaves in the attic, new weapons to fight off the carpenter ant army) of which Mr. Blandings never dreamt. Aunt Rebecca was laughing audibly up her cotton corduroy sleeve from her hideously efficient West Sea condo.

If it had not been for the measly ten thousand dollars Keny Blue gave him per book and the occasional local decorating/ design commission, Dickie would have been drowning in severe financial waters. As it was, he was floundering.

On that drear Wednesday afternoon, after overspending his luncheon budget—Baby's looked but was not inexpensive— Dickie was supposed to be working on the plans Lettie Browne had commissioned for a chic New Federal rooftop café.

The New Federal Inn was a plain if endearing Victorian brick building with little to distinguish it except for the mansard roofs, one of which Lettie wanted eliminated. This was exactly the cut of meat the mayoress, the Cole sisters, and the other appointed members of the village's Historic Architectural Review Committee (HARC) loved to get their yellowing teeth into and rip apart. As if they had even the most rudimentary knowledge of architecture, much less preservation, Dickie harrumphed.

Dickie's harrumph was actually a snort, and he let another fly as he removed his Ralph Lauren tortoiseshell-framed glasses, which he wore at home, the new contacts too irritating for full-time use. Looking for solace, he went to the bookcase that housed his excellent miniature stereo system and his nicely displayed compact disc collection. His musical tastes leaned toward decayed and fey romanticism, great upsurges of sound undercut by death. Tempted by Mahler, in the end he chose Richard Strauss.

Music filling the small, insecure house, Dickie returned to his work and studied the preliminary drawings. Only Lettitia Browne, backed up by Wyn Lewis's legal expertise, could get this cockamamie plan past HARC. If Lettie wanted a Burger King franchise in the middle of Main Street, she would have one.

She was formidable, Lettie. Right up there in the same league as Mildred Venue and Keny Blue. Every time he thought of Keny Blue, Dickie's delicate tummy turned. He was aware that the time had come (actually, had long passed) for a confrontation. Ten thousand dollars had seemed a great deal of money when, years before, Keny—remembering Dickie's adroitness in composing her high school papers—approached him to ghostwrite a sexually explicit romance. She gave him the plot (it opened with a bra burning and ended with the heroine's first multiple orgasm) and mandated pages of foreplay and foreskin. Dickie sat down and wrote it in what he imagined Keny Blue's inner voice to be. It had taken him six weeks. It took her agent three years to sell it.

Underestimating Keny's ambition and public appeal, Dickie had not had a clue that *Midnight Matinee* would become the best-seller that it had. Three increasingly popular efforts followed, along with a miniseries, a career as a talk show guest, and twenty-five thousand dollars per lecture. Keny was a multimillionairess. Dickie was left with his paltry, demeaning ten-thousand-dollar-per-book contract.

In his fantasies of revenge, such women as his mother, his Aunt Rebecca, Mildred Venue, and Rhodesia Noble were more or less interchangeable. But Keny Blue had her own position in his galaxy of Evil Women—at the pinnacle.

He found himself looking forward to the imminent face-off with fear, loathing, and a tiny glow of excitement. "If that bitch doesn't come through," Dickie said, wondering if it would be too tricky to save the framework of the mansard roof and house the café inside it, "I'm going to wring her neck."

Peter Robalinski was taking a break from his on-the-job training at the Symposium office, since Jane (his trainer) had to meet with the FALAS calligraphy committee. He had decided an afternoon siesta was just the ticket and thus he was sprawled full length in an oversized butter-soft navy blue leather Stendig sofa. Rhodie had authorized the extravagance from California when Dickie ffrench was redoing her father's suite in the Bay Street mansion. It had already been decided that Peter was to return with her. Dickie had retained the thick bookcases that lined three of the walls but had them painted ochre, one shade lighter than the new gold carpet. This was a detail lost on Peter, who viewed all houses and rooms and paint jobs as either rich or poor, comfortable or not. The sofa, wonderfully commodious, had proven ideal for his diurnal nap, but on this day his enviable facility for falling asleep under any and all circumstances was failing him.

When he had first learned that Keny was going to speak at the Symposium, he had laughed (to himself), thinking it might be fun. Even after all these years, the thought of Keny produced a tingling sensation in the pouch of his black Calvin Klein boxer shorts. But now that the reality was upon him, Peter wasn't so much tingled as, well, discombobulated. You never knew what Keny was going to do or say. There were certain revelations—he looked at a thick silver-framed photo of Rhodie, given to him by her—best left unrevealed.

The bottom line was that Keny could upset his apple cart. Not that he was going to let her. A rare, vicious look came over Peter's benign athlete's face. He put his thumbs in his braces (decorated with quail and deer, another present from Rhodie) and stretched them, letting them rebound against his nicely developed Asher-and-Turnbull–shirted chest. He was thinking Keny had better watch her big mouth. Or he was going to have to do something about it.

Jane Littlefield was overseeing the winter women committee skilled in a simplified form of calligraphy. They were copying the names of the Symposium attendees onto color-coded name cards: green for paying customers; yellow for speakers; blue for media; hyacinth for organizers.

Instead of providing them with the usual (tea and chat), Jane was ignoring them. She stood at the insubstantial windows of the second-floor Symposium office, her arms wrapped around one another, ignoring the mild stomach cramps and light nausea that she perversely enjoyed. She was looking down on the mixed-use buildings of Washington Street, thinking of Peter Robalinski. He had changed in the past few days; that innate sunniness, such a nice antidote to her own chronic pessimism, had dimmed. Jane, no dummy, as her Aunt Lucy often pointed out, had a fair idea of what—or who—was doing the dimming. Turning her attention to Barbara Ann Perloff, who had run out of ink (what does she do with it, drink it?), Jane went to refill the inkwell, telling herself she would murder anyone who made Peter unhappy.

Sondra Confrit was reclining in her messy bedroom-studio in the Water Street house she shared with her husband, Rupert "Ginger" Hale. Rupert (Sondra was not amused by nicknames) was typing away in his bedroom-studio on the far side of the meager hallway. Rupert's quarters were supposed to have been soundproofed—at enormous expense—but the piercing racket of his hoary Remington defied even fortified paneling.

Sondra herself should have been working on a piece she intended for *Lear's*—"The Graying of the Free Sex Movement"—but the green screen of her PC was blank. Not so the black screen of her mind, which contained a particularly graphic memory of the Barbara Walters interview with Keny Blue in which La Blue regretted the fact "that every uprising has its victims. Think of the women who were involved at the start and look at where they are now, eking out livings lecturing and writing regurgitated, dated dogma."

Barbara wanted to know if Keny had anyone in mind and Keny said, well, she didn't like to name names but there was poor Sondra Confrit, living in a remote corner of the world, forgotten by everyone but the most loyal of her coital colleagues, churning out rehashed ideas in seldom-read articles. "And imagine, Barbara: the founder of the Feminist Free Sex Movement, married. In desperation, no doubt. No, poor Sondra hasn't had an original position in decades."

Poor Sondra was on the phone with her Manhattan attorney in seconds, but the attorney said she didn't think Sondra had the time or the money to go through what might very well be a pointless lawsuit. "This call alone is costing you one hundred and fifty dollars." Sondra hung up and seethed.

Now Keny Blue was coming to Waggs Neck, to Sondra's

Symposium—Feminist Literature had been her concept, after all—to heap more scorn on the mother of the free sex revolution.

Sondra, unable and unwilling to keep her anger bottled up, stormed into Rupert's inner sanctum, disturbing the genius at work on his magnum opus, *Deuteronomy.* "I'll be fucked by a jackhammer," she said, "if I'm going to let that nymphomaniacal egomaniac screw up my Symposium. I'll see her in hell first."

Rupert Hale, used to these small storm warnings, sat quietly with his fingers poised on the keys of the Remington, waiting for this, too, to pass. While Sondra ranted, Rupert permitted a small private smile to appear on his moon-shaped face. He so often felt about Sondra the way Sondra felt about Keny Blue.

Rhodesia, claustrophobic in her twenty-room house—not a good sign given her unstable past—bundled herself up in her mother's old sable coat and strolled over to Main Street.

As usual, she had forgotten appropriate gloves and grabbed the yellow leather ones she used for rose clipping from the shelf in the enormous foyer closet. The sharp and chilling wind from the bay was invigorating and she decided she didn't need gloves after all. Stuffing them in the commodious pockets of the coat, she nearly cut her hand on the "proper hanging equipment" she had promised Dickie she would pick up so the lacquer-framed China trade mirror he had unearthed could be properly hung. If Dickie used the word *proper* one more time, she was going to smack him.

She suddenly felt, for no reason, happier than she had in days. She was not unused to mood swings, but this ray of sunshine seemed not so much medication-induced as genuine. "All your fears are foolish fancies, baby" was a line from an old song Annie Kitchen had been singing along with the TV as she'd done her ironing that morning. Perhaps it was true.

Rhodie stopped in front of Frank E. Taylor's Antiquarian

Book Store and looked in the window at the New Book section, wondering if there was anything she should read. Keny Blue's intrusive face stared up at her from the back of her latest effort and Rhodie's momentary good spirits evaporated.

Frank shouldn't carry books like that, thought Rhodie, who often took the fascistic approach to censorship. Then she decided that wasn't fair. Books like that, she amended, shouldn't be written, much less published.

A group of winter women were just coming out of the Japanese restaurant and looked as if they might speak to her. Rhodie wrapped the oversized sable collar around her head and made a sharp about-face, taking the New Federal Inn parking lot shortcut to Bay Street and home.

Peter's Miata was parked behind the building that housed the Symposium office. He must have cut his nap short and returned to the office. So California, driving what was a five-minute walk. But he was taking his job seriously. He is a good boy, she reassured herself.

She trudged on, her mind back on Keny Blue. "Women like her," she said aloud as she exited the parking lot onto Bay Street, "shouldn't be."

Chapter

6

After the long lunch at Baby's with the FALAS executive committee, Wyn skirted the village parking lot puddles and entered her Main Street office through the back door. She was immediately comforted by the *click click click* of Liz Lum's computer keyboard. Liz Lum's everywomanness was just the antidote to the executive committee's feline high bitchiness.

"*Qué pasa?*" Wyn wanted to know, knocking on Liz's open office door.

"I left a few messages on your desk, nothing earthshaking." Liz swiveled around, pushing her drooping electric-curled Clairol No. 3 Ash Brown hair away from her soft round face, adjusting the slipping shoulder pad in her flowered pantsuit jacket. Wyn was wearing a short black wool skirt and sweater to match under an ancient camel's hair polo coat and looked, Liz thought, ready for a *Vogue* cover.

That Wyn felt herself on shaky ground in the fashion department invariably surprised Liz. When Wyn stuck to simple black and/or white classic outfits, no one in town could beat her for innate chic. Wyn only fell victim to fashion when she allowed herself to be enticed into the cutting-edge dress shop known as Sizzle, where she was hopelessly intimidated by Dicie Carlson into buying what she shouldn't.

Liz, who thought that Wyn could wear anything as long as Dicie Carlson hadn't designed it, often was deluded by the same fancy as Wyn: youthful high-color, imaginative runway clothes would make her into something she clearly wasn't. Nightmare memories of the sea-green culottes (her legs appeared even shorter cut off at the calf) and the burgundy two-piece formal pajama ensemble that played up her lack of a significant midriff came to mind.

When Wyn had returned to Waggs Neck and established herself in her father's old real estate office, Liz (likewise newly divorced, from that bastard, Mike Lum) had nervously resigned from her teller's position at the bank to become her old friend's receptionist, secretary, and general dogsbody.

Wyn engaged in a perennial motivating crusade to convince Liz that she didn't have to be a dogsbody forever, that she possessed genuine and persuasive sales talents, that she should go for her own real estate salesperson's license. Liz— firm in her belief that the only thing missing from her life was a man—had, with a marked lack of enthusiasm, signed up for the Real Estate I course at the college.

"How's the Heidi chronicle?" Heidi was Liz's sixteen-year-old big, beautiful, and somewhat brutal daughter. Wyn thought it sad the way Liz's old-dog-Tray smile evaporated at the mention of her child's name. Liz removed her half-moon reading glasses and looked into space with the troubled-eyed expression she reserved for inquiries regarding Heidi.

"Her highness did not turn up until five A.M. yesterday morning from her Saturday night date with Dax Fiori." Liz took a breath and asked the question that had long been on her mind. "You don't suppose Heidi's sleeping with Dax, do you?"

"You don't suppose they're not."

"Heidi says Dax is confused about his sexuality."

"Right. And Heidi is helping him make sure of it. As long as she's on the Pill, they're using condoms, and don't have multiple sex partners, I wouldn't worry about it."

"Jesus, Wyn."

"As I recall, you slept with the late, not-so-great Mike Lum when you were a junior in high school."

"We were affianced."

"Perhaps Heidi and Dax are *affianced,* a truly terrible word."

"Bite your tongue."

Wyn moved on into her office—a large book-lined room—and adjusted the wooden venetian blinds so that she could look out at Main Street through the plate-glass window. Main Street was empty and gray, as it should have been on a forlorn January afternoon. The New Federal Inn, directly across Main Street, looked solid and secure in all its repointed redbrick glory. Reassured, Wyn sat at her inherited and much scarred partner's desk and read through the messages Liz had collected.

Betty Kunze, the village pharmacist/mayoress (Betty, not holding with newfangled ideas, insisted on the *ess*), wanted to list the often-flooded, stick-furnished house she owned on Water Street for a three-month summer rental. That she wanted several thousand dollars more than she could get for an annual five-year lease presaged a repeat of last summer's last-moment, in-the-nick-of-time, twelve-hundred-dollar rental. That call, Wyn decided, could easily be put off at least until spring.

LeRoy Stein requested a return call. He was founder and president of Grasslands, a Waggs Neck Harbor–based housing development corporation that had purchased (through Wyn) Lucy Littlefield's Swamp Road acreage for an ecologically hip town house site. Wyn tried and was told by Stein's woodwind-voiced secretary that Mr. Stein hadn't returned from luncheon but he would be certain to call as soon as he did. Two weeks of phone tag would ensue, Wyn decided, wondering if the elusive LeRoy wanted to put the property back on the market. Not that there was much of a market for unimproved swampland, the environmentalists currently holding sway while demand for townhouse condominiums had waned.

These thoughts were interrupted by a call from Wyn's feared and detested ex-mother-in-law, Audrey Meyer. "Darling, we never see you anymore."

There didn't seem to be any right answer to that so Wyn remained silent.

"Anyway, darling, I only called to keep in touch and to mention that a dear, dear friend of mine, Myra Statler, is actually attending that little seminar you people put on in that sweet little village. Darling, would you be a perfect dear and look after Myra? Take her to lunch or dinner, whichever's more suitable. Of course, send the bill to me. I know how much you Realtors make."

"Audrey . . ."

"Do call me 'Mother.' "

"I have a mother and even when you were my mother-in-law I didn't call you 'Mother' and for the last several years you've had a new daughter-in-law to call you 'Mother' and you have your own daughter and that unnatural son to call you 'Mother' and isn't that enough, Audrey?"

"Well! Nicky said he thought you had a new therapist, but I must say you seem just a teensy bit shrill, darling. You know I only want what's good for you."

Wyn suppressed a need to scream and instead asked, "What's the point of this communication, Audrey?"

"The point is, darling, that my dear friend, Myra Statler, is dying to meet your Keny Blue and I said, in a moment of weakness, that if anyone could introduce her, it would be dearest Wynsome. I am sorry if I spoke out of turn."

Wyn had a mini-fantasy in which she confronted Audrey Meyer in her palatial, truly vulgar chintz-on-chintz Park Avenue triplex and said, "I demand that you keep out of my life, and if you don't, I'm going to get a court order mandating it. And that goes for your son and new daughter-in-law and all other members of the Meyer lineage who feel a small event like a divorce doesn't merit their attention and continue, year after year, to treat me as a poor but personable member of the family. Get out of my face, my hair, and my life, Audrey."

But she had tried similar if less hysterical entreaties before and had been regally ignored. So Wyn put the fantasy aside and told her former mother-in-law that she'd be glad to say hello to Myra Statler, but as she had her own volunteer role to play in the Symposium and as she didn't know Keny Blue, luncheon and dinner were probably out of the question. Cross out "probably."

"Darling girl. I know you. You'll arrange it somehow."

She had no sooner finished with Audrey than Jane Littlefield called to remind Wyn that she was Keny Blue's "village host." She was dropping off Ms. Blue's schedule this afternoon and Wyn should be sure to look at it.

"I'll commit it to memory." Wyn was increasingly unhappy about her assignment. As so often was the case, what had seemed duck soup when she agreed to be La Blue's host in the early fall now, in the winter, looked like entrée to the third circle of hell.

At this point Wyn thought it was time she did some potentially income-earning work. Deciding she didn't need her coat, she ran up the block to the Municipal Building, a large, ugly, redbrick edifice, circa 1889, which brought to mind the worst excesses of nineteenth-century factory architects.

The lightly mustached village clerk demanded and received ten minutes of small talk before she allowed Wyn access to the battered second floor room where the plat books were kept. According to the latest plat book, title to the property Rhodesia was interested in was being held by something called the K.B. Trust. The microfiche tax files, kept in a neighboring room and requiring the clerk's presence once more (she held all the keys), gave Wyn more information about the property: the village taxes were paid; the cottage contained nine hundred and fifty square feet of interior space; the trust had a Fifth Avenue address and had held the deed to the cottage since 1982.

By the time she emerged, the rain had turned to sleet. Wyn, regretting her efficiency, decided that she'd better do the job right and drive over to the title company in West Sea, look up the deed, and get the full history of the house.

"What are you doing running around without a coat in weather like this, Wynsome Lewis?" Ruth Cole asked as Wyn emerged from the Municipal Building. Ruth and Camellia looked like Mussolini wanna-bes in their new sheep-lined storm coats, wool trilbies, and winter galoshes.

"We've had to put the Persian lambs away," Camellia said, and for a moment Wyn thought she was talking about the Coles' infamous, incontinent King Charles spaniels. "The enviro-lunatics made such mean comments last winter whenever we wore them. It wasn't as if we had gone out to Persia and slaughtered the lambs ourselves."

They were coming from Woody's IGA, Ruth explained, having returned, with a great deal of indignation, a Gouda cheese that was decidedly off. The new dairy manager had been persuaded to return their investment, but not, Ruth Cole said ominously, with grace. Woody should have left him in produce and she was going to tell Woody so.

Wyn, who by this time was very cold, allowed herself to be carried along to the Eden, where a cup of tea was prescribed and produced. Sipping at it, she realized there was no immediate need to drive over to West Sea for information when an equally reliable source was sitting across from her. "Do you know who used to live in the house Rhodie wanted to turn into the Seminar offices?" she asked.

"Of course I do and so do you," Ruth said. "Sad Mrs. Bleuthorn lived there for years, until she died in, oh . . . when did Mrs. Bleuthorn die, Camellia?"

The younger Cole sister, deep into a blueberry muffin, wiped her dainty lips and said, "May of 1970." Camellia had an idiot savant knack with dates.

"You remember Mrs. Bleuthorn, Wynsome," Ruth said with some asperity. "You must. Poor Mary, everyone called her. The last of the once illustrious LeBow family. She had trained to be a nurse and married an accountant from West Sea named, of course, Bleuthorn. German extraction, it was claimed, though the shadow of the Israelites hovered over him.

"When their marriage broke up, Mary stayed on in the cottage that once had housed the LeBow servants and did odd household sort of jobs for the Nobles."

"She, too, had a wee drinking problem, did our Mary," Camellia broke in, putting on a broad, humorous Irish brogue. "But, aye, all the LeBows did."

"Oh," Wyn said, setting down the china cup on its thick saucer, seeing the light.

"The cause of your consternation, Wyn?" Ruth asked, carefully putting down her spoon.

"Wasn't Poor Mary Keny Blue's mother?"

"Of course she was," Ruth answered. "When Keny was two, Mr. Bleuthorn divorced Poor Mary, received custody of Keny (a big deal in those times, father getting the child), and took her to live with him in Brooklyn. When he remarried, he decided—as you can well imagine—that Keny was an impediment to his newfound happiness. It was Mary's turn, he said. Mary Bleuthorn was probably certifiable at that point but Keny could take care of herself."

"She was our only flower child," Camellia put in, looking up from her hot chocolate. "It was already 1964. Waggs Neck would have missed the entire era if it hadn't been for Keny."

"Her clothes came from the Methodists' thrift shop," Ruth said disapprovingly. "Straw hats with artificial cherries; lace gloves; glass bracelets."

"And do you remember the barrette? She always had it stuck somewhere in her hair. She still wears it. I saw her on 'Donahue' last week and there she was, barrette and all, big as life and twice as audacious."

"What's it like?" Wyn wanted to know.

"It's a wide band of aquamarines set in what appears to be gold," Ruth answered. "I think the stones may even be real . . ."

". . . there was such a vogue for barrettes in the forties . . ." Camellia said dreamily.

". . . but," Ruth continued, not liking interruptions, giving her sister her own version of the evil eye, "whatever Keny wore, she always managed to invest it with a cheap pruriency.

"She was, to give the devil her due, extremely bright in many ways and very motivated," Ruth went on, attempting to be fair. "I was still teaching math and Keny was one of my best students ever. Very quick. But English was her downfall. Maggie Carlson, may she rest in peace—she certainly didn't live in it—was teaching English then but she never could get Keny to understand basic concepts.

"Which was why her scholarship to that college in California came as such a surprise. We more or less forgot about her after she went to California and Poor Mary died. I don't think anyone, Wyn, would have realized that poor, snubbed Keny Bleuthorn, who had spent her high school years in the village, and Keny Blue, the glamorous, liberationist feminist novelist, were one and the same. But then that first novel was published and Dickie ffrench went on about it ad infinitum, ad nauseam, and the *Chronicle* featured her in a Waggs Neck Harborite of the Month column."

"Why didn't you mention Poor Mary when we were going through her old house this morning?" Wyn asked, thinking if she heard the name Keny Blue one more time today she would lose it.

"Rhodesia is so unhappy with Keny Blue coming to the Symposium, I was being protective," Ruth said, draping her storm coat around her shoulder.

"Ruth's always been Rhodie's apologist," Camellia said, not entirely with approval.

Ruth ignored her sister and made those economic movements that indicated she was readying herself to depart. "Now, Wyn," she said, adjusting her hat, "I want you to go straight to your office and don't dare come out again without adequate winter protection." With surprising grace in a woman her size, Ruth made her way around the many laminated tables and chairs that made up the noncounter section of the Eden.

David A. Kaufelt

"Maybe your young man can call for you," Camellia said, patting Wyn's shoulder, sailing off in her sister's wake.

Wyn, stuck with the check, decided she had gotten, after all, good value out of the four dollars and change it had cost for the afternoon refreshment. She had a reluctant Selma Eden issue a receipt—Wyn was careful about accounting—and returned to her office, holding out her tongue to catch snowflakes, wondering who was going to answer the telephone at the K.B. Trust office in Manhattan.

No one did. A doubtful recorded voice suggested that she either write or fax any query she might wish to make. Her query, which she had Liz fax to the trust offices, was simple: Was the Waggs Neck Harbor Bay Street property the K.B. Trust held in trust for sale and, if so, would the appropriate party please send particulars?

Rhodesia Noble called to ask for a progress report as Wyn was preparing to leave. I only started this afternoon, Wyn thought. She took a deep breath and said that she was in touch with the trust that held the deed and would have an answer for Rhodesia as soon as they returned her communication.

"Who are the owners?" Rhodie wanted to know.

Wyn told her that the deed was held by an organization called the K.B. Trust, which satisfied Rhodie for the time being but wasn't exactly the answer. It didn't take a decoding genius to figure out who the owner was.

Scarred veteran of many a real estate battle conducted solely on the basis of opposing personalities, prescient Wyn foresaw big-time aggravation. She just didn't know how big-time the aggravation was going to be.

Chapter

IT WAS THURSDAY MORNING, THE ANNUAL LITERARY ARTS SYMPOSIUM was about to begin, and the FALAS members were in full preliminary spin. Liz, laying a long-in-coming fax on Wyn's desk as if it were road kill, waited for Wyn to look up before she asked, tremulously, how she looked.

She was wearing a copy of a copy of a Chanel suit that featured a number of crisscrossed imitation brass chains and a color somewhere between mud and plum. Her hair, treated with dark red rinse, had been glue-gunned into place by Guido (né Ricky Bell), billed for the past half decade as the hot new stylist at Waggs Neck Harbor Coiffeurs.

"I told Guido I wanted something new and today," Liz said and Wyn agreed, mendaciously, that Guido had done a pretty good new-and-today job. Privately she thought that the extreme reverse flip Guido had managed to create only exacerbated Liz's soft chin; the frizzy bangs evoked the song about the surrey with the fringe on top.

"I've got to go," Liz said, doing a Lady Macbeth with her hands. "I'm a wreck. How do I really look?"

"Swell," Wyn said, wanting to go over to Waggs Neck Coiffeurs and pistol-whip Ricky Bell with his hair dryer. Then she thought of Ricky's younger brother, Billy, who had been killed two years before and felt, as she often did when confronted with the Bell progeny's many miscalculations, a little shot of guilt.

"Heidi said I looked like shit."

Wyn, now wanting to go over and attack Heidi, said Liz looked terrific. Liz accepted that, taking a phone call from Patty Batista at Wyn's desk. Patty was a diminutive, solid winter woman who had moved to the village some years before and had used her divorce settlement wisely. She had bought the old railroad station (the train had stopped coming to Waggs Neck in 1939), moved it to its present site on Washington Street, and transformed it into what she called the Old Railroad Spa.

The spa was, in reality, a hardscrabble gym where Patty Batista and other New Age followers taught, with stern determination, yoga (spiritual and physical), aerobic dance, vegetarian nutrition, and tai chi for "those interested in balancing their minds and bodies."

Patty and Liz were co-chairs of the committee responsible for getting food to various Symposium events and Patty was calling to say she had borrowed Dax Fiori's mother's van (Angela Fiori was the town florist) and was ready. The first official Symposium get-together was an afternoon Meet the Participants cocktail party in the public rooms of the New Federal. Finger foods and beverages were to be served while the speakers and the organizers and the hundred and thirty-eight paying members of the audience (gathered together from Manhattan, New Jersey, and Connecticut) commingled.

Liz said, again, that she had to run. She and Patty Batista faced a long morning, having to pick up finger foods from such varied sources as Peggy Kunze (the mayoress's sister-in-law), who had persuaded the Daughters of Italy to provide the tuna, ham, and macaroni salads; the two new women who lived way out on Madison and were, single-handedly, in a doomed effort to win acceptance, doing the cucumber and watercress sandwiches; Selma Eden, whose kitchen had agreed to donate the Eden Café's exotic egg salad, curry being its secret ingredient; and the Ladies of the Presbyterian Church, who were supplying the brownies and frosted lemon wedges.

Liz was feeling guilty about leaving the office unattended and her conscience took some time to be assuaged. After Liz finally departed, Wyn called Rhodesia. "I wasn't certain," she said somewhat diffidently, "that you'd want to be bothered with this while the Symposium . . ."

"Don't be ridiculous, Wynsome. The Symposium, such as it is, is under control. Jane is not stupid about organization. What news?"

Wyn read her the terse fax Liz had dropped on her desk from the K.B. Trust: "There is no interest in selling the property in question at this moment or in the foreseeable future."

"Wait until Monday and then offer forty thousand dollars, cash, with a thirty-day closing. That should pique their interest. And, for God's sake, use your noodle: Find out who's behind this trust fund. I might know someone on the board."

Wyn, teeth clenched, thought Rhodie was being especially thickheaded. The K.B. Trust board hadn't been remotely coy in the communication it had taken three weeks to make: The property was not for sale. What's more, forty grand was not enough, in Wyn's opinion, to change their position. She was about to couch this in diplomatic terms when Rhodie hung up without, as was her wont, saying good-bye.

"Is that steam coming out of your head?" Tommy asked, strolling into her office a second later, seating himself in the visitor's chair. Teeth clenched, Wyn said she had been talking to Rhodesia Noble and Tommy said oh. He was wearing his brown leather bombardier jacket, stonewashed jeans, and carefully weathered boots, items usually reserved for sacred occasions. "How do I look?" he asked, and Wyn wondered if the entire village was going to stop in this morning for a wardrobe consultation.

"Like a newborn pup. Why?"

He reminded her, as if he needed to, that he was Annie Vasquez's host and that he was picking up her and her kid at the Bridgehampton train station. "As a Symposium representative, I want to come off . . . you know."

Wyn did know. Tommy had a fan's crush on Annie Vasquez. She was one of the authors he was studying in the New American Short Story, his latest night class at the West Sea Community College. Tommy, after he and Wyn "got serious," began auditing English Lit. courses in the spirit of the housewife who takes up golf to share her spouse's interests. Wyn, a dedicated reader, had once believed she was going to spend her working life instructing college students in the joys of Jane Austen, but that was before Nick and reality set in.

Tommy, to everyone but his mother's surprise, became an avid reader and fervid course-attender, genuinely moved by what he would have missed if it hadn't been for Wyn: the magic of the written word.

Wyn, while always delighted to listen to Tommy's often original views on, say, J. D. Salinger, lived in fear of the day when he took the inevitable next step and started writing himself.

She moved into Liz's office and sent another fax to the K.B. Trust, detailing Sophie's offer and asking for the names of the trustees, all the while feeling unsettled. Perhaps it was the stale health bar ("POWER UP!") she had persuaded herself was breakfast. As she watched the fax machine digest her communication, she wondered if Annie Vasquez was as nice to look at as her press photos led one to believe and if the accompanying daughter belonged to a husband in good standing.

Catching sight of the oversized clock in Liz's object-filled office (she collected miniature pottery penguins often engaged in purportedly humorous human activities), Wyn realized she had better get moving if she was going to be on time picking up Keny Blue at the East Hampton airport.

*   *   *

The helicopter, descending from the cloudy sky like a drunk bird, arrived, as promised, exactly at two P.M. Five cashmere-coated male passengers deplaned and silently headed for their chosen modes of transportation: Land Cruiser, Land Rover, Jeep, truck, chauffeured limousine. No Keny Blue? The pilot affirmed, ma'am, that Ms. Blue was not on board today.

Wyn uncharacteristically slammed the door on her Jaguar, despite knowing she was once again risking the collapse of the electrical system. She sped back to the village, parked the Jaguar in the garage, and strode into her house. Probity demanded and received a paw shake but otherwise kept out of her mistress's way, having a keen appreciation of her more sour moods.

"I know," Jane Littlefield said, answering the phone on the first ring, her voice fruity with pacification. "I know. You wasted your entire afternoon but Ms. Blue did have someone call a few minutes ago. She has decided to skip the Meet the Participants cocktail party and is coming out tomorrow, first thing. She'll be arriving at the airport at nine."

"And I won't."

"Wyn . . ."

"Tell the bitch to take a taxi."

"Wyn . . ."

"Get someone else to pick her up."

"Like who?" Jane said, letting the tension shine through.

"Like Peter Robalinski in his new racing green Miata. A poor man's sports car if I ever saw one."

"Peter's busy and so am I and anyone else we might send will be eaten alive. Wyn, we need Keny Blue, distasteful as she may be. The media people are only coming for her. Most of our paying participants are only coming for her. How Rhodie and Sondra Confrit would crow if she didn't show."

"What about Dickie 'little f' ffrench? Isn't he her collaborator?"

"I tried. Dickie says it's bad enough he writes her books. He's not going to be her driver as well. Wyn, I'm having enough trouble with Rhodie without your . . ."

"All right," Wyn said with ill grace. "I'll pick the bitch up."

"And we'll see you very soon at the Meet the Participants," Jane prompted. "It's important the board turns out."

"You'll see me eventually at the Meet the Participants."

Grudgingly, Wyn got into the winter white skirt and the gray silk blouse that nearly matched what Jackson Hall once called her spit-colored eyes. Thinking of that artist's early painting that hung over her mantel, regretting his madness, she put on the camel's hair coat, ran Probity up and down School House Lane, and departed for the New Federal.

Stopping for a moment at the V where Madison met Main Street, she took a loving, exasperated sweep of her village thoroughfare. The weathered statue of the Union soldier presiding over an elderly cannon stood beside her, looking in an easterly direction. The redbrick shops and the hotel and the monstrous Municipal Building were near-perfect illustrations of nineteenth-century-after-the-fire building style. The shingled ex-Carlson mansion and the futuristic barn attached to it (both now comprising Dolly's elegant B&B) sat squarely at the far end of Main Street, blocking the view of the bay but not the winter winds.

Normally, on an early Thursday evening in February, there would be half a dozen cars on Main Street, mothers and retirees getting in their weekend shopping, maybe taking a cup of coffee at the Eden before closing time (six P.M.). But today only a couple of brown town dogs were strolling past the shops while every parking space was filled with costly foreign runabouts. The runabouts belonged to the mostly female participants, come to combine a love (well, at least a like) of literature with the titillation of hearing the outspoken Keny Blue speak on such celebrated new feminist topics as self-induced orgasm and multiple sex partners and the brave new world of sexual freedom as depicted in her novels.

Wyn walked east on Main Street, following several pairs of attractive, middle-aged women dressed in tweeds and suede into the expertly Victorianized New Federal lobby. Flocked wallpaper, Turkish carpets, chesterfield sofas, and a fire in the fireplace created a Sherlock Holmesian atmosphere that even the most diehard modernist found hard to resist.

The only person Wyn knew who disliked the New Federal was her ex-husband, Nick, who disdained charm, preferring the efficiency and anonymity of an AAA-approved chain motel. On their honeymoon in Hong Kong (grudgingly paid for by his mother), Wyn had longed for the venerable Peninsula; Nick had booked them into a suite in the Sheraton.

Wyn, who normally viewed any sort of sentimental arrangement—furniture or otherwise—with suspicion, admitted to herself that she was a sucker for the sort of Victorian charm the late mayor and hotel owner, Phineas Browne, had managed to create.

Today the lobby was organized chaos. Her fellow FALAS executive committee members plus half a dozen winter women were doing their duty: greeting the paying participants; leading them to the appropriate sign-in desk (Unpaid or Prepaid or Media); helping them with the hand-lettered, color-coded badges; providing them with Xeroxed maps indicating their lodgings (either the New Federal, the Carlson B&B, or the budget choices out on the highway); escorting them to the large dining area where Liz Lum, Patty Batista, and other FALAS members presided over an extraordinary array of finger food.

Soon after she inherited the New Federal from her brother, Lettitia Browne had had a cutting-edge electronics system installed and the ground floor's nonbearing walls replaced by artfully designed (Dickie ffrench) folding wall panels. Thus, the entire first floor could be turned into one large public space, ideal for meetings and such. But it rarely was, the convention planners Lettie courted drawn to larger, more accessible hotels.

The conversion, however, worked for ALAS; most Symposium social gatherings, aside from panel discussions, took place in the New Federal.

Wyn was immediately pressed into service by chief hostess Ruth Cole, who passed on David Kabot as if he were her partner in a square dance. Kabot had a deliberate two-day growth, a sweater with a hole in its sleeve, and a gold stud in his ear. The rumor was that he was having trouble giving birth to his fourth novel. Kabot, who had once lusted after Wyn, only to be rebuffed, refused the proffered badge (red ink for authors) somewhat abruptly.

"So refreshingly modest, David," Wyn said, handing the badge to his wife, the raven-haired beauty and Main Street dress shop owner (Sizzle), Dicie Carlson. Dicie, more than a touch pregnant, her black curls cut short, and her film vamp's lips painted Real Ritz Red, rolled her eyes behind her husband's muscular back. "Thank you, Wyn," she said in her child's whiskey voice. "The boy's worried that the baby will take his place in my affections."

"Yeah, right," David Kabot said, turning around. "Sorry, Wyn. I hate these things."

Wyn didn't ask why he attended because she had already seen, set up in the small dining room, the long table with local authors' works piled on it, David Kabot's prominently featured. "Would you sign my copy of *Six Months,* Mr. Kabot?" a woman with a diva's bosom asked. "Pretty please. It's my favorite novel of all time. That peanut butter scene. Do make it something personal. My name is Iris."

A *Chronicle* photographer took a photograph of David Kabot signing his book, a heavy-breathing Iris looking on. "Kabot Smiles" should be the cutline for that photo, Wyn thought, wondering not for the first time how Dicie stood him.

Iris broke out in uncontrollable giggles. "Look what he wrote," she said, holding the book under Wyn's eyes. " 'For Iris, In memory of that night in Chicago.' Bad boy," Iris said, clearly delighted. Wyn's mood darkened.

The lobby was turning stuffy, what with the fire and two hundred or so women swarming around. Three local authors who had gone to the trouble and expense of having their books privately printed were haranguing poor Frank Taylor (of Frank E. Taylor's Antiquarian Book Store), demanding to know why he hadn't stocked their efforts for the Symposium sale.

Frank, very tall and very adept at slipping out of tight situations, suggested they have a natter with Rhodesia Noble about the ALAS policy of not purveying privately printed books. While angry and righteous, none of the three felt quite up to facing Rhodie, as Frank well knew. He dodged Sondra Confrit, winked at Wyn, and faded toward the bar.

Wyn, taking care not to touch his shedding sport jacket, escorted Rupert Hale to his place behind the sales table. "I never do this," Ginger said, as they all did, searching his pockets for a pen. Wyn supplied him with one that had the Lewis Real Estate Company logo on it. She left him to his fate between a cookbook writer who specialized in local dishes (e.g., baked tuna fool) and a deranged-looking woman who had written a cautionary paperback on the dangers of radar ranges, electric toothbrushes, and other household apparatus.

Making her way across the room, which smelled increasingly of Estée Lauder's venerable Youth Dew, Wyn caught sight of Tommy. He was leading Annie Vasquez to the more exclusive sales table, a half round reserved for the three principal speakers.

Sondra Confrit had found her own place there and was lecturing four women with spiked haircuts who said they had come by truck from Elizabeth, New Jersey, and were great admirers. "So buy a book," Sondra said, holding up a copy of her *One Woman's Sexual Manifesto* (Cannabis Press, 1967). Cowed, they bought books while Tommy introduced Annie to Sondra.

"Very nice to meet you," Sondra said, concentrating on autographing the recently purchased books. "Love your stuff."

"I love your stuff, too," Annie said, and for a moment Sondra really looked at her.

"You do?"

"You're a brave woman and we all owe you a great deal."

Oh, no, Wyn thought, coming up to be introduced. She's

sincere, too. As well as long and lean and glamorous in a dark, retiring, confident way. She was wearing jeans and a jacket to match and a white lacy blouse underneath and red high heels and a big, fat turquoise and silver bracelet on her elegant wrist. Though they were about the same age, Wyn felt years older. She also felt a burning desire to race home and put on red high heels, if she only owned a pair.

What's more, Annie Vasquez radiated integrity and niceness and Tommy was looking at her in a way that Wyn acknowledged she didn't like. Worse, Annie was deferring to Tommy in a way Wyn absolutely despised. Wyn said a few words of welcome and asked after Annie's child. Caitlin was upstairs, Annie said, watching what was probably a triple X-rated film on the VCR. "She's twelve. The hormones are raging."

Wyn commiserated and then moved off as Annie Vasquez's admirers, realizing she was present, started buying her books as if they were original Gutenberg Bibles. Irene Handwerk, Tommy's mother, was swamped at the cash box. Sondra, whose only sales had been the four she had brokered—*One Woman's Sexual Manifesto* had, after all, been in print for a number of years—said she'd had enough and was going to help Rupert, who "couldn't give away free gold."

Her only comfort, she went on to say, was that Keny Blue was not present. "That woman can suck the life out of any room she walks into, just like that." Sondra snapped her long fingers, making a castanet sound. That was when the lights were dimmed for a moment and, in the silence that followed, Jane Littlefield's clipped, amplified voice asked everyone to pay attention: the Symposium's chair had been persuaded to say a few words of welcome.

Rhodie was standing at the podium between Jane Littlefield and Lettitia Browne. Behind them were Peter Robalinski and the executive committee members: Dolly, Dickie, the Cole sisters. Ruth Cole gestured impatiently for Wyn to join them. Wyn did so while Rhodie was giving what she described as an informal welcome to Waggs Neck Harbor's fifty-first Annual Literary Arts Symposium.

She had arrived at the part that her dead mother had really loved—asking those who had been attending the Symposium for more than ten years to raise their hands—when the outer doors to the lobby noisily opened. A short woman, buxom in the great Dolly Parton tradition, strode in.

She wore an ill-advised floor-length blue fox kimono coat that emphasized her lack of stature despite (this gave Wyn a second of happiness) her red high heels. Her mass of expertly disarranged Wonder Woman blue-black hair featured a vintage blue aquamarine barrette over one ear. With all the artifice—huge, blue-shadowed eyes, expertly bobbed nose, inflated lips—Wyn wondered if anyone knew what she really looked like. It didn't matter, she supposed: the impression was extravaganza—all brass, no strings. She was as out of sync in the New Federal, Wyn thought, as Rhodesia would be in Caesars Palace.

The newcomer stared into the awed silence facing her and, taking her time, counting the house, finally allowed her gaze to settle on Rhodie, Peter, Jane, and the FALAS executive committee. They were fast-frozen at the far end of the large space, looking as if they had been caught engaged in some naughty activity.

"Well, look who's here," she said in a voice that was one part Tallulah, the rest Brooklyn, waving a short, be-ringed hand with very long, painted fingernails. With the gesture, her coat fell open, revealing a skintight blue snakeskin-print jumpsuit and an oversized bleached bone necklace with a crucifix resting in her considerable cleavage. ("It couldn't be human bone," one thrilled attendee whispered. "Could it?")

Lettie Browne, possibly not realizing that the microphone was still "live," said, "What—in God's name—is *that*?"

"How quickly they forget," the newcomer said, proving she didn't need amplification. "This is a Keny Blue, dolls. So hello, girlfriends. That includes you, too, Dickie love."

Chapter

8

LONG AFTER KENY BLUE HAD BEEN SHOWN TO HER SUITE AND HER HALF-dozen matching pieces of Louis Vuitton (blue) brought up and her rented Saab Turbo convertible (blue) stashed in the hotel parking lot, the tongues wagged.

"She could be worse," Jane Littlefield said hopefully in the back booth of the Nonesuch Bar, sipping at one-star brandy, taking her pink eyeglasses and placing them on the stained oaklike table. "She apologized again for not turning up this afternoon. Said she decided at the last moment to drive herself out here and save everyone time, trouble, and money. Of course she's billing us for the rental car."

"She's a model of economy and consideration." Wyn's voice was steady but her insides felt like jelly on a plate. Though she had no rational right to, she felt betrayed. As she and Jane had escaped from the New Federal and made their way up Main Street to the Nonesuch, she had glanced into the window of the new Japanese restaurant and hated what she saw.

Tommy, his mother, Annie Vasquez, and presumably her

issue—a devastating twelve-year-old strawberry blonde named Caitlin—were seated at the round table, laughing and eating what Tommy had always heretofore considered inedible.

It had looked like a happy family gathering, Tommy's good-natured and somewhat dizzy mother, Irene, chatting away to Annie Vasquez while Caitlin—clearly and forever enthralled—talked up to Tommy. Wyn could imagine Annie's and Tommy's private smiles to each other as they patronized one another's closest relative.

"Ms. Blue expects you to pick her up at one-thirty P.M. tomorrow and escort her to the library," Jane was saying, folding her hands prayerlike on the table, closing her eyes, looking wan, taking refuge in minutiae. It had been a long day. "I can count on you, can't I, Wyn?"

Wyn, hearing hysteria in Jane's no-nonsense voice, said, "You bet. Where's Peter?"

"I don't know. He disappeared right after Ms. Blue came in. As did Rhodie. Perhaps he drove her home. After Ms. Blue went to her suite, I went up to see if there was anything she needed. She said, imitating Mae West, I suppose, that all she needed was a bad man and a good night's sleep.

"I left only to find Dickie climbing up the rear stairs. He was knocking as I was descending but Ms. Blue wouldn't open the door. Shouted that she'd see him in the morning. 'Too tired, babe, even to talk to you.' Dickie agreed, loudly, that he'd see her in the morning, but he wasn't happy and made a lot of noise coming down the stairs.

"I went out through the first floor. Lettie and Dolly were at a table in the corner of the small dining room . . ."

". . . a dangerous liaison," Wyn suggested.

". . . and the Cole sisters had a bunch of women gathered around them in the lobby . . ."

". . . launching their Keny Blue attack, no doubt."

"They were having tea and everyone seemed to be listening to Camellia very carefully. Auntie took a group over to the Blue Buoy."

"I would have liked to have witnessed Lucy and her followers displacing the rummies at the bar," Wyn said wist-
fully, imagining a triumphant Lucy ordering cream sherry,
staunchly defending Keny Blue in her own contrarian way.
"Well, by now every parlor in the village is ablaze with winter
women having the time of their lives dripping venom over
Keny Blue's reputation."

"Not to mention mine," Jane said.

"Yours?" Wyn asked in genuine surprise. She hoped Jane
wasn't going to cry. There was a suggestion of poor-me-pink
around the pale blue eyes; the long patrician nose threatened
to leak.

"Sondra Confrit had been suggesting the feminist theme for
years but it was me who actually sold it to the board. And it
was me who invited Keny Blue. The Symposium is a disaster
and it's all my fault."

Wyn wondered why it so often happened this way. Just
when she was ready to engage in a bout of self-pity—she was
forever being chastised for not "sharing" her feelings—her
chosen confidant one-upped her. She said a great many sensible, calming things to Jane. The most prescient was that the
Symposium was going to be the most discussed ever, certainly the one with the best media coverage.

Jane, unconvinced, paid the modest bill and drove Wyn
home in her Aunt Lucy's old De Soto, notable for its push-
button drive. Wyn's house, a white wooden nineteenth-
century balloon construction that sat high on a small hill, was
dark and empty behind its wall of privet hedges. Wyn crossed
the porch, opened the door, and aborted the alarm system she
had installed when it seemed as if someone were routinely
breaking into the house. She then led a manic Probity—her
teeth, Wyn thought, must be floating—down a deserted
School House Lane to the village park, where Probity liked to
do her dainty business.

Home again, Wyn switched on lights and treated the vegetarian Probity to a broccoli-laced canine biscuit and herself to
a frozen Milky Way. She left the candy wrapper on the kitchen

counter where Tommy, a recent convert to health food, couldn't miss it.

At three-thirty in the morning, when a cautious Tommy, reeking of garlic and soy sauce—and was that a hint of a discreet, alien perfume?—crept into bed, she pretended sleep. It was either that or what Natalie, her therapist ex-sister-in-law, called a confrontation and Wyn called a screaming, drag-down how-could-you brawl. She had been there before and didn't have the energy.

She lay awake for some time, reminding herself that after Nick she had sworn that she would never let another male make her miserable. But there she was, in this modern, open relationship she had devised, as miserable as could be.

She fell asleep at the far edge of her side of the bed, hugging her pillow, wondering what the hell Tommy was smiling at in his dreams.

Dickie ffrench was Wyn's first visitor on Friday morning. "Fun last night, wasn't it?" He took a moment arranging himself in the green leather visitor's chair. Flanneled legs crossed, blazered arms enfolded, his wedge of reddish brown hair in place, he looked much as usual except that his freckled skin seemed a shade whiter than normal.

Most of the time Dickie, who had taken the late Phineas Browne's place in her life, amused Wyn with his evil patter and sharp insights. But occasionally, especially of late, he had exasperated her with his recherché egomania. It looked as if recherché egomania was running rampant this morning.

Wyn asked if he wanted coffee or tea and he said no, he was here on business. Wyn said they could still discuss business over coffee or tea but Dickie wasn't listening. "I have learned from reliable sources that Zero's is going belly-up," he said, digging in his side pocket for a Lucky Strike, lighting it with his gold Cartier lighter, letting an exquisite smoke ring rise in the air, this despite the No Smoking sign in four languages that sat above the round clock on the wall facing him.

"Moving to East Hampton," Wyn said, getting out the

chipped, mean, green glass ashtray she saved for insensitives who insisted on smoking. "Freddy Zero has decided it's a better market for upscale sporting merchandise."

"I could care less about Freddy Zero's take on the economic scene. What I want to know, Wynsome, is how much it would cost to buy his lease and get myself a good, new, long one. I'm thinking of opening a shop. Decorative oddments and such. You see, I've got to earn a living now that that woman has cut me off."

"Off?" Wyn, knowing Dickie, was aware that one word would suffice.

"I'm no longer La Blue's ghostwriter. She fired me this morning when I managed to beard her in the lobby. She fired me in front of the blue-haired ladies who make up the FALAS Food Committee while they were setting up the complimentary breakfast Lettie was too cheap to provide.

"That bitch utterly and totally humiliated me and she did it between interviews for the *Post* and the *Chronicle*, the subject being a book for which she claims authorship and I wrote."

Dickie issued an harrumph. "Just when our contract stipulated that I was to begin getting a share of the royalties. I was about to become, Wynsome, if not rich, at least comfortable for the first time in my diminutive, disconsolate life."

"Why don't you write a book under your own name?"

"She dictated the sex scenes. I can't do sex scenes."

"So many people can't."

"She's going to write the books herself. She says it doesn't matter what they read like now. Women only buy them because her name is on them and the formula is always the same." Dickie sighed deeply.

"Why did you trust her in the first place?" asked Wyn, who was losing patience as well as her morning. "The lady doesn't exactly possess a reputation for loyalty."

"She's exactly like Mildred Venue, my former employer. Incredibly seductive. She promised that as soon as she was established, I would start making real money. I signed a contract that gave her all rights. What do I, little Dickie ffrench,

ex-darling of the demimonde decorators, know about con-
tracts?" He put his cigarette out and lit another. "You have no
idea how I hate, loathe, and despise her."

Wyn, eyes on the clock, not comfortable with Dickie's pal-
pable desperation, said in her mother's sunny-side-of-the-
street voice, "A decorating shop sounds like a good idea."

"It's my only idea. Besides taking a hammer to Miss Blue's
barrette-bedizened head."

Wyn, really not liking the look in Dickie's eyes, began talking lease arrangements and Dickie, bored, stood up, shot his
linen cuffs, and told her to go ahead with whatever she had to
do to secure him the store. Wyn said she'd talk to Freddy Zero
on Monday and, if all went well, she might have a contract for
him to sign soon after. "You don't want time to think it over,
do you, ffrenchy?"

"I've thought it over," he said, sitting down, deciding he
would have a cup of tea after all. "You know my father kept
a shop . . ."

". . . ffrench's Fine Shoes . . ."

". . . and his father kept a shop . . ."

". . . ffrench's Fine Wines . . ."

"And now I'm going to keep a shop," Dickie said, adding
sugar and milk to the cup Wyn handed him, sipping noisily.
"Do you suppose it's genetic?"

"ffrench's Fine Furniture?"

"Keny Blue's Revenge? Not. Anyway, I'm going to carry a
lot of fine American pine along with essential froufrou like
ball fringe and fabric for shirring and needlepoint pillows. A
fitting end to a less than spectacular decorating career. It may
actually be fun. Not as much fun as getting what that sex-
obsessed harridan had been promising me for the past decade, but sure as my name is Richard Harrison Xavier ffrench,
I'm going to see to it that Keny Blue gets paid in kind."

"You're not going to knot her up in ball fringe?" Wyn
asked, now looking directly at the clock on the wall and, after
a moment, the one on her desk. "Tickle her to death with an
ostrich feather?"

Dickie, oblivious to time and irony, rather thought he'd have another cup of tea. He looked so forlorn, Wyn agreed that he might. For the next half hour he talked desolately about decorative oddments, wondering if Wyn wanted to sell her father's old ("and not in very good repair, either, my dear") mission bench.

Wyn poured herself a cup of tea, resignedly. Dickie lit another cigarette and reminded her that he was now in the market. During her travels through houses old and new, if she happened to run across a fun Chinese carpet or a clever set of white pine chairs . . . well, they might come to some sort of arrangement.

That was enough for Wyn, who told him that she had no intention of going into the antique scouting business. She would pursue Freddy Zero and the lease as soon as she could, and what time was it, anyway?

Dickie, sighing, departed, giving Wyn just enough time to put on lipstick and pat down her hair before fulfilling her obligation to the Symposium.

As it happened, she was a few minutes late but in time to witness most of the great "slanging match"—as Ruth Cole put it—between Sondra Confrit and Keny Blue.

By rights Keny Blue should have been exhausted. She had thrown her all-enveloping foxes over her peignoir and driven herself out to the Swamp Road location of WWAG for the seven o'clock talk show. The zany morning host hadn't gotten in one word after she began. Keny was great at monologues. She returned to the hotel, fired Dickie ffrench in the lobby to the immediate gratification of a gaggle of local women, and then went upstairs to her suite. Changing into a body-sculpting black and blue strapless and marginally daytime dress, she repositioned her trademark barrette so that it sat dead center in her coils of blue-black hair.

Back in the lobby—its folding walls replaced—she had taken over the small dining room, breakfasting with a Bright Young Journalist from *Newsday*. This interview was immediately followed by coffee with an earnest, nail-biting stringer from the Long Island Section of *The New York Times*. She finished the morning with a taped interview that was to air on local cable that evening.

"Give me one good reason why you shouldn't use your vibrator in your morning bath to get the day going? I do." The interviewer, an out-of-work humanities professor, could only come up with accidental electrocution. "But what a way to go, dolls," Keny had replied, causing the cameraman (Angela Fiori's brother-in-law, Vincent, who videotaped weddings and confirmations and other social events) to laugh out loud, ruining the take.

Mayoress Betty Kunze arrived at noon, wearing a new and sprightly red-and-white polka dot dress under her good fur-collared winter coat. She was leading the less spectacularly attired Waggs Neck Harbor Official Welcoming Committee.

The mayoress did not subscribe to any aspect of the feminist movement. Nor had she read more than three of the four Keny Blue novels. "Filth," she maintained. "Pure and pristine filth." Still, she featured them prominently in the paperback racks situated next to the Russell Stover candy display at the front of her drugstore.

Despite her feelings about the writings of Keny Blue—"we must separate the artist from the work," she maintained—she had come equipped with a gigantic plastic-made-to-resemble-brass Key to the Village, complete with village crest. She planned to present this to Ms. Blue in a brief ceremony in the New Federal lobby. The mayoress performed this service, at the expense of her valuable time, for all visiting celebrities, it being one of her innovations when she took office. Lucy Littlefield, Jane's aunt, a welcoming committee member, opined that Mayoress Kunze toted that key around in the hope that she would get her name in the national press. So far, no luck.

This was academic in the Keny Blue case because Ms. Blue, having learned that no member of the press showed interest in the ceremony, sent word via housekeeper Viola Bell that she was canceling. "I want to talk to her right this minute,"

Betty Kunze said. "We've left our jobs and homes and this has been planned for over a month and I've even had her name engraved on the key . . ."

"Hear, hear," Lucy Littlefield said, undoing her plastic rain kerchief. "Get the woman out here."

"Yes," the mayoress said. "Where is Miss Blue?"

A grim Viola replied, "Left the back way. Said she'd return in an hour. If you want to wait."

Lucy said she wouldn't mind waiting but Betty said that waiting was out of the question and Viola could pass on a message to Ms. Blue: The mayoress and the entire welcoming committee, book buyers all, were extremely miffed.

Keny Blue was returning via the back entry from her un-explained absence as Sondra Confrit entered the lobby, look-ing for her. "There you are. Heard you stood up the welcoming committee girls. Bad form, Keny."

"Tough titty, Sondra."

"I've come here for a peaceful powwow," Sondra said, showing extraordinary restraint, her mouth very tight. "What if we have a cup of coffee in the small dining room and I fill you in on the drill. No explicit sexual language, appropriate deference to the founders of the Feminist Free Sex Move-ment . . ."

"Too, too kind, Sondra. Going to all this trouble to 'fill me in on the drill.' Maybe if your nerdy husband, or someone, or anyone, filled you in with their drill, you could stop playing Susan B. Anthony and get real."

"How dare you?" Sondra asked, and it did look to Wyn, who had come in a few moments before, as if she were going to hit Keny Blue. "You fifth-rate TV personality with your ghostwritten potboilers and your Vegas face-lift and your sil-icone breasts. If it weren't for women like me, women like you would be sitting home in a concrete-block ranch house, darn-ing socks, changing diapers, and waiting for hubby.

"I was in the trenches, you filthy, opportunistic bitch, fight-ing for our sexual rights, while you were in the grandstands getting laid. Now you're making a dirty joke out of what we've fought so long and so hard to achieve. I'll see you six feet under before I let you undo what I've done."

There would have been applause from the women gathered in the New Federal lobby, but Sondra was wheezing, so there was a general fear that she was about to have a heart attack. And Keny Blue was quick to kill the mood. "Someone get her a glass of water before she implodes," Keny said. "She's not as young as she used to be. But then again she never was. Is there someone named Wynsome Lewis here?"

Wyn raised her hand, studentlike, and Keny said wasn't she supposed to escort her to the library, not that she needed an escort but she was a great one for going along with the program. Sondra had been led to one of the leather chesterfields and was being hand-fed a glass of water by Lucy Littlefield. Wyn waited while Keny Blue got into her furs and approved of herself in the lobby mirror. "Come on," she said to Wyn, "we're out of here."

But before they left, Keny turned and looked at Sondra Confrit, sitting alone with her glass of water and Lucy, the other women hurrying to get to the library for seats. "Later, sweetie," Keny said.

Sondra, with a dismal visage, said she would see her later in hell.

Chapter

9

⚜

THE BRICK AND CONCRETE WAGGS NECK HARBOR PUBLIC LIBRARY HAD
been donated to the village by Rhodie's maternal grandmother soon after she began summering in Waggs Neck, in
1901. Considered a village treasure by old-timers and a Victorian aberrance by the lately arrived architecturally hip, it
resembled an elaborate Victorian police station, complete with
iron bars on narrow slotted windows, oversized lamp lights,
and near inaccessibility.

The imposing main double doors were reached by a mon-
umental number of wide, shallow concrete steps to which
green-painted iron handrails had been affixed just after the
First World War, when a number of unfortunate accidents
occurred involving veterans. Inside, a small glassed-in anteroom with wooden racks held outer clothes, umbrellas, and
galoshes and was the source of chronic aggravations stem-
ming from lost/stolen/forgotten property.

The main reading room was a large, confused space, presided over by a professional librarian (the popular, apple-
cheeked Mrs. Levinson-Cowen) and a number of poorly paid

winter women. They favored severe hairstyles, cardigan sweaters, flat shoes, and Barbara Bush pearls. They often stood about socializing in small, cozy groups, sipping at cups of tea brewed in the narrow pantry off the reading room, complaining about the lack of heat in the winter and the over-enthusiastic air-conditioning (installed in 1971) in the summer.

Each of the village schools (high, middle, and grade) had excellent libraries and thus the only children who came were under five, accompanied by parent/guardian adults and quickly consigned to the remote, cell-like Children's Room.

Most of the adults who regularly patronized the library were interested in popular novels or guides to help them plan real and imagined winter vacations.

During the summer months historians and historical novelists wandered in, optimistically looking for Waggs Neck Harbor archives. A section had been set aside under the windows facing the cemetery featuring the pamphlets and privately printed books of remembrance that came—Mrs. Levinson-Cowen hoped—under the archival rubric.

There was a permanent exhibit of local authors' works; Melville, reputed to have spent a winter at the original Federal Inn, was represented as were David Kabot and Rupert Hale. Less well known village authors' works (e.g., *A History of Table Manners, The Economic Potential of E.S.P., Let Your Juicer Be Your Drugstore*) were also on display. Soon after Sondra Confrit had come to live permanently in Waggs Neck, a bookcase had been grudgingly set up near the ladies' room for feminist writings. Explicit sexual tomes—including those written by Sondra—were kept behind the desk. The acquisition committee did not consider Keny Blue's novels appropriate public library fare.

The roof of the library featured a green glass dome that sat sturdily over the second-floor auditorium and allowed for a certain amount of sickly natural light. This large, round, and difficult space held a narrow stage and myriad metal folding chairs and was reached via an adventurous circular marble stairway. Halfway up was a niche that held a sculpted head of the library's benefactress.

Martha Comfort looked so smug and happy in her perch that Wyn had wanted, ever since she was a girl, to write something despicable on her marble brow. Too late now: Plexiglas had been installed to frustrate the potential graffiti artist.

As Wyn and Keny climbed the stairs to the Dome Room, followed by dozens of anxious latecomers worried lest they wouldn't find seats, Keny stopped at the niche and laughed. "I forgot about Mrs. Comfort. She really is asking for it, isn't she?" And, allowing the women to queue up behind her, she took her purple lipstick and drew a crude representation of "the miracle of the male erection" on Martha's Plexiglas shield.

Wyn wondered if the essential difference between Keny and herself was that she *thought* of doing such things and Keny *did* them.

Tommy Handwerk turned as Wyn and Keny entered the Dome Room closely followed by what seemed like a conga line of attendees. Tommy, sitting in the midst of a sea of women, stuck out, taller and broader and blonder than anyone else, with the possible exception of Selma Eden's Swedish cousin, Ingrid. Tommy gave Wyn a shy, guilt-laden smile. Next to him was Annie Vasquez, scheduled to speak on the following morning. Annie's Lolita-esque daughter, Caitlin, sat on his far side, sporting heart-shaped sunglasses.

"Yo, Wyn," Tommy said as Wyn walked up the ragged aisle, Keny Blue in tow.

"Yo yourself, Handwerk," Wyn said companionably but letting him know with tone and body language that she wasn't happy to see him, that there would be a conversation, perhaps a confrontation, between the two of them before the day was out. In the meanwhile, she conveyed that she had better things to do. This assumed sangfroid cost her a certain effort but she felt it was worth it.

Rhodie was already sitting on the stage with Jane Littlefield in a pair of chairs that looked as if they had been stolen from a school administrator's office. Jane, a nervous wreck the night before, seemed composed, giving a half wave to Wyn and somewhat more of a smile. Wyn decided she must have taken a Xanax. Rhodie almost certainly hadn't. Her pink silk toque (matching her dress) brought to mind the Queen Mother, not an image Rhodie could have been striving for. She was attempting a benign smile as the audience sat in a state of anticipatory titillation, whispering to one another. The acoustics of the Dome Room encouraged sotto voce confidences.

Rhodie waited, with a noticeable lack of humor, for Keny Blue to make her way through the admiring audience and climb up onto the stage with as much grace as she could muster under the circumstances (more challenging steps). Rhodie indicated a lone chair, a match to the other two, situated by itself at the far side of the stage. When Keny, amused, sat in it, Rhodie took her place behind the podium and called the Symposium to order.

She introduced Jane Littlefield, who made a few "housekeeping" remarks. No one would be admitted to Symposium events without proper identification; attendees were enjoined to wear their badges at all times, especially if they wanted to take advantage of the discounts being offered by Main Street merchants; there was a correction to the printed program: the Waggs Neck Harbor Poets Society reading would take place at four, not three, P.M., in Frank E. Taylor's Antiquarian Book Store, refreshments to be provided by the Friends of the Annual Literary Arts Symposium.

Jane asked Liz Lum and Patty Batista to stand up so they could be personally thanked for the grand job they were doing with the finger foods. Liz blushed and Patty beamed as appropriate applause rang out.

Rhodesia sailed back to the podium to make a few more welcoming remarks and to introduce literary figures from the audience. Sondra Confrit wouldn't stand but she did wave her hand. Rhodesia went on to alert the attendees that next year's Symposium would be devoted to the Art and Craft of the Historical Novel. Oohs from the crowd, perplexity from the executive committee to whom this was news. All inquiries for early and reduced-price reservations should be made to the incoming executive director, Mr. Peter Robalinski. The latter stood but Wyn thought his salesman's smile was not up to its usual thousand-kilowatt beam.

Wyn was sitting between Peter and Dickie ffrench in the first row along with the other members of the executive committee. Keny Blue, Wyn noticed, was staring down at Peter with a lip-smacking expression on her lascivious mouth. Dickie noticed as well. "Dear, dear. Methinks Keny sees you as her midafternoon snack, Peter," he said in a loud whisper, leaning across Wyn. "Best be sure and bathe thoroughly." Peter looked as if he might punch Dickie in the head and in the interest of peace, Wyn pointed to the stage.

"Our opening speaker needs no introduction," Rhodie was saying, glancing in the general direction of Keny Blue. "Her liberated novels, not to mention her lectures and television appearances, are famous for their frank language. She is known personally to a number of us, having spent her high school years in Waggs Neck Harbor. I know she is going to temper her language today, given the audience"—here Rhodie acknowledged the audience with a grim smile—"and that she is going to thoughtfully illuminate the subject of her talk, New Sensuality in the American Woman's Novel. Please welcome our principal speaker."

Keny Blue took the podium as Rhodie, avoiding contact, went stage right and off into the wings. She appeared a few moments later among the audience, taking the front row seat reserved for her next to Jane Littlefield.

"Thanks, Ms. Noble, for that rousing welcome," Keny said in her hoarse Brooklyn delivery. "What Ms. Noble in her anxiety to get things right forgot to mention is my name— Keny Blue—and the fact I never stick to the subject—I don't even know what the hell New Sensuality in the American Woman's Novel is supposed to mean and I don't think she does either.

"Now for the program warning: If words like *fuck, cunt,*

cock, pussy, blow job, suck, cum, cajones, and *muff diving* offend you, you'd better get out now. I wouldn't want to offend anyone."

Lucy Littlefield tapped Jane on the shoulder with her arthritic faux-diamond–bedecked forefinger. "What in God's name," she asked in a voice loud enough for her words to bounce twice around the rotunda, "is muff diving?" Lucy was roundly and immediately shushed. Otherwise there was silence.

Keny Blue spoke for forty-five riveting minutes, detailing for the middle-aged, middle-class women her own early repressed sexuality, her sexual awakening, and the new insights and life it gave her. She did not, as promised, mince words. She talked undramatically but with real feeling about her longings, her needs, and the sexual techniques that helped release them. She said she knew that most of the women gathered in the Dome Room shared those feelings and those needs but had been conditioned by a frightened male-dominated society to deny them.

"My dad, that bastard, remarried when I was fourteen and sent me to live with a mother I didn't know. I came to Waggs Neck Harbor as a teenager with an accent I wasn't aware I had and all the complicated, warring inner needs that go hand in hand with postpubescence. Waggs Neck Harbor took one look at my braless T-shirt and my platform heels—I've always been a snappy dresser—and turned away. Luckily I was more interested in my sex life than my social life. Though I was a touch confused.

"My mom, who had her own troubles, was about as repressed as they come. High school teachers were no help. Sex was something called *intercourse* and if you thought about it, much less engaged in it, you were one sick little chicken. I was thinking about it all of the time.

"It was the sixties and flower children were having group sex at high noon in the fountains of Central Park. Waggs Neck, bless its heart, was still into sock hops and church socials.

"I got myself out just before I went bananas with a scholarship to an Episcopalian, yet, college in southern California. It was the old frying-pan-into-the-fire number. The school officials expected a proper WASP virgin and they got me, a Brooklyn bagel baby in all her thrift-shop glory.

"I had a piece of luck, though. I met a boy with a man's needs. An hour after we met, he was playing me like Paderewski strummed the piano. He was a virtuoso lover and I was his prize student. We acted out one another's fantasies, and though he was smug and arrogant and not a nuclear physicist in the brains department, he was the best sex I have had, ever. To say that together we left no avenue unexplored is an understatement."

Keny went on to detail some of those avenues and to discuss other lovers, male and female. She closed by saying, "I shlepped out here to the middle of nowhere in freezing cold for a couple of reasons—some personal—but mostly to tell you it's not too late. Liberation is here, dolls. It's been here for nearly thirty years and too many of you are still whistling in the dark with your thumb up your nose. Put it in another orifice, I'm begging you. Or get a man. And if there's no man around, try a woman. After all, who knows your wants and needs better than another female?

"And if there's no woman, go down to the mayoress's drugstore and get yourself a fourteen-inch vibrator and a thick lubricant. Give yourself a good time. You deserve it and who's going to care?

"If you don't know where to start, read my novels. My latest and greatest, *Reflected Glory*, is for sale in the hotel lobby, and I'll be more than glad to sign it for you. Listen, ladies: I don't care if you're twelve or if you're ninety. Today's the day to say hello to your body and your fantasies and your needs. Any one of you sitting in front of me who's not having sex is not really living. I'm warning you: Tomorrow morning I'm going to take a poll to find out just how many of you have a climax tonight.

"And now, if there are any questions . . . ?"

"Shame on you," Sondra Confrit shrieked so loud that the library custodians feared for the glass dome. "Shame on you." Marching toward the staircase, the tall, shapeless woman in the big Reeboks and the velour jumpsuit continued to rant. "Betraying the sexual revolution for profit and neurotic sensuality, trying to destroy the work of women like myself. Vermin like you must be destroyed."

As Sondra stomped down the tricky stairs, Keny Blue said, "And there goes the drugstore's first customer. Make it the Big Bob deluxe, extra-strength model, Sondra. And hurry. Now," she said, facing the audience, "any more questions? Or answers?"

Camellia Cole raised her hand and stood up. She had taken off her new sheepskin coat but was still wearing the matching Mussolini-esque trilby. "I want you to know, Miss Blue," she said in her clear, high voice, "that I have felt many of the things you have said today. I always have believed that I was, as you put it, one 'sick little chicken.' I have, since I was a young girl, tried to repress all sexual thoughts and needs. I am realizing, today, now, that I have lived as stunted a life—if I may be so dramatic—as those Asian women who once had their feet bound. In my case, it was my emotions that were crippled.

"I want to thank you from the bottom of my heart, Miss Blue, for saying the things you said today. You have made me understand what I have missed. But you have also helped me feel a little less lonely. I never dreamt that anyone but myself had those feelings."

"It ain't over till it's over, you know." Keny Blue was moved, as was nearly everyone in the audience.

"I'm aware of that, thanks to you. I've made several resolutions. As soon as this is over, I'm going to get in line at the Waggs Neck Harbor Pharmacy and buy myself a vibrator, whatever that is. Then I'm going to purchase a copy of your new novel, though I understand it's not very good, and then I'm going to lock myself in my bedroom and see what I can do to enjoy myself.

"What's more, I'm going to use a word that has been on my mind for well over six decades and that I never, in my wildest dreams, thought would pass my lips. The word is *fuck.* Fuck. Fuck. Fuck. There, I've said it and I'm glad."

Camellia Cole burst out crying and sat down, burying her head in her older sister's shoulder. Ruth, rare tears in her own steel-gray eyes, tried to comfort her.

"That's a terrific start," Keny Blue was saying. "Now I want every well-brought-up, nicely educated woman in this room to bite the bullet and say the F word. Shout it out or mumble it to yourself but for God's sake, for your own sake, say it."

There was a moment's silence, followed by a chant. The two winter women who had selflessly volunteered to skip Keny Blue's talk and man the reading room desk stopped their busywork (erasing pencil marks in travel guides). They looked at one another in disbelief and then up fifteen feet at the plaster ceiling. "We misheard," the more established of the two said, wringing her hands. "We most assuredly misheard."

Chapter

10

WYN LED KENY BLUE DOWN THE SERVICE PASSAGE AND OUT THROUGH THE wheelchair entrance. Mandated by the state, it had cost the village twenty-six thousand dollars and was only used by the town's most celebrated hypochondriac, Mrs. Morrell, when she was in her electric wheelchair mode. Other disabled citizens preferred to take advantage of the library's excellent home delivery service rather than scale the Everest-style ramp.

"Wasn't that a giggle?" Keny Blue said, removing her fox coat, stabilizing her barrette, making herself as comfortable as she could at Baby's only table by the window, the one that faced the parking lot. "You guarantee that mob's not going to crowd in here, watching my every bite, clomping over to the table in their Mary Janes to ask me the best way to achieve vaginal orgasm after sixty?"

Wyn assured her "they" wouldn't be coming to Baby's when the food (finger) was free at the poetry reading at Frank E. Taylor's bookstore. Wyn was wearing a charcoal-gray suit left over from her Manhattan days, nicely severe but more

Saks Fifth Avenue than cutting edge. She had on lipstick and blusher and her blond-white hair was combed and she guessed she looked okay. But next to Keny's blue-black coiffure and Kabuki-esque war paint, she felt dowdy. Hanging up her old camel's hair coat on an unstable clothes tree, she wondered if it weren't time to acquire a baby-blue fox and pretend she had bought it before the foxes had rights.

They ordered sandwiches and coffee from the home-permed and multiwrinkled May Potter, one of the startled owners. (The other, wee Bishie Sundergaard, had run upstairs to their apartment, where she remained until Keny Blue departed.) Stalwart May moved off to the sandwich counter, crammed into the closed-in former front porch, mumbling that she thought she had seen everything. Keny's décolletage would provide May and Bishie with several weeks' worth of small talk, especially in light of upcoming events.

"You look like your old man," Keny said, studying Wyn. "Always did. Angelic face. *Alien III* eyes."

"I thought you didn't remember me."

"How the hell could I forget? Like, your mother was the assistant principal at the high school and, like, I was her fave problem student. Woman couldn't get enough of me. I was such a challenge. I had a hundred and thirty-six IQ, aced every subject but gym and English, and yet for some reason—my sassy mouth, my Dale Evans cowgirl blouse, my pink Double Bubble—I drove already shaky teachers round the bend and gave the demivirginal co-eds palpitations. They were still wondering if titty-fucking could make them pregnant while I routinely carried Trojans in my alligator purse. They knew I was light-years ahead of them. So did the teachers who got off on sending me to the office. Where yo' mama was drumming her fingers. I guess she was bored out of her box with being assistant principal, waiting for old lady Reilly to have that final paralyzing stroke so she could take over. 'You're never going to fit in, Keny,' she used to tell me, and I used to tell her that, like, maybe I didn't want to fit in. Like, she was really listening.

"She was rapping away about my clothes, my tits, my walk, and my talk and my lack of interest in anything having to do with Waggs Neck Harbor. According to your ma, if I didn't make immediate and big-time changes, I was going to spend my life alienating everyone I came into contact with and wind up in the hard-core wing at the Federal Penitentiary for Habitual Sex Offenders.

"While she mouthed off, I'd sit there schlumped down in the prisoner's chair, gum parked in my cheek, keeping my imagination busy with a big framed photo of you and your dad facing me. You were on his lap, staring straight into the camera with that take-no-enemies expression while Hap was hugging you as if he'd never let you go. Ultimate *goyim*. You know what *goyim* means, right?"

"A pejorative for non-Jews," Wyn answered, thinking she sounded like her mother again. She always did when faced with hostile witnesses.

"Such consummate belongers. Has anyone ever had a straighter nonsurgical nose? Blonder hair? A peachier complexion? Your eyes save you. That pale color is just weird enough to make you interesting and maybe a bit dangerous.

"Then, I hated your guts. But I loved your old man. Like he ever said two words to me. I used to hang out on the bench in front of his office after school to watch him come out on his way to the golf course, your perfect *Saturday Evening Post* stud.

"Saturday mornings you and he took your stroll down Main Street, hand in hand, a dog running in front of you, all three of you sedate, smiling, happy to be who you were, everyone saying hello, how are you, what's new, glad to see you. Please, you golden family, touch me with your radiance so maybe I could have some good luck, too.

"They looked the other way when they saw me. I would have traded places with you in a heartbeat, Wynsome Lewis."

"You say that now . . ."

"Think about it. My *bubbie*—grandma to you—brought me up on the front stoop of the two-family house she owned in

Flatbush, wallowing in chopped liver and schmaltz. When I was thirteen she died from what had to be acute indigestion and I moved upstairs with my old man, who started to shake whenever we happened to pass in the living room, incest on his mind. Truth is, I wouldn't have minded. Harry was hot, even in old age.

"He married his bookkeeper so he'd have an excuse to dump me on his first wife, that marginally sane lady at the end of the civilized world, Waggs Neck Harbor. Drove me out here in his puke-green Sedan de Ville and didn't say two words the entire trip. Poor Mary met me at the door, salivating. He took off but not before handing me this."

She undid the blue-stoned barrette and handed it to Wyn. "Said he got it years before from a fine woman he had been in love with. Said he wanted me to have it. Like it meant so much to him, it was going to have major significance for me.

"Bastard turned out to be right." She took it back from Wyn and held it up to the yellowed globe light. "My own little phallic symbol. But get this: turns out it belonged to my mother."

Reaffixing the barrette to her hair, Keny went on, intent on her autobiography. "So there I was, your basic hysterical thrift-shop junkie, Fanny Brice in costume for *Secondhand Rose,* standing on Main Street, U.S.A., lusting after your wonderful dad. Don't tell me if he wasn't, okay?"

Wyn said he was wonderful.

"Man didn't realize I existed and neither did you."

"Stop. Every single person in this village was aware of your existence. I thought you were great. I remember those gold shoes . . ."

"Joan Crawford fuck-me specials. I used to do my toenails with car paint."

"It never occurred to me that you were unhappy. You were letting it 'all hang out.' You were doing 'your thing.' Which is what we were all supposed to be doing, though some of us were having trouble figuring out what our thing was."

"Or where it was," Keny said. "Jesus, if you knew how many times I thought of offing myself."

"Your mother was no help?"

"Poor Mary, the Drooler? I don't know what she was like when Harry married her but there wasn't much left when he dumped me on her. She dealt with me by ignoring me. I wasn't there. Puff, the Magic Dragonette.

"I used the guilt money Harry sent to buy clothes, food, the occasional joint. I single-handedly kept the five-and-dime makeup counter in business for three years. When your relentless old lady called my demented old lady to take a meeting, subject being my behavior, Mary slipped quietly over the edge like a melting Dali watch and went to bed for a month. The woman needed serious testing.

"And living in the shadow of the Noble mansion wasn't all that much fun either."

"Sophie?"

"Yeah, Sophie. She was interested in me, though she took pains to hide it. I'd catch her watching me from her sitting room, but when we came face-to-face in the street, I'd barely get a hello. It must have been my second Christmas when Princess Rhodie came home for her annual visit and Sophie had her housekeeper of the moment come over and ask if Ma could help in the kitchen. When Ma said she didn't think so, I was invited to join the scullery girls, working our asses off to feed Rhodesia in style. I nearly went for Rhodie with my potato peeler when she deigned to come into the kitchen and complain about the temperature of the tea water, but the cook ran interference.

"After I left Waggs Neck, Sophie kept in touch. Hard to believe, but there were, like, fan notes when my books came out and postcards from rich-bitch spas. It was weird. I couldn't imagine why she bothered. I mean if *I* was on her postcard list, so was Charlie Manson. I finally figured out why. It blew my mind."

Wyn asked why but Keny had stopped talking, staring off into the parking lot. Wyn did not like the way Keny's calculating eyes were narrowing and, to distract her, asked how she had won her college scholarship.

"Grades were, like, not a problem. But I'm a helluva lot better at talking than at writing. Dickie was the class writer. I taught him to smoke grass, he wrote my papers. I let his muscle magazines—guys with shaved pecs in jock straps stuffed with salamis—come to our post office box and he came up with this terrific essay that helped win the scholarship. Or so I thought.

"In gratitude, I took him to bed just to prove it doesn't smell like fish—at least mine doesn't—and to take his mind off magazine body builders."

"Dickie ffrench?"

"Don't knock it till you've tried it. You'd be surprised how much oomph that cocksucker had in him. Not that I want to give cocksucking a bad name. Anyway, now he's having a sissy fit because I'm not renewing his contract. Dickie is not hip to the fact that he always got more than he deserved. I mean we're not talking *War and Peace* here. The books sell thanks to the sex scenes, which I orchestrate, and the round-the-clock promotion I give them. Not only don't I need 'little f'any longer, I never did.

"That essay he wrote? I could've submitted 'Mary Had a Little Lamb' and won the scholarship. Sophie's cousin was the only member of the Cadmus scholarship committee. Sophie was my silent angel. Dickie was—still is—a Class B *putz*."

"You unspeakable bitch." Dickie exploded into the dining room looking as if he were going to attack Keny with the two-foot-long loaf of delicious potato bread for which Baby's was much celebrated. "It's one thing to publicly fire me but it's another to slander me to the world."

"I haven't slandered you to the world, yet, Dickie. Give me time to get to a fax machine . . ."

"You know, I could just kill you, Keny. I could just wrap my fingers around that short, stout neck," Dickie ffrench said, clutching the bread as if it were Keny Blue's short, stout neck. "I could . . ."

"No you couldn't, Dickie. Face it, sweetie. You don't have the testosterone.

"What can I tell you?" Keny went on as Dickie, murdered bread in hand, strode out. " 'Little f' was always a touch meshuga." They munched for a while and then Wyn, putting Dickie and his rage out of her mind, asked, "Why did you come back? ALAS wouldn't seem publicity-generating enough to be worth your while."

"After your husband dumped you, why did you come back?" Keny sidestepped the question while proving the infallibility of Waggs Neck's system of providing instant background research for anyone interested. "You had a law degree and a Realtor's license, you're hip and cool, and you look like an angel in disguise. Hey, with the right clothes, you could have married Donald Trump."

"Gee."

"You would have had your own real estate empire."

"I couldn't think of anyplace else I wanted to be," Wyn said. "I was hurt and scared and Waggs Neck was safe and familiar. I'm glad I came back," Wyn went on, knowing she sounded defensive, wondering for a moment what would have happened to her if she hadn't returned. Certainly not the Donald.

"If it's any consolation, I'm glad I came back, too," Keny Blue said. "And maybe not just for your long weekend. You know, I might consider a house here. Strutting my stuff up and down Main Street. Introducing my New York mob to the joys of village life. Getting into everybody's face. Wouldn't that just make them nuts?"

Wyn thought that Keny Blue, under all the "now" bravado, was not nearly as sure of herself as she sounded. This slim vulnerability didn't make her any the more endearing. "Your vindictive streak is showing," she said.

"Vindictive, Wynsome-ette, is my middle name. Wait till tonight. The winter women are going to have what to talk about."

She repositioned the barrette again, checked her cleavage, and asked a hovering May Potter for the check, which she handed to Wyn. Wyn paid it, requesting a receipt. May, taking her time, wrote out the receipt with a last-straw sigh. She handed it to Wyn, who scribbled a reminder on the back to apply to Jane for reimbursement. "Careful little sweet-ums, aren't you?" Keny Blue said, wrapping herself in the blue furs, which Wyn decided she wouldn't wear on a bet.

Wyn, in her Realtor capacity, had convinced Tony Deel—the saturnine son of the late painter, Jackson Hall—to give Dolly Carlson a five-year lease-option on the enormous barn he had inherited. The barn, once part of the now greatly diminished Carlson holdings, had been turned into a futuristic home and studio by Jackson Hall shortly before his death.

Tony Deel, loathing Waggs Neck Harbor, had asked Wyn to sell all of his property in the village. Save for the barn, this was easily done. But the barn was too special and too expensive to be salable. "I want to get out what we put in," Tony Deel, like many other real estate innocents before him, said from his Paris gallery.

When Dolly evinced interest but then decided she didn't want to tie up too much of her cash, Wyn had proposed the lease-option. Tony had finally agreed, with the proviso that Dolly make no important changes. "I can imagine what that provincial beauty would do to it if she had carte blanche," Tony had said.

The provincial beauty had taken Jackson Hall's upstairs glass-walled studio bedroom for herself and had been forced, by the terms of the lease-option, to keep the huge, sensational open space that took up most of the ground floor as it was. Providentially, the ground floor also contained six bedrooms, each with its own bath. Thus, Dolly was able to offer deluxe accommodations in addition to the twelve "superior" bedrooms she had carved out of Carlson House's original seven.

Tony Deel, learning of this, was not happy. But as Wyn reminded him in one of several transatlantic phone calls—his nickel—Dolly was keeping to her end of the bargain and no structural renovations had taken place except for a tasty, closed-in walkway. "Trust Dolly Carlson to turn one of America's most important artistic shrines into a tatty B&B annex," Tony had complained from afar.

The Friday night Meet the Authors Champagne Reception was being held in the Jackson Hall Memorial Barn (as Dolly had the plaque inscribed). Even with the two hundred and some literary lovers who turned out for the event, the reception room was as cold and spare and magnificent as it had been when Jackson Hall had briefly lived there.

The glass doors fronting the town were closed in deference to the chilly weather. The view of the bay through the thick glass gave the illusion of being inside a black marble space-ship, about to take off for outer space, the red lights in the near distance on Shark Channel Bridge blinking out a Martian message.

Dickie ffrench, who wore an angry expression and a custom suit, had been working off his fury by helping rearrange furniture and other objects all through the late afternoon. He stood with Dolly at the door as the guests arrived. Dolly said the evening was a veritable fashion show. "A cautionary fashion show," Dickie amended.

Ruth and Camellia Cole, in their good black dresses with accompanying jet earrings, had arrived early to make certain they sampled the canapés and secured their rightful place in the receiving line.

Liz Lum wore a tight brown and orange ankle-length woven wool dress equipped with a cowl. The dress severely constricted her movements. "Slinky?" Liz had asked her daughter, knowing she shouldn't have. Heidi had observed that a garment that resembled a homemade macramé plant holder could only look slinky to an aspidistra.

Heidi herself was present, having won one of the two Symposium scholarships offered by FALAS to Waggs Neck Harbor High School students. (Heidi had been the lone applicant.) She wore a turquoise sweater dress purchased on time from Sizzle, where she worked on Saturdays and during school holidays. The dress suited her too well, Liz thought but was wise enough not to say.

Heidi and the Rudolph Valentino look-alike, Dax Fiori, were helping serve hot and cold canapés and tiny meatballs. "Every single women's group in the village has been tapped out of finger food," Patty Batista said with pleasure.

She and Liz were serving cheap champagne. Patty was resplendent in what Dickie ffrench described as "thirteen yards of coffin crepe and still not enough."

Annie Vasquez, accompanied by her daughter, Caitlin, and her official Symposium escort, Tommy Handwerk, declined champagne. Annie wondered if there was any Mexican beer (there wasn't) and Caitlin wondered when they were going to get "out of this place." All three, in variations of blue jean fashion, strolled around the room. Annie said she felt wonderful vibes and Caitlin rolled her eyes.

That singular anomaly, the Important Artist's Widow, was represented by two charming examples, one a bit overweight and overbearing in outrageous red, the other trim in faded mauve velvet, both filled with oft-told tales. They took up their places at opposite ends of the room.

Dolly, in her twenty-year-old forever chic St. Laurent, stood greeting guests and guarding the door from party crashers. Dickie, still at her side, thought it more likely people would want to crash out than in. The winter women, he went on, had done what they could with what they had, which wasn't much. "Such a fatal predilection for pantsuits. Just what do they think their derrieres look like draped in baby-poop green wide-wale corduroy?"

The local novelists and short-story writers all arrived twenty minutes late and gathered around the Writer's Widows in small, homogeneous groups, complaining about the lack of attention they were receiving. That ill was not to be redressed by the widows, who launched into anecdotes ("I remember the night that Klaus . . .") even before they were certain of their audiences.

The poets, who felt they had had the most successful readings in years and were still high from the excitement, mingled as they had been instructed to do.

David Kabot, his usual surly, attractive self, wore a black

leather jacket, his dark hair in a ponytail, an emerald stud in his left ear. "Don't you think that look's getting old?" Dicie, his wife, wanted to know. She was wearing a black-and-white patterned dress that made the most of her maternity.

"Something's getting old, Crabby," Kabot said, kissing his wife's neck, much to the irritation of the mayoress. Betty Kunze, resplendent in what Dickie identified as a Kmart picnic tablecloth, did not approve of public displays of affection.

Sondra Confrit and her husband, Rupert Hale, were blocking access to the miniature meatball dish. Spearing bits of darkened meat with dull blue-dyed toothpicks, they were popping them into their mouths as if this were their first food in months. Washing them down with the low-end New York State champagne, they simultaneously and dispassionately argued about the time it was taking Rupert to finish his novel.

"If you didn't make me attend affairs like this, I might get some work done."

Sondra laughed theatrically at the word *affairs* and, spotting her New Jersey admirers, crammed half a dozen more meatballs into her mouth. Blood-red sauce flowed down the crannies of her chin, negotiated the downhill crevices of her neck, and continued to ride down the zipper line of her neon-green jumpsuit as Sondra left Ginger in midsentence.

A statuesque woman known professionally as Dagmar played her own ethereal compositions on an electronic harpsichord that had been set up next to the main bar. What with the food and the space and the music, virtually everyone, many with an eye on the door, agreed that "this is lovely." They were waiting with anticipation for Keny Blue's entrance.

As were Jane Littlefield and Peter Robalinski, standing under the sculptural staircase and attempting to follow the conversation of Jane's aunt Lucy. Lucy had ruined the effect of her pink angora sweater and skirt (purchased from the home-shopping channel on Easy Pay) by wearing pink bunny slippers on her long, narrow feet. "Forgot, to tell the truth," she admitted. "They're so comfy." She removed one of the offending creatures and held it up for Peter's inspection. "Pinch Bunny's nose. It squeals and glows in the dark. Go ahead."

Peter did not pinch Bunny's nose because at that moment Wyn Lewis came in and was greeted by Lettie, who had managed to usurp Dolly's place in the lineup. Lettie was magnificent in a yellow and red Galanos and rubies the size of robins' eggs. Wyn wore a winter-white bouclé suit she had purchased, in a fit of fashion insecurity, at Sizzle that afternoon. The skirt was short and the braided jacket formfitting. Dicie had said she looked like a 1930s film star, the sort with fabulous shoulders and insurable legs. The kind who played wacky heiresses.

Wyn felt about as wacky as the aging usherette she feared she resembled. She caught sight of Tommy sandwiched between Caitlin and Annie Vasquez, leaving, heading—she guessed—for the Nonesuch and veg burgers. La Vasquez, she thought meanly, would let no meat pass her environmentally pure lips. For a moment Wyn feared she might cry—they looked so casual, so hip, so secure—but Lettie, teeth bared, fixed that by saying, "Darling getup, Wynsome. So very, very, very young."

"One tries not to overdress," Wyn said, glancing at Lettie's five-figure gown and the possibly genuine rubies.

"You succeeded admirably, my dear."

Giving Lettie the set, Wyn wondered why she let herself get into these things and, willing herself not to think of Tommy and Annie and Caitlin, she moved on to the Cole sisters as a penetrating silence infiltrated the room. Only Dagmar's fulsome strumming of that old favorite, "By a Waterfall," disturbed it.

Keny Blue was making her entrance, wearing what looked like a blue-tinted cellophane body wrap, the aquamarine barrette riding high on her hair, a clunky necklace depicting the sex act as interpreted by ancient Mayan goldsmiths enlivening her décolletage. Her eyes were surrounded with black kohl and, of course, blue shadow; her lips and nails had a bluish tinge. Her breasts, bundled together with some secret mechanism, looked like Miracle Gro grapefruit displayed to best advantage in a good grocery store.

The crowd took this all in and were about to break their

silence in a big way when the clatter of custom heels down the steel steps got their attention. Rhodie, ladylike yet sensual in one of her pale silk dresses, descended the Jackson Hall staircase, coming to rest in front of Keny Blue.

Rhodie was wearing diamond clips in her hair and just the right amount of makeup. She managed to look—Dickie had to give her this—both upper class and sexy. "Very Mary Astor."

"Ms. Blue. How fortunate," Rhodie said in her most clipped transatlantic accent, Queen Elizabeth being gracious to a belly dancer. "You've saved me a trip. Here is your honorarium plus something extra that should cover all your expenses." An envelope was produced and proffered. "Thank you so much for giving us your time, but knowing how busy you are, the board realizes there is no need for you to stay on. We'll arrange for someone to turn your car in—Hertz, is it?—and tomorrow morning Wyn Lewis will drive you to the airport for the early helicopter ride back to Manhattan. I must say you've been extremely interesting. Good-bye."

All eyes and ears were focused on the two women as Keny Blue took the proffered envelope, folded it, and stuck it between her legendary breasts. "You really think I'm going to dust off this town because you have decreed it, Rhodie?" She turned to the crowd and said in her clarion voice: "Fasten your garter belts, girls. I've got a couple of announcements that are guaranteed to wig out the entire Waggs Neck Harbor establishment."

She waited while everyone else waited and then allowed herself a slow smile as she went on. "But tonight, I'm afraid, is what the purists call a dry fuck. I'm holding off until the morning. I've had my publicist call a press conference in the New Federal lobby for ten A.M. and you're all invited. So until then, ta-ta, Rhodie. Ta-ta, Peter. Ta-ta, Dickie. Ta-ta, Sondra. Ta-ta, girlfriends."

"Magnificent," Camellia Cole said, before everyone else got their breath and rushed headlong into speech. "A triumph. I only hope she doesn't catch her death of cold walking back to the New Federal in that costume."

Chapter

II

ONCE AGAIN TOMMY DID NOT ARRIVE HOME UNTIL EARLY MORNING, AND then he slept in the guest bedroom. The guest bedroom mattress had not been aired in some time; the sheets hadn't been changed since Wyn's ex-sister-in-law, Natalie Meyer, had visited over the Christmas holidays. Natalie favored the pulsating scents of Jungle Gardenia—a perfume that made Tommy gag—and Wyn hoped the sheets still reeked of it. She heard him toss and turn as she lay corpse still in her big, lonesome bed.

Tommy performed none of his usual Saturday morning capers. He rose early, showered, and quietly went downstairs, feeding Probity her disdained but healthful and wildly expensive vegetarian breakfast purchased from the health-oriented pet shop in West Sea. Wyn could hear him opening and closing the old Kelvinator door, preparing his own roughage-laden cereal breakfast.

She sat up in bed, uncertain how to proceed. A screaming fit had its attractions but, in Wyn's experience, usually didn't do much but delay the inevitable.

Besides, it wasn't her style. Maybe it was time for a new style. She stared up at the wooden ceiling, remembering a peppy Judy Garland song about a trolley that her father had liked. But Judy had been high on new love while Wyn was experiencing the painful zing of the strings of her heart breaking, one by one.

She forced herself to get out of bed, determined to present a business-as-usual face, telling herself that women of the nineties didn't cry. Brushing her teeth vigorously with a *Consumer Reports*-recommended toothpaste, she felt moisture around her eyes and decided that, all right, she did love Tommy after all. She had been loath to show it, to make too much of her involvement, in case of just such an eventuality as faced her now.

"Bastard," she said, finding a small release in controlled anger. Damn Mother and, yes, damn Hap for all those sane, polite conversations about control around the dinner table. Wyn knew what Keny Blue would do in the situation: she'd stomp all over Mr. Thomas Wainwright Handwerk with her stiletto heels and then go have Annie Vasquez and issue for breakfast.

Getting into her leopard-print leotards and her Nike Airs, Wyn marched noisily down the stairs lest Tommy remain unaware she was up and ready. Stopping at the door to the dining room, she felt her anger ooze away as self-pity and a terrible longing seeped in.

Tommy sat at the round pine table in the French-doored octagonal room, drinking tea stewed the way he liked it, chomping on his Granola. Wyn couldn't stand looking at the sympathetic back of his head and the way his ears stood out, so she went into the kitchen and got her caffeine from an open diet Coke can before returning to the dining room doorway. Wishing Tommy an early baldness—no man deserved that corn-blond hair—she resisted the urge to put her arms around those knobby shoulders and nuzzle one of those protuberant ears.

"Morning, Wyn," he said in his deepest, dolorous voice, not turning around.

David A. Kaufelt

"I have three requests for you, Tommy," Wyn said, as casually as she could manage.

"Wyn . . ." he began, but Wyn wasn't to be stopped.

"Well, two are hopes. I hope that Caitlin has her own bedroom at the New Federal."

"Jesus," Tommy said, turning but looking just above her at the molding atop the doorway. "Do you think that I . . ."

"And two, I hope you're using what we modest ones call precautions. That was our pre-living-together arrangement, was it not? That we were absolutely free to have sexual relations with anyone we wanted as long as we used the above-mentioned precautions." She knew she was sounding like a hybrid between her academic mother and a Bush Supreme Court nominee, but she couldn't stop herself. "Not that I ever intend to sleep with you again, Handwerk."

"Wyn . . ."

"My last request is that you remove your belongings from my household as soon as possible and no later than noon today."

"Wyn, I love you . . ."

"You have a remarkable way of showing it."

"I thought we had this agreement . . ."

"It's null and void."

"Wyn . . ." Tommy said, looking at her with helpless, pleading eyes, so handsome and appealingly manly in his own boyish way that she almost gave in. But the last two eon-length sleepless nights and all the long-ago sleepless nights she had endured waiting for Nick the Rat kept her from going to him. "Listen, Tommy," she said, "I want you to have a great life and Annie Vasquez may just be the one to give it to you."

"Wyn . . ."

"As always, I'm overwhelmed by your way with words, Tommy."

He stood up and she knew if he touched her, she was going to lose her resolve and they would only be going through this again in a week's time, so she turned and fled out the kitchen

100

door. He and Probity, salivating on Tommy's bare feet, watched as their mistress jogged down School House Lane toward the Old Railroad Spa for whatever solace or distraction the red-eye aerobic-step class might provide.

"You okay?" Dicie asked as Wyn joined the dozen other aerobic animals—mostly of the younger winter women ilk—prepared to give their bodies and souls to Patty Batista for the next sixty minutes.

"Is this a coffee klatch or you here to work?" Patty shouted, obviating the need for Wyn to answer Dicie, whose New Wave obstetrician encouraged exercise. As the rock sound of "Have Mercy" reverberated through the not insignificant stereo system Patty had had installed, Wyn, catching a glimpse of concern in Dicie's memorable green eyes, wondered what had happened to her own famous poker face. And then she wondered aloud what she was going to do next.

"Tai chi, dear," Charlotte Cherry, the new chair of the Presbyterian Women's Club, advised. "We do step aerobics until we're sixty and then we switch to tai chi. Billy and I saw ninety-year-old women doing it in a Chinese park last year . . ."

"Shut up, Charlotte," Patty Batista enunciated beautifully, hitting each *t* with tremolo, "and move those sorry buns."

After class, rather than face Dicie's interested empathy, Wyn went home. She found it not unexpectedly empty, save for a bewildered Probity. She showered, changed into an all-purpose dress, and got the Jaguar out of the garage, noting that Tommy's motorcycle and truck were gone. I won't think about it now, Wyn told herself. Tomorrow is another day. Et cetera.

Tommy's mother, Irene, had recently realized a lifelong dream and had become the Swap 'n' Shop announcer on WWAG. She was a great success, airing music she liked between sale announcements of flatbed trucks and nearly new washer-dryers. This morning she was playing a lugubrious Peggy Lee rendition of "Am I Blue."

David A. Kaufelt

"Lordy," Wyn said, shutting off WWAG, deciding this was not going to be her day (month, year, or decade). She drove around into the New Federal parking lot, the Symposium attendees and area book lovers having taken up all Main Street spaces. Frank E. Taylor—tall, handsome, and a well-intentioned cook (his specialty: veal tonnato)—was hosting yet another event, an early morning coffee at his Antiquarian Book Store.

Wyn, occupying her mind with nonessentials, noticed Sophie's vintage Mercedes and Peter's new Miata occupying their accustomed spaces. They *could* walk, she thought, despite the fact that she also had chosen motorized transportation.

She sat in the car for a moment, not wanting to go into the New Federal's lobby. Knowing my luck, she thought, Tommy and Annie will be coming down the main stairs in wedding whites, Caitlin throwing brown rice in their wake.

Packing up her troubles in her old kit bag, as Camellia Cole would advise, wondering what the hell a kit bag was anyway, Wyn used the New Federal's never-locked rear entry, which led to a long and narrow wainscoted corridor, which in turn led to the lobby. The entry also contained richly carpeted back stairs that at one time had been the private ingress to the late mayor's spacious, high-tech apartment. It had taken up most of the mansard-roofed New Federal attic and had been a source of wonderment to that fellow's friends.

Lettie, soon after inheriting the inn, had Dickie design and oversee the creation of several suites carved out of her brother's former "aerie." Dickie had "done" the new suites in what he called Billy Baldwin Victoriana ("tons of leopard-skin throw pillows").

Keny Blue had demanded and been given the most lavish of the suites. Wyn ascended the steep stairway in what she assumed was the vain hope that overnight Keny had seen reason, that her Vuitton was packed and that she was ready to take the helicopter back to Manhattan, where she belonged.

She might have called first, but keeping on the go was the

prescription for the day. The image of Tommy and Annie and Caitlin strolling hand in hand through an urban wonderland was permanently acid-etched in her mind.

Wyn knocked on the door where a pink-beige rose-encumbered ceramic plaque read Suite Sue. Phineas, she thought, must be having conniption fits in decorator heaven. There was no response. Perhaps Keny was in the shower, an elaborate hydra-headed "minispa." Wyn thought about trudging downstairs to the main lobby and trying the house phone, but then she heard Tommy's voice coming from the neighboring suite's (Suite Pea) half-open door and, finding Keny's door unlatched, she escaped into Suite Sue.

Keny Blue was not in the minispa. She was in an elaborately canopied bed, nude, a thin black wire twisted around her neck, red seeping out from around its edges staining the pillows. Her trademark aquamarine barrette had been repositioned once again. It now adorned her pudenda.

Chapter

12

LATER AND SURPRISINGLY, WYN'S MOTHER, LINDA, COMMENDED HER FOR coolheadedness under fire, for strength in adversity. Her uncle Fitz—Linda's older brother and a retired New York City police commissioner—assured Wyn from his Key West vacation bungalow that she had done everything according to the letter and intent of the law.

Maybe, but she still had felt inadequate. She had not used the suite's novelty telephone (antique white with gold trim) and had only touched one item: the oversized brass key that lay on the pickled pine credenza, using it to lock the door after her. Tommy and his new women had chosen that moment to exit Suite Pea.

There was a long moment of silence in the upholstered New Federal Inn suite floor foyer finally broken by Wyn. She said hello to Tommy, to Annie, and to Caitlin. Tommy, appearing confused—one of his ploys—wanted to know if Wyn was feeling okay. Another of his ploys.

Wyn said she was feeling dandy and Tommy started talking compulsively, as he did when he was nervous. He said they were skipping the book signing at Frank E. Taylor's and were going to have a *nosh* (a new word, *nosh,* Wyn thought; how quickly Tommy learned) at the Nonesuch and then go on to the library to get seats for Sondra Confrit's lecture and would Wyn like him to save her one since seats were going to be hard to get because everyone wanted to hear what Sondra had to say about Keny Blue.

Wyn thanked Tommy for sharing all of that with her and said, no, don't bother, there were reserved seats for the executive committee. And then, feeling simultaneously light-headed and heavyhearted, she carefully walked down the main steps into the lobby. She thought she had carried that one off well enough, avoiding Annie V's you-poor-dear expression.

Wyn found Lettie turning the full charm onto a nice pair of feminist travel agents. They wore Frieda Kahlo facsimile pins on the broad collars of their plum-brown suit jackets and confessed they had recently, in the light of the movement, changed their names from Sandy and Ramona to Oak and Skye.

Watching Tommy & Co. stroll by, Tommy looking back at her with one of his quizzical expressions, Wyn thought that there was nothing like coming upon a murder victim to put one's errant lover out of mind.

It must have been quick, she hoped. That wire garrote around Keny's neck had nearly sliced through it. Wyn felt her own neck and wondered if she was going to be sick in the laps of Oak and Skye. She said, with some urgency, that she had to see Lettie immediately.

"Don't be dramatic, Wyn. Not your long suit. Oak and Skye are thinking of booking the New Federal for a women's retreat in early March. They might be interested in a petite village getaway cottage. Isn't that grand?"

"Grand," Wyn agreed, adrenaline helping to settle her tummy. "You don't mind if I use your telephone?"

Lettie bathed Oak and Skye in the warm smile that had beguiled a generation of theatergoers and then turned to Wyn.

David A. Kaufelt

"Yes, Wynsome," she said with resigned asperity. She wondered what the hell had got into Wynsome this morning. She should have been all over Oak and Skye, setting up appointments to view. "Do use my telephone. And I believe there's a bottle of tranquilizers in the desk drawer. Help yourself, I beg you."

Wyn made her way through what seemed like an acre of winter women cum Symposium attendees spiritedly putting on dispiriting outer garments. They were readying themselves to brave the chilly weather and the library's treacherous steps for the thrill of hearing the "midwife of the new sexuality" drip righteous venom over the revolution's enemies. As an added incentive, yet more finger food was to be served in the main reading room.

Several wondered aloud if Keny Blue's promised revelations were ever to come. Not bloody likely, Wyn said to herself. Standing in Lettie's claustrophobic and heavily scented office located under the stairwell that led upstairs to the suites, Wyn punched in 911. She found herself looking upward as if blood might be dripping down.

Meanwhile, Lettie had second thoughts about listening to Wyn's communication. Wynsome Lewis was not the kind of gal to have hysterics over a crooked hemline. Nor was she the kind of businessperson to cold-cock a pair of prospective fish. Lettie expertly shed herself of Oak and Skye and snared Wyn as she was leaving the office. "What's up?" Wyn told her.

Waggs Neck Harbor's newly promoted sergeant, Ray Cardinal, had answered the call from Wyn and asked a lot of questions. It was one of his jobs to protect Chief Price from the numerous and unnecessary communications he daily received from women who had nothing else to do but call for help to remove the robin's nest discovered in the air conditioner.

The truth was that Homer Price, six foot four, with skin the exact shade of the African statuettes sometimes found at area flea markets—the most beautiful man in town, Lucy Littlefield maintained—hadn't much else to do. Waggs Neck was,

106

in general, a law-abiding village aside from traffic violations, teenagers smoking grass behind the movie theater, and Saturday night brawls at the Blue Buoy.

There had been initial opposition to his appointment by local bigots, but after five years Homer Price had become an accepted figure of authority. He was known, sub rosa, as Captain Midnight.

Having experienced one village murder case, Homer Price was not keen for another. Yet he responded quickly to Wyn's clearheaded account, directing Raymond to call Hauppauge and request the crime lab techs and the coroner to be on standby. Feeling a melancholy déjà vu set in, Chief Price strode over to the hotel in his size thirteen regulation Corfam shoes.

Following Wyn's advice, he avoided the lobby and took the rear stairs, finding Wyn sitting on a lacquered Chinese chair in the suite floor foyer, pale but composed. Lettie, wearing the most expensive trouser suit in town, was with her, pacing.

Homer Price let himself into Suite Sue, closing the door after him. "What's the damage?" Lettie asked, hands on trim hips, when Homer came out again.

"You can maybe get the blood out of the mattress, Ms. Browne, but the pillows are write-offs." He and Lettie had never got on.

"I didn't mean that and you know it. Listen: I'm aware it's not 'done,' but is there any way we can move the body? I don't think that's too much to ask, do you? We can put her in that rented convertible. What difference does it make where she was killed?"

". . . as long as it wasn't in the deluxe suite at the New Federal Inn?"

"The publicity would kill me and damage the village. We are, after all, Captain, lest you forget, a tourist economy. We don't," Lettie went on, dotting her *i*'s, "want to be known as Murder Village, U.S.A., do we? The Main Street Business Association would be forever grateful and I would certainly make it worth your while."

The dialogue, Wyn knew, was from a seldom-seen film

Lettie had made some years ago, now appearing on cable networks. Homer Price did not know this and gave Lettie a look that quelled even her. He would undoubtedly have gone on to say something that he might have regretted but was distracted.

The redheaded Ray Cardinal came bounding up the stairs at that moment, excitement lighting up his appealing young face, a serious and more measured Dr. John Fenton behind him. The county coroner was otherwise occupied and had deputized Fenton to take his place.

A short time later, when Homer once again exited the suite, he asked if he might not have a private—here he looked at Lettie—word with Wyn. Lettie said that it would have to be in the afternoon as they were late for Sondra Confrit's talk. It was imperative for board members to be there.

Homer said later would be fine, after the crime scene mob had come and gone. An unbowed Lettie said, "Make certain they don't create a mess. They are not to be allowed in the lobby under any circumstances. Discretion, Captain, *s'il vous plaît.*"

A few moments later a protesting Wyn found herself propelled quickly up Main Street, Lettie's slender hand on her arm, as she thought out loud in her usual rat-a-tat style. "You'll have to make the announcement. After the talk. Let Sondra bury herself deep in the *merde.* Appear *très, très triste.* Mention an unfortunate accident. Don't say where it occurred. But, you know, after thinking it over, the publicity may do us some good. There wasn't much mess, right? So the suite will appear luxurious and unsullied on TV.

"Eventually we'll do a mystery weekend. Over Halloween. Charge the earth for Suite Sue and lead a tour through what's left of the convent . . ."

"Lettie," Wyn began as they clattered up the library steps, knowing she was sounding like her mother, not able to help herself. "Lettie, a human being has been killed. Don't you think it might be appropriate if you . . ."

"Stop," Lettie said, projecting loudly into the silence, en-

108

tering the Dome Room as Sondra Confrit was opening her Spaghetti-O of a mouth, about to speak. "Half the world—the civilized half—hated that bitch. It was a matter of time before someone knocked her off. Do go on," Lettie said to the still open-mouthed Sondra. "Sorry for the interruption. Where are the seats reserved for board members? Way over there? No, please. Don't bother. We'll sit here on these tiny folding chairs. No, you musn't. Please go on, Sondra. Do."

"Who was murdered?" Sondra asked.

"Wyn has an announcement to make right after the Q and A. Go on, Sondra. Please. We're all riveted. Aren't we?"

"What's going on, Wyn?"

"Keny Blue is dead," someone said, and Wyn wondered who had spoken before realizing it was herself.

"You don't say. By whom?"

"No one," Lettie put in, "said she was murdered."

"But she was," Sondra, who prided herself on being no-body's fool, said. "Who iced the bitch?"

Wyn said she didn't think the police knew yet.

"Well. This does add a certain spice to the soup." Sondra ran her hands through her mane of canary yellow hair, which needed a touch-up, the roots going dingy gray. "Might as well go on, don't you think? Not much we can do." There was silence in the Dome Room as Wyn exited and Sondra Confrit launched into her familiar diatribe against the enemies of sexual liberation, ending with her usual histrionic rendition of its beginnings and her own salient role.

Wyn found herself in the library's basement ladies' room, a dark and drippy place that invariably brought to mind "A Cask of Amontillado." She threw up in an appropriate vessel, washed her face, looked at herself in the cracked and blackened mirror, and wondered if she were going through what Natalie blithely termed a psychotic experience. Perhaps Keny wasn't dead at all. Perhaps it was all an elaborate practical joke staged by Caitlin Vasquez. Perhaps she should go knock on the doors of some state-funded sanatorium and beg for admittance.

She thought of a story Camellia Cole had written and read aloud during the Short Story Symposium, some years back. It had ended, "And Cordelia awoke and realized it was all a beautiful dream."

It wasn't a dream, Wyn knew, emerging from the basement and catching sight of Lucy Littlefield's rabbity face. Having heard Sondra speak many times before, Lucy had volunteered to take over the desk during what she termed Sondra's same old sermonette.

"There you are, Wyn." This was uttered in a piercing, conspiratorial whisper just loud enough to be heard over Sondra's basso profundo, echoing throughout the building. "Captain Midnight called, looking for you. You'd best call him *tout de suite.* It sounded *très serioso.*" Lucy tended to use her limited foreign vocabulary creatively during times of extreme excitement.

"I don't suppose," she asked coyly, putting her mittened hands (there was a chill in the library reception area) to her long chin, "that *you* killed Keny Blue?"

Chapter
13

❧

"YOU DIDN'T KILL HER, DID YOU, WYN?" HOMER PRICE PROPPED HIS BIG shoes on his excessively neat government-issue green metal desk and smiled. This prompted Wyn to say great minds think alike, and when he asked what the hell that meant, she told him of Lucy Littlefield's comment, which caused Homer Price to light up a White Owl cigar.

Cigar smoking was an affectation Homer had picked up from Wyn's uncle Fitz, and though she feared for her lungs, Wyn didn't object to the old-timey aroma wafting across the desk. It added humanity to an inhumane space and reminded her of Fitz, who had, in his own way, stepped in when her father died.

Homer Price missed Fitz as much as Wyn did. Waggs Neck's first black police chief and Fitz Robinson, the grizzled retired commissioner of New York City police, had become unlikely pals after a series of murders had traumatized the village two years before. Wyn, who had scorned Homer and his political ambitions then, liked him better now because, against all odds, he seemed to have a sense of humor under all that beauty and brawn. Besides, if Fitz liked him . . .

"I wish Fitz were here."

"Ditto," Homer Price said, failing in an attempt to blow a smoke ring à la Fitz. Fitz was spending his second winter in Key West, recovering from a difficult flu, fishing, finding he liked the subtropical weather, discovering that the island city denizens, while outwardly far more outrageous than anyone in Waggs Neck, provided the same kind of human comedy Fitz liked to observe. Wyn had received this pronouncement with half-closed eyes and a pinched mouth. She suspected the worst: a woman.

"I spoke to him a quarter of an hour ago," Homer admitted.

"And?"

"He suggested I bring you in."

"Why?"

"Because you found the body and because you know everyone and because you think you know everything and because you're not stupid and because it was you who more or less solved the Fat Boy murders and because, goddamnit, I need someone to talk to." Homer, exasperated, stood up and paced the low-ceilinged, cell-sized office, talking around his White Owl.

"County tells me to handle it myself, they're going berserk over a rape serialist; State won't touch a celebrity murder with a ten-foot pole. Ray's a nice kid but his longest sentence starts with *yes* and ends one word later with *sir*. The truth is I need Fitz but you'll do."

"All right," Wyn allowed in the same gracious note. "Talk to me." Homer outlined what the crime scene technicians had come up with so far—dozens of sets of fingerprints; the weapon was a wire used to hang heavy pictures and mirrors.

"The wire was embedded an inch into the victim's neck. Probably a 'crime passional,' the M.E. says."

"Keny would be glad to know she died in the heat of a moment."

"That's all it took. According to the Hauppauge boys she was sitting on the bed when the perp walked up behind her, wrapped the wire around her neck, and jerked it tight before she could react. She was then arranged as you saw her."

"The barrette was a nice touch."

Homer ignored this. "Given the fact that nearly any man or woman in the village could have chilled her, off the top of your head who do you like?"

"Do you think I could have coffee and a couple of slices of Baby's banana bread, Homer? If I don't eat something soon, I'm going to pass out."

Homer suggested calling over to the Harbor Café, which delivered, but Wyn said she had lost her taste for oily coffee and Teflon Danish and she would pay for the added expense but it had to be Baby's. Homer, trying not to grit his teeth, sent his secretary, Yolanda, that blue-and-yellow-spike-haired individualist with attitude to match, over to Baby's for refreshment.

Homer took a call from Hauppauge and Wyn used the respite to sit at Yolanda's desk and check in with Liz Lum. Liz had delegated her finger food activities for the day to Heidi so that she might take care of real estate business.

LeRoy Stein had returned her call and wanted to know if she could "take" a meeting on Tuesday morning, the subject being the watch factory condominiumization. This was another long-term LeRoy Stein project Wyn suspected would never go anywhere, especially in the current market. But LeRoy liked to waste his and her time talking about it.

"Your boyfriend from New Delhi," Liz went on, "wants to see the School House Lane house *again* first thing Wednesday morning. He's driving out and this time Dr. Singh swears on his word of honor that he's going to make a decision. I suggested he bring his wife but he said he didn't know what Shamali had to do with it. I probably shouldn't have, but I asked Dr. Singh why he was taking so long to make up his mind—this is, what, his tenth viewing?—and he said in that sweet singsong voice that he couldn't decide whether he wanted to buy the cottage because of the cottage or because of your personality. Do you have a comment on that?"

"No."

"He's great-looking."

"There's Shamali."

"Yes. To go on, Madame Rhodesia called and wanted to know what you had found out about the cottage she wants, and I'll bet dollars to doughnuts it has nothing to do with your 'personality.' "

"Rhodie called this morning?"

"Twenty-two minutes ago. I gather she skipped Sondra's talk and hadn't heard the news. I took it upon myself to inform her but there wasn't much reaction beyond tsk-tsk. The Nobles always were a warmhearted bunch."

Wyn thanked Liz as Yolanda returned with the takeout and her attitude and asked if she couldn't have her desk back as she had work to do.

Wyn said that would make a nice change and went back into Homer's smoke-infested office. She wolfed down her coffee and the banana bread while she watched the chief pick the raisins from his bread pudding and stack them in a neat pyramid. They discussed potential murderers.

"The M.E. says she died no earlier than midnight. He said he'd be more accurate once he got her body in the lab but it doesn't matter because everyone's going to have the same alibi for the wee hours in Waggs Neck: they were asleep."

"They might have been sleeping with someone who could offer corroboration."

"Yeah. Anyway, Mr. ffrench looks most likely to me, and if he was sleeping with someone, I don't want to know who. The weapon is right up his alley, so to speak. A picture wire, virtually untraceable, the kind you can buy in every hardware store up and down the East Coast. ffrench must have yards of it. He also has a nice motive, or so I hear."

"How do you hear, Homer?"

"In the usual way. Liz Lum's girl, Heidi, told her best friend, Dawn Cardinal, about the scene in the New Fed lobby, and Dawn told her mother, who told Raymond, who finally told me. He doesn't look it, but Ray Cardinal has a great nose for news."

"All that village inbreeding. What does Ray do, come in every morning and you and Vampira and he have a little gossip?"

"It's taken me a while but I have learned that there's no way I'm going to be police chief in this town if I don't tune in on a regular basis to the village hot line."

"And the village hot line says that Keny Blue humiliated Dickie ffrench publicly in the New Fed lobby, cutting off a good portion of his livelihood and his claim to fame. But, Homer, be honest: Can you see Dickie ffrench garroting Keny Blue?"

"Oh, yeah."

"Trouble is, so can I," Wyn admitted. "He was, poor thing, terribly proud of writing those awful novels, no matter how he disdained them publicly. And then he thought he and Keny were about to negotiate a new and profitable contract, one that would finally cut him in on the money she was making. It wasn't only that she was telling him there was no new contract—she did it with so many witnesses!"

"Yeah, the bitch cut off his balls and the winter women stood around chewing on them."

"Lovely visual, Homer," Wyn said, invoking her mother. "But there are other possibilities."

Homer mentioned two of them: Sondra Confrit, who saw Keny Blue as a threat to her lifework and threatened her in front of a couple hundred witnesses. Rhodesia Comfort Noble, herself threatened, and not so subtly, by the deceased with revelations now never to come. At least from Ms. Blue.

"What I don't get," Homer said, "is why Blue and Confrit were at war. Weren't they both on the side of 'giving it away'?"

"Sondra said it first and, for a long time, loudest. She thought free sex and free love were synonymous. Then Keny came along and said they had nothing to do with one another."

"Who cared?"

"They did." She stood up and stretched, thinking about

lunch and then thinking how could she be thinking about lunch after she had just put away a quarter of a pound of May Potter's banana bread, the man she loved had left her, and she had discovered a woman brutally murdered.

"Keny Blue was famous for making enemies; more are sure to surface," Homer said, bringing her attention back to the matter at hand. "What'd you think of her?"

"The funny thing is," Wyn said, one arm in the sleeve of her camel's hair coat, a torn lining impeding her way, "I liked her. She was awful but she had guts and then some. I think the human kindness gene might have gotten lost somewhere between the catatonic mother and the sex-fixated dad, but kindness isn't everything, I have learned. And whatever one thought of her books or her philosophy, she was her own woman in a way that a lot of her critics can never be. I'm sorry Keny's dead and I hate the way she was murdered. She deserved better." Wyn finished getting into her coat.

"You going to cry?" Homer wanted to know.

"Yes. But not in front of you."

" 'Men!' " Homer said, trying a falsetto and failing. "Before you have your private breakdown, you have any other ideas we should be pursuing? Hauppauge's computers are at my command."

"Well, you'd better get a list of the Symposium attendees from Jane and see if there's a famous garroter among them."

"Being done."

"Peter Robalinski's sports car was in the New Federal parking lot this morning, and though he might have left it there last night and walked home, he's a Californian, and Californians don't walk."

"He do it?" Homer asked hopefully.

"It's possible. Keny had something on him, I'm pretty sure. For an incoming Symposium director, he was especially scarce at important events where you'd think he'd be politicking his butt off. Whenever Keny appeared, he faded."

"What about Annie Vasquez?" Homer asked as Wyn was opening the thin door with the beaded-glass inset. "She and the deceased shared a landing. And who knows what else?"

"Homer, every time I think you might be borderline human, you bring me back to reality. All right, Annie and Tommy are seeing one another in the broad interpretation of the phrase; and it would be conceivable to a mind like yours that Keny, with her voracious appetite for casual sexual encounters, also 'saw' Tommy. But if you can build an eternal triangle around Tommy and Annie and Keny, all coagulating in the space of three days, I'll eat your White Owl."

The door slammed with such force that Homer Price feared for the inset glass.

Chapter

14

❧

"YOU MAY FIND IT IN YOUR HEART TO DISAPPOINT ALL THOSE WOMEN," Rhodesia was saying, presiding over a hastily convened executive committee luncheon meeting in the Symposium's Washington Street office. "But I cannot."

She was wearing an ice-blue cashmere trouser suit with a turban to match. Lettie had to admit that Rhodie looked splendid, though Dolly said she appeared too Lana Turner-ish for her taste. Wyn was more interested in the argument Rhodie seemed to be having with herself. No one had proposed canceling the remainder of the Symposium.

"Besides, there's only two major events to go," Jane, the voice of reason, put in. She looked healthy for a Littlefield, aglow with a curious inner well-being. Passing out Eden Café homemade processed turkey sandwiches on Miracle Whipped white bread, Jane seemed, well, maternal. (No, Wyn—still in denial—said to herself. I refuse to believe this.)

"Annie Vasquez's reading should be calming and noncontroversial," Jane went on, not looking at Wyn. Everyone by this time was well aware of Tommy's new interest. "Tomorrow's panel is another matter."

There was a moment's silence as the FALAS executive committee realized that the concluding Symposium main event would be shy one speaker. "We'll be fine," Peter Robalinski said, setting down his orange plastic tub of limp coleslaw. "Ms. Vasquez and Sondra can field questions with the best of them."

"And Peter has had a great deal of experience as a moderator, haven't you, dear?" Rhodie asked possessively. Peter, impressing the assemblage with his ability not to look like an idiot when pressed with such a question, gave his all-purpose, whatever-you-say-is-all-right-with-me smile.

"Don't you think, Rhodie," Ruth Cole asked, one chin in the air, the others quivering slightly, "that something must be said about Keny Blue in a formal sort of way? We can hardly ignore the fact that she died while she was under our auspices."

"You don't think we can be sued?" Dolly asked.

"I suppose we must," Rhodie allowed, ignoring Dolly. She looked down the long yellow wood Symposium conference table that also served as Jane's desk and once graced Dolly Carlson's father's dairy barn. It took up most of the constricted space in the second floor Symposium office, and Dickie ffrench, at the far end, seemed removed in more ways than one. "Dickie, since you knew and worked with the woman, don't you think it's only appropriate . . . ?"

"No, Rhodie, I do not," Dickie said decisively, adjusting his pale mauve linen cuffs, which sported a pair of links featuring the Hapsburg coat of arms. He pushed up the smoked-lensed tortoiseshell frames on his thin nose. The new contact lenses continued to give him trouble. Wyn wondered if Dickie thought it inappropriate because he had murdered Keny Blue. For a second, she found herself looking at his small, beautifully kept, capable hands.

"I assumed," Lettie put in, arranging her own hands gracefully, one atop the other, just the way she had toward the end of the curtain-raiser in her one-woman Edith Wharton show, "that you'd want to write the biography. True crime and celebrity scandal. You'd make a fortune, Dickie, not to mention the *New York Times* best-seller list. It doesn't have to be sensationalistic; it could be an in-depth study of a phenomenon of our time, sort of a Mailer-on-Marilyn thing."

Dickie, a quick study, allowed that perhaps he might say a few words about his association with Keny. After all, they had grown up together in this very village, and who knew her better than the man who wrote the books on which her reputation would stand. Or fall.

"The world could be your oyster." Lettie, Wyn thought, was laying it on thick, but Dickie, his freckled cheeks aglow with possibilities, didn't seem to notice.

"Well, then," Rhodie said, "perhaps Jane will utter a few words this afternoon about the accident and Dickie will make brief pre-panel remarks tomorrow morning about the, um, tragic loss."

The matter settled and the sandwiches disposed of, the committee dispersed, agreeing to meet later in the afternoon at the library for Annie Vasquez's reading. Dickie said he might be late; he had to put in a call to his agent.

Rhodie asked Wyn to stay on for a moment as Camellia Cole, following her sister out the door, bumped her knee on the sharp edge of the narrow davenport that took up the space in the office not commandeered by the table. Camellia, beaglelike, stopped for a moment and, pert nose in the air, sniffed several times. "I smell something exotic and unclean," she said in her eerie Madame Arcady voice. Deep down, Camellia genuinely believed she had Powers. "I smell the distinct odor of sex."

Ruth, who believed the Symposium had been too much for her sister, took her arm and led her out the door. "Camellia," she asked, "how on earth would you know?"

"Really!" Rhodie said, sitting at the head of the yellow table. "I think Camellia Cole has finally crossed over the thin

120

line between sanity and madness that she's long trod." Peter, hurriedly leaving with Jane to help set up the Dome Room for the afternoon session, kissed Rhodie's cheek.

"Dear boy." Rhodie looked after him as if she meant to say something more, changed her mind, and took off her turban, running her large hands through her expensive hair. It fell around her face, making her seem softer, more accessible. But that softness was a beautician's expertise, an illusion belied by her next words. "Now that the woman is dead," she said, lighting a mentholated cigarette, unburdening Jane's pencil jar of its contents and using it as an ashtray, "her estate may be interested in selling the cottage."

"So you've known all along that Keny owned the cottage."

"I assumed that she did. I wanted you to find definite proof, but since you couldn't, I did my own digging via my extremely competent Manhattan attorney. Well, one gets what one pays for, as Annie Kitchen likes to say. The unimaginatively named K.B. Trust was a tax dodge the late Ms. Blue had set up for herself. My mother, in a fit of rare sentiment, gave Poor Mary the cottage over forty years ago and Poor Mary must have passed it on to Keny. It doesn't matter, does it? Now that Ms. Blue is departed, do you think you're up to getting the trustees—her publisher and a couple of well-positioned men friends—to consider selling?"

"It's a little premature," Wyn said. "I doubt if the trustees would be able to move as quickly as you'd like from both moral and legal points of view." Stung by the success of Rhodie's Manhattan attorneys, Wyn wondered why she was surprised at yet more evidence of Rhodie's iron-willed determination to get what she wanted.

"I shouldn't like it stolen out from under me, Wynsome."

"It's not exactly Park Place."

"Look, if you don't want to pursue this, I can always get that Realtor with the rheumy eye—what is his name? Bradford?—over in West Sea to handle it. I'm merely asking you to make some queries, not desecrate the dead. The more information we have about the cottage, the more pressure we'll be able to exert on the trustees. I don't want to tell you your business, but it seems to me a look at the most recent title search might be appropriate."

Wyn, resisting the need to tell Rhodie to put the most recent title search up her fine-nostriled nose, agreed, but without fervor. Having left Rhodie contemplating her turban, she stood on Washington Street; the chilly breeze coming from the cove cleared her head.

For one moment she was tempted to go back upstairs and tell Rhodie, fine, use H. Harold Bradford to pursue the cottage. The commission wouldn't amount to much, but expensive trouble was already mounting.

On the other hand, she thought, her father's sunny genes getting the upper hand, it would be nice to leave the village for a couple of hours. She could avoid the sights and sounds of Annie Vasquez reading one of her exquisite short stories, Tommy and the unnatural daughter salivating in the front row of the Dome Room, the winter women oohing and aahing, taking delicious joy in the romance that was a nonpublicized bonus of the Symposium. Wyn shuddered when she thought of the waves of "discreet" sympathy that would wash over her at her next public appearance.

She made a few calls from her office, told a sympathetic but restrained Liz where she was going, and got the Jaguar out of the garage. Heading west on Lower Main, she took the turnoff to West Sea Road. It was cold and clear and sunny, the leafless trees and the brown landscape and the black macadam secondary road providing a pleasant if somewhat dour landscape. A very young Bing Crosby, singing via the tape deck, lifted her spirits with such oldies as "Please (lend a little ear to my pleas)," "Thanks (again for taking me on that trip to paradise . . .)," and that old masochistic favorite, "Prisoner of Love (. . . "too weak to break the chains that bind me . . .").

The West Sea Title Company was a boon for Wyn, who, before its recent establishment, had had to drive all the way into Riverhead for real estate information. Its offices were located in a sorry strip mall erected in the hopeful midseventies. A Disney-inspired yellow brick castle motif predominated over its facade.

The title company owner-manager was a twenty-three-year-old Waggs Neck Harbor native who insisted on addressing Wyn as Ms. Lewis, making her feel a hundred years old. Millie Rotz was as efficient and wired as her disreputable brother Jeremy, who owned the Blue Buoy Bar in the village, was sloppy and laid back.

Millie led Wyn into a small, windowless chamber where a monitor screen was aglow with what Millie assured her was the most recent title search for the property in question. It had been completed in 1980, when the property had last changed hands, Millie said, pulling at her thin brown hair, which tended to crimp and curl in unnatural patterns. Ms. Lewis's hair was always so nice and straight.

The fact that there had been a title search as late as 1980 was a surprise. Wyn had assumed that Keny had inherited the cottage when her mother died in 1970. Now it looked as if Keny had bought it from a third party.

Tantalizing as this information was, Wyn found herself distracted. The dark room was warm and soporific and she had trouble concentrating on the monitor's small yellow print. An indelible image of Tommy Handwerk was on the screen in her mind and it wouldn't go away. She felt as alone and abandoned as she ever had. Wyn, who loathed self-pity, started to cry.

Some moments later, after blowing her nose in an antique Kleenex found balled up in her pocket, she ordered herself to concentrate on the monitor. She loved reading deeds of purchase and title searches, finding them as interesting as any Dickensian novel and sometimes as bizarre. This one was no exception.

Keny Blue did—as Rhodie deduced—inherit the cottage when Poor Mary died in 1970 but almost immediately quit-claimed it to another party for a token remuneration. The new owner had been—now hold on to your bloomers, girls, Wyn thought, reading the tiny type several times to make certain she wasn't hallucinating—Peter Paul Robalinski of Pasadena, California.

Wyn opened the door and asked for the plat map book, which Millie brought to her, opened to the page Wyn wanted. According to the plat map, Keny Blue (or rather her estate) still owned the cottage.

Wyn returned to the monitor, summoned up the quitclaim deed, and held her breath, enthralled. She forgot about her troubles, using Millie's telephone. She located Peter Robalinski on the first try, at the library, but then had to convince Rupert Hale to call him to the phone.

"I didn't know you got involved in FALAS activities," Wyn said to him, distracted. Ginger Hale was notoriously unsympathetic to village goings-on and considered all local literary endeavors, other than his own, somewhere below Sylvester the Cat in intellectual relevance and content.

"Only quiet spot in this godforsaken place," Ginger said in his plaintive, telegraphic style. "Sondra's Women on Women Group have taken over the house for an impromptu wallowing in horrendously read Sappho and h.d. as a protest against Annie Vasquez's mainstream writing. Motorcycle jackets and decorative, one hopes, whips and chains abound."

Everyone, he indicated, was either attending Annie Vasquez's reading or lolling around Sondra's house, smoking filterless Lucky Strikes and using foul language. For this privileged place of relative serenity, he had agreed to man the library telephone. Implied was that he hadn't agreed to fetch people to it.

Wyn said it was important, and Ginger said, what did she think his work was, Sondra's ravings? In the end he agreed to find Peter, who, after a longish time, picked up the Dome Room extension and said engagingly, "Howdy." He listened while Wyn spoke and then he said he really didn't see how he could get away until after the reading and couldn't this be put off until the next day? He was supposed to help set up Rhodie's ballroom for the Saturday night Meet the Authors buffet.

Wyn said, no, it couldn't wait, and she would meet him in

her office in forty minutes. Peter objected, saying her office was awfully public. Wasn't there someplace where the village wouldn't have the opportunity to speculate on what cabal they were putting together. Wyn said, all right, they could meet at her house.

"May I know the subject of the meeting?" Peter asked, Rhodesia-like.

"Real estate."

Chapter

15

"THAT'S THE VEHICLE I WANT TO GO TO HEAVEN IN." PETER ROBALINSKI was staring out through the French doors that led to the garden and the driveway where the Jag was parked. "I lust after it," he said with some feeling.

"You have your Miata," Wyn said meanly.

"That pussy car? When are you going to let me drive the Jag? It's not like I don't know how."

"In the spring," Wyn said mendaciously.

Peter Robalinski reminded Wyn of the young men in her pre-Nick set in college—intellectual jocks, feminist fellow travelers, equally enthusiastic over the Bloomsbury Set and the Boston Marathon and repression in China. They had tried to seduce her softly with their sensitivity, a line Wyn easily had resisted.

She had remained an aesthetic virgin until Nick—that Rat, that muscular, black-haired campus celebrity, greedy for social status and instant gratification, about as subtle as an orangutan, sputtering recently learned Yiddishisms—had walked into her life and taken her to bed, and everything (even Jane Austen—well, maybe especially Jane Austen) had changed for her.

Nick grabbed. Peter asked softly before taking. He sat nonchalantly in the rigid ladies' chair Wyn's mother had bought on sale in another age at Sloane's, perfectly content in his relaxed California way to stare undisturbed at the automotive object of his desire.

Nick (would she ever, Wyn wondered, stop comparing all men—even that traitor, Tommy—to him?) would have been whirling around the room, lifting objects, asking the price of this, the value of that, demanding amusement and attention.

Not Peter. His muscular legs crossed, his cordovan tasseled loafers nicely shined, he looked like a racquet-ball-playing member of the Young Republicans, perfectly at home in the neglected room. Wyn didn't like him but she had to admit the guy was sexy. For a second she wondered what it would be like to make love with Peter and then asked herself if she were nuts.

"Is that a Jackson Hall?" he wanted to know. Wyn had gone into the kitchen to avoid her thoughts and to play gracious hostess—fat chance. Saying yes, it was a Jackson Hall, she wondered what the hell Tommy had done with the corkscrew (he wouldn't have taken it—not his style). Feeling helpless, she was ready to sob again, this time over Tommy's granola jar sitting forlornly in the dark refrigerator (the bulb had burned out that morning and Wyn knew she was never going to replace it) along with three bottles of Premium O'Doul's nonalcoholic brew and one of strawberry-flavored designer water. Tommy had fallen a recent victim to the recidivist health theories (i.e., nuts, excepting walnuts, and margarine out; beer in controlled amounts in) being forcefully promulgated by David Kabot in the wake of Dicie's pregnancy.

Wyn had a minifantasy in which Dicie and her soon-to-be-born baby and Annie Vasquez and Caitlin were sitting in the cheering section at the annual Waggs Neck Harbor Artists and Writers Baseball Game, watching David and Tommy and Peter play. Wyn herself was on the sidelines.

"Listen, Peter," Wyn asked, slamming the fridge door, going into the living room, "do you mind if we dispense with refreshments? Someone, probably me, stored the wine next to the hot water heater and I can't find the corkscrew and . . ."

"Don't worry about it." He gave her that chipped-tooth smile, which was, Wyn had to admit, attractive. "Since the damn Symposium got started, I've been refreshed to death." He leaned forward, leather-patched elbows on cashmere knees, and said with Dan Quayle-like sincerity, "I haven't much time, Wyn. What did you want to talk about?"

Wyn sat next to a snoozing Probity on the beloved, oversized green sofa. She had rescued it when Dolly was throwing out "everything old and dowdy" in preparation for the construction that turned Carlson House into its current incarnation as a five-star (Dolly's rating) B&B. "I told you. Real estate. What made Keny sign over her rights to her mother's cottage to you?"

Peter laughed. It was a good laugh but it wasn't as good as his smile. And he knew Wyn wasn't buying it so he stopped in mid–ha-ha and said, "I didn't kill her."

"No one said you did."

"We were at school together. You know about Cadmus College in beautiful Pasadena, California?"

"Small, private, boring, what passes for exclusive. Turns out would-be CEO's and their future wives who favor Orange County for their mini-estate home sites."

"You got it. This may take a while. You mind if I smoke?" he asked, reaching into his pocket.

"Yes."

"You have to understand the background of Cadmus College," Peter went on, unperturbed, putting his hands back on his knees. For the next quarter of an hour he regaled Wyn with the history of his school.

Charles Cadmus, a poor Pasadenan—his Greek émigré father had run a shoe repair shop—had been rejected for a scholarship by Columbia University in the 1930s on the grounds of abysmal grades. Thanks in part to World War II, Charles went on to make a fortune in the manufacture and distribution (primarily gas station dispensers and PX's) of condoms.

After the war he got even with Columbia by founding his own school of higher education. Each year he offered one full scholarship that was to be given to a resident of New York State. He had gotten it into his bovine head that Columbia had rejected him in favor of a local student.

By the mid-1960s there weren't all that many New York State residents who wanted to attend, free or otherwise, a fiercely pro-government, Episcopalian-run (Charles Cadmus was a convert from Greek Orthodoxy) liberal arts college where hemline length had been fixed in 1952 and facial hair on males—who had to wear school ties and school blazers at all times—was proscribed.

Keny Blue had seemed the perfect scholarship recipient to the Cadmus directors. Her grades and her boards were excellent, her entry essay was absolutely moving, and if her teacher recommendations were somewhat tepid, the elderly Cadmus alumnus who interviewed her in his Westchester County house gave her a glowing report. Dickie ffrench had dressed her for the part (navy blue dress with white collar, navy-and-white shoes to match, no makeup, no jeweled barrette, white gloves) and told her to keep her mouth shut.

"She would have gotten the scholarship anyway," Wyn said, explaining Sophie's interest and connection. "It must have been tough for Keny, going from one exile to another."

"She had to adhere to the dress code, but as you can imagine, she found ways around it. She scared them. She was so bright. Like sunshine being let into a long-boarded-up closet." Peter was banal yet sincere.

"They wanted to get rid of her immediately but they couldn't. Now I know why. Still, her grades were terrific and she found me, early on, to write her papers in exchange for certain favors. What's more, the local newspapers made a big deal of a New York girl winning a Cadmus scholarship and even the L.A. papers carried a feature on her. Naturally, with that mouth, she wasn't all that popular on campus, but she wormed her way onto a local TV show for a guest spot, and the next thing anyone knew, she was doing a weekly half hour devoted to the college. The Cadmus Guardians couldn't do much but twirl their fingers for four years.

"When her mother died, Keny was worried that the Guardians were going to have their big chance to get rid of her. The scholarship rules were predictably rigid and her inheriting the cottage would have disqualified her immediately. The day after she formally came into possession of the cottage, Keny quitclaimed it to me for one hundred dollars."

"And you kept it?"

"Why not? I finally got to see it when I came to Waggs Neck with Rhodie. Not much, is it? Back then, I needed money— girl trouble—and looked up Keny and offered to sell it to her. She had this trust she had set up to buy it but she wasn't exactly cordial. She said someday she was going to get back at me for making her pay for what she had given away. It's not like I hadn't paid ten years' of taxes and it's not like ten grand meant anything to her then. Right?"

Wyn ignored the invitation to condone Peter's behavior, saying she had one more question. "Why does the quitclaim deed read Keny Bleuthorn Robalinski?"

He looked away, up again at the Jackson Hall. It portrayed a pair of cherubic boys attached by what seemed an umbilical cord, standing disconsolately at the edge of a dolorous beach. "That's a cheery thing to have in your living room."

"You want to answer that last question or maybe I should ask Rhodie? As your aunt, she probably has a good idea . . ."

"All right. Keny and I were married. I was in love with Keny in a way I've never been in love with anyone else. We spent a lot of time in bed. I mean our skin was rubbed raw."

"Spare me the details, Peter."

"At the end of the first semester it looked like she might be preggers and I said, trying it out, let's get married, and she said sure. We drove out to Vegas in a Rent-A-Wreck and did it.

"Not that anyone knew, because if the Guardians had found out, Keny and I would both have been kicked out, Sophie's cousin and my dad notwithstanding. Neither of us wanted to leave Cadmus. I liked the military deferment my dad wrangled for me and Keny was determined to get her degree.

"Anyway, there was no baby and the marriage lasted right up until graduation, when Keny split, telling me she was going to Mexico for a divorce. I remember asking her why. I mean I was still in love. The only word she said to me was 'Please.'

"I went to graduate school to keep up the deferment and got a master's in education and ended up where I began, at Cadmus, teaching freshman English. All the time I thought I was divorced. The idea of marriage, until recently, didn't tempt me."

"Who is tempting you?"

"That would be telling. Anyway, I was a little nervous at seeing Keny again, and when I found she was definitely coming, I wrote her a friendly note warning her I'd be in Waggs Neck, asking her to keep what I believed was our former marriage a secret . . . like I did for her when we were at Cadmus."

"Tit for tat."

"Exactly. First thing she tells me when she shows up on Friday is that we're still married. After she left Cadmus, headed for Mexico, she found temporary love in a Houston cocktail bar, and she said she was sorry but she never did make it to Mexico."

"It's a good thing you didn't get married again," Wyn said.

"Sure is," Peter replied, unconvincingly.

"I guess now you're a rich man."

"How do you figure?"

"You're the surviving spouse. If the estate's settled in California, you get half of her assets whether you're in the will or not. In New York you'd get a third."

"Gee, I never thought of that." Peter, Wyn decided, would make a lousy actor.

He glanced pointedly at his recently acquired gold and

chrome Rolex, took another look at the Jackson Hall, shook his handsome head, and made his exit. Wyn, opening up one of the bottles of fake brew, took a swig, made a face, and mixed it with a generous portion of Wonder Health Chow in Probity's ceramic dish.

Watching Probity lap the mess up, Wyn wondered if anyone could possibly be as naive as Peter Robalinski. Despite his rubbed-raw tales, he did not seem a passionate fellow, the sort who would garrote an ex-squeeze unless she had a Jaguar in the garage.

But Keny—a dead Keny—had the wherewithal to provide him with a lot of Jaguars. And alive she had had the power to seriously damage Peter's current arrangement with Jane. Not to mention his current arrangement with Rhodie. Auntie Rhodie would assuredly not have welcomed Keny as her niece-in-law.

Perhaps Homer was wrong. Perhaps Keny had been killed not in passion, but with measured, cold-blooded forethought.

The phone disturbed these ideas. Homer Price's mellifluous voice said, "I've got some news for you."

"And I've got some news for you, too."

There was a moment's silence and then Homer Price asked Wyn if she were going to the Meet the Authors Buffet at Rhodie's. Wyn said she'd rather die young. Then Homer hesitatingly asked what she was doing about dinner and she asked if he were offering. Claire and the kids, he explained, were visiting her ailing mother in Montclair and he thought maybe he could buy Wyn a pizza and they could talk.

"The least you can do," Wyn said, arranging to meet him at La Pizzeria in a quarter of an hour, thinking it was a shame that most of the loose tongues of Waggs Neck would be wrapped around miniature meatballs, missing out on some choice potential gossip. She poured what was left of the O'Doul's into Probity's water bowl, gave that grateful dog a distraught pat on the head, and vowed that she was not going to think of Annie Vasquez's new boy toy.

Chapter
16

THE MAIN STREET BUSINESS SOCIETY (MSBS), FOR ONCE WORKING HAR-
moniously with the Waggs Neck Harbor Historical Association (WNHHA), had successfully lobbied the village board to
quietly append an anti-neon addition to the code of violations. This measure passed at a specially called board meeting, of which few members, if any, of the public had prior
notice.

For once the Preservationists (newcomers who wanted
to close the historic architectural gate after them and certain well-heeled, culturally up-to-date old-timers) and the
development-prone (longtime village residents who would
have razed Main Street to make a buck) saw eye to eye. Only
the brashest entrepreneurs, Ruth Cole and her fellow historical association members maintained, wanted to radically de-
tract from the "quaint old village atmosphere of Main Street"
with dread and modern neon.

The next village board meeting was a well-attended event.
The Municipal Building board chambers were packed, Lucy
Littlefield observed, like a fat woman in a tiny woman's dress.

133

Tuesday night was a slow television evening and the acrid scent of acrimony was in the air. After the Marjorie Main Launderette management (Mrs. Snow and her Elvis-inspired fifty-year-old son, Marco) agreed to replace its dim neon (with near-naked light bulbs), the only holdout was the fellow known as Pizza.

"Pizza" was the nom de guerre for Bobby Joe Gibbons, who hailed from West Texas and came with appropriate size (three hundred twenty-five pounds in his birthday suit) and regional accent. He cannily had his name legally changed to Pizza when he emigrated to his wife's hometown of Waggs Neck and went into the pizza pie business, not being a man of half measures. "Just one name," he had told the presiding judge. "Pizza. Like Garbo." The court had insisted he retain his last name but Pizza disregarded this injunction.

The owner-manager of the heavily neon illuminated La Pizzeria, Pizza had brought along Wyn to the board meeting to argue his case and to show that he meant "business."

Wyn, no neon lover she, made it a point to put aside personal preferences when representing clients with legal rights. She therefore argued before a rapt audience that the new law could not be retroactive, that the La Pizzeria lighting system had been in place for the past seven years and not a word had been said against it in all that time. In short, Pizza's neon was grandfathered in and she didn't see how the board had legal grounds to force him to replace it.

Rather than risk a lawsuit, the board, unsure of grandfathering laws but certain that Wyn would know what she was talking about, caved in. Pizza thereupon stood up to his full six feet three inches and loudly said to Wyn, "How much do I owe you, ma'am?"

Wyn said they could discuss it in the morning but Pizza was insistent, balancing his ledger on his thick hands. "How much, ma'am?"

Wyn, irritated at being drawn into Pizza's personal melodrama, said, "Two hundred and fifty dollars now; one twenty-five if you wait till the morning."

"I'll pay you now. Then I'm going to hire you to sue the village for all the money and aggravation this monkey shit is costing me."

Mayoress Kunze, not at all liking where this was headed, decided it was time to apply her infamous tact. Marcelled head held to one side in what she thought was a winning way, harlequin glasses charmingly askew, she asked in her most reasonable voice, "Now that you've won the argument, Mr. Pizza, why don't you do the right thing and replace your hideous neon lighting with something that would win you lots of friends? Gas jets would be lovely."

Pizza thereupon had a Rumplestiltskin-like fit, claiming anti-Texan bigotry, threatening terrible and even physical abuse to Dickie ffrench. Dickie had added oil to the flame by suggesting that Pizza move his entire establishment to the premises of the recently bankrupt WhaleBurger way out on Lower Main Street. "You could become a beacon to hungry wayfarers. You could change your name again, and more appropriately, to Moby. Or Whale."

"You little fucker," Pizza said, losing it. "I'm goin' to kill you five ways to Sunday." Raising his Brobdingnagian fist, he went for Dickie, but his domineering wife and oversized sons dragged him away. Everyone gave Dickie credit for showing spunk under fire, raising only one quizzical corner of his exquisite lips.

In any event, La Pizzeria's neon—more ghastly blue-green than ever—was ablaze as Wyn made her way through the village teenagers, a motley set. Under the unforgiving light they looked like extras in *Night of the Living Dead*. She closed her ears as best she could to the Nashville sound emanating from the low-tech jukebox and acknowledged Pizza with a determined smile. Pizza waved his ham hock of a hand without conviction, concentrating on scowling at his thirty-year-old married son, who was having a prolonged conversation with an underage siren.

Having run the gauntlet of the Saturday night pizza counter, Wyn found Mrs. Pizza (Charlotte Cherry's niece,

Rita) at her usual spot, guarding the white plastic arbor that was cleverly decorated with green plastic ivy. This was the entry to the rear dining room, "La Salle à Manger." Mrs. Pizza rarely left this site lest some adventurous front-room patron try to sit at a table reserved for those who required and were able to pay for service. The diminutive, strawberry blond Mrs. Pizza's generic hostility was legendary as was her ability to make poor Pizza and their sons quiver and quail.

"Table for one, Ms. Lewis?" she asked, looking as if she were having difficulty swallowing. She was ill disposed toward Wyn, unfairly blaming her for the inflated cost of the neon conflagration and rightfully suspecting that she starred in Pizza's lurid fantasies about her.

Wyn, who had long ago had enough of Rita Cherry and all the Pizzas, said in her mother's carriage-trade voice that she was meeting Chief of Police Price. La Salle à Manger, underlit by bug-repellent candles in colored glass jars, was as dim as the front was illuminated and Wyn took a moment to find him. Homer was sitting in a corner under a niche artfully filled with an arrangement of Chianti bottles. He was the only diner.

"*Bon appétit*," Mrs. Pizza said, giving Wyn a huge plastic menu as if it were a death notice, disappearing into the neon of the front room to tell the teen vamp taking up her eldest son's attention that it was time to eat up and get out.

"I ordered two medium pizzas," Homer said, "with everything on them. Okay by you?"

Wyn said that it was and asked the skulking, gum-cracking waitress—one of the famous Bell progeny—if she could have a beer, and the Bell girl said she guessed so.

Mouth full of first-rate pizza, sausage and pepperoni exploding delightfully on their journey through her digestive tract, Wyn asked what Homer had got.

"A line on Peter Robalinski," Homer Price said, somewhat more fastidious in his pizza-eating habits, using a knife and a fork to tame the elasticity of the mozzarella.

"Me, too," Wyn said indistinctly, wondering (without really wanting to know) what predilection toward masochism made her invariably shove oven-hot pizza down her throat. "You go first."

"The guy's not Ms. Noble's nephew," Homer said, spearing an anchovy with his fork, popping it into his mouth, chewing thoughtfully, enjoying himself. Homer was a judiciously slow eater.

"What is he, her grandpa?"

"He's her husband. They were married two months ago in Vegas in what the boys in Hauppauge said was described as 'a simple, very private candlelight ceremony.' "

"Robalinski must like Las Vegas."

"Want to explain that?"

Wyn told him the results of her title search and her recent conversation with Peter.

"I guess Robalinski's been confirmed as numero uno in the suspect department." Homer gave himself another slice, carving at it as if it were a T-bone steak.

"No hard evidence," Wyn put in, looking at the two lusty slices remaining on Homer's tray and the last twisted piece of unadorned crust on hers.

"But great circumstantial," Homer countered. "Keny Blue, discovering he's married to Rhodie—I suppose the fool told her—announces that they are still married and threatens exposure, disgrace, and hard jail time on a bigamy charge.

"Assuming this is all true—I'll get the Hauppauge boys to check it out—getting rid of Ms. Blue and her big mouth would be as good a way as any to avoid prosecution. What's more, he gets to stay on as Rhodesia Noble's secret but nicely set up husband, living just next door in the Poor Mary cottage, inheriting big time when Ms. Noble dies."

Homer had fastidiously started on his next-to-last slice when he looked up and asked, "Why do you think Ms. Noble kept the marriage secret in the first place?"

"Are you nuts, Homer?" Wyn asked, wondering if he would split his last slice with her; heartache always made her hungry. "Rhodie Noble is morbidly involved with the image she presents to the world. Which is a grand American aristocrat of the old school, socially and culturally responsible, a mature woman past menopause and above sexual desire. She has paid her dues with her all-but-forgotten first marriage. That she has now, at nearly age sixty, married a man fifteen years younger, is not something she's all that ready to advertise.

"Can you imagine what the winter women would do with such news? The arched eyebrows of triumph? Rhodie is reluctantly admired now; married to Peter Robalinski, she'd seem pathetic. And Keny, who had a long list of grievances against women like Rhodie and the Nobles in particular, wasn't about to keep it under her barrette."

"Do you think Rhodie chilled her?" Homer asked, polishing off his last bite of pizza, shaking the ice in his glass of Coke before chug-a-lugging it.

"Maybe. But at the moment I like Robalinski better. 'Neath all that anxiety to please, I get the feeling he's genuinely ruthless."

"I think I agree with you. I'm going to have Ray Cardinal bring the boy in to help with the investigation. We can always hold him on the bigamy charge."

"He's one of those men," Wyn said, "who will marry anyone. It's who he sleeps with that he's particular about."

At that moment a starched and perfectly uniformed Ray Cardinal, backlit with grandfathered neon, stood stooped under the plastic arbor, trying to adjust his pale pink eyes to the perpetual midnight of La Salle à Manger. He was looking for his commander and chief and idol; finding him tête-à-tête with Wyn Lewis gave him pause.

"What's a matter?" Homer asked, wiping tomato sauce from his face with the thin, bile green paper napkin Mrs. Pizza provided for her elite guests.

"I think we finally got us a serialist, chief," Ray said, as if that had been his lifelong goal.

"What?"

"There's been another murder. This time the killer stuck a cameo pin in her privates."

Chapter

17

AN HOUR BEFORE SHE FOUND THE BODY ON THAT MEMORABLE SATURDAY evening, Lucy Littlefield had stood on the extravagantly porched Noble house, peeking through the shuttered windows, watching the Friends of the Annual Literary Arts Symposium entertain the many women and occasional man who had come to the Symposium from near and not so far.

Lettie Browne, hair tortured into a French knot, wearing a breathtaking, formfitting matte black Galanos, was allowing Dickie ffrench—in a breathtaking, formfitting navy blue Armani—to serve her a glass of champagne. Jane, in billowy yellow chiffon, and Peter, in casual gray flannel, were moving from group to group, ensuring that all was serene. Occasionally they made eye contact as if they shared some amusing secret, which of course they did.

Ruth and Camellia Cole, in their best black dresses with the jet-beaded bodices, were talking to John Fenton (generic dark suit) and Dolly Carlson (unbecoming purple), whose attention was haphazard. Her pregnant daughter, Dicie, and Dicie's husband, David Kabot, were making a discreet and early departure through the French doors that led to the garden and then to the circular drive. Lucy hoped all was well with Dicie (in a turquoise tent dress) but assumed (correctly) that she and her exotic husband (ponytail, Gypsy earring, Hungarian officer's shirt) were simply bored.

Most of the other attendees were lining up for the extensive Lilliputian buffet (tiny meatballs, tiny Vienna sausages, tiny quiches, tiny lemon tarts) the food committee had provided for this final evening event. "A triumph," Charlotte Cherry proclaimed. Liz and Heidi Lum served from behind the buffet tables while Patty Batista and Dax Fiori worked the room with trays. An all-female string quartet—imported from Great Neck—wearing bottle-green tuxedos, was playing from a second-floor landing.

Lucy, her Zenith hearing aid turned up, could detect the strains of "Tales from the Vienna Woods" coming from inside the handsome, half-round room that took up most of the ground floor of Rhodie's house. Everyone looked peppy and excited and Lucy would have bet her eyeteeth (if she still had them) that the hot topic of the evening was Keny Blue's murder.

The temperature was moderate for February but it was still nippy, and Lucy, wanting to get out of the cold, was glad to observe Rhodie leaving the salon, crossing the foyer and entering her office. Lucy opened the ten-foot-high coffin-shaped doors. There was supposed to be a FALAS volunteer in attendance but Lucy knew her winter women, and whoever was responsible (well, irresponsible) was probably lined up at the Vienna sausage table. As the string quartet segued into "The Blue Danube," Lucy wondered if the theme of the evening was Sigmund Freud's birthplace and, if so, why she hadn't been notified so she could have dressed more harmoniously?

To add insult to injury, the cloakroom attendant was also absent (really, Lucy was going to have what to say at the next FALAS meeting). This dereliction was not, however, of real import as Lucy was loath to part with her newly acquired

Pepto Bismol pink fun fur with its extravagant raglan sleeves, matching muffler, and copious, detachable hood.

She paused at the door to Rhodie's office, scanning the pamphlets some of the publication-happy women's groups had arranged atop a blond wood console. "*You* Can Make a Difference," one of them was entitled, giving Lucy confidence. She knocked and, hearing a muffled summons, opened the door. Rhodie was seated behind her imposing desk, a single overhead light illuminating her, creating a chilling stage effect.

She wore a dark green beaded, high-collared sheath; she reminded Lucy of Madame Chiang Kai-shek and Imelda Marcos and the daughter of Fu Manchu, all rolled into one Anna Mae Wong-ish creature. She looked hard and handsome and ruthless sitting there by herself in that wintry room.

Lucy asked if she might come in and Rhodie, who tended to patronize Lucy, said by all means, how may I help you?

"I've come to plea-bargain," Lucy said, sitting in a modern steel chair that felt as if it had been modeled on the iron maiden.

"I didn't know you were accused of anything." Rhodie placed her large hands on the naked desk as if to balance herself. In the unforgiving light, Rhodie's ironed-away wrinkles and tightened jawline did not make her look so much younger as simply better preserved, mummylike.

"Actually, I've come to plead not for myself, but for two perfectly swell kids who deserve all the happiness they can get." Lucy spent a number of her hours watching the movie classics channel and had finally, in late life, come to appreciate Barbara Stanwyck's performance in *Stella Dallas*.

"Lucille," Rhodie said, "I have a serious migraine and a roomful of winter women and inquisitive strangers all hopped up on this morning's tragedy, and each and every one of them wants to talk to me about it." She put those large hands to her forehead. "What in God's name are you talking about?"

"My niece, Jane, and your nephew, Robalinski."

141

"What about them?" Rhodie said this in a dangerous voice, lighting a mentholated cigarette with a jeweled lighter Lucy had long wanted to pinch.

"They're in love."

"They're not in love, my dear dope. They're in heat. Lest it escape your notice, there's a difference."

"They want to marry, Rhodie. I heard them talking."

"Listening in on the downstairs extension?"

"No, I was behind the pantry doors just off that dear little winter porch Mother added to the house after the 1948 hurricane. Listen, Rhodie, Peter's desperately afraid that you'll cut him off . . ."

"And well he might be. He started sleeping with Jane two weeks and a day after we arrived. I didn't bring him all the way from California so he could fuck—well, that is the word of the hour, isn't it?—your spinster caretaker niece. And if this doesn't stop soon, I plan to cut Peter off in more ways than one. Now take your futile meddling and your monstrosity of a rabbit coat out of here while I try to bring myself to go say hello and good-bye to those pathetic creatures in my salon."

"I've always thought you were hard-boiled, Rhodesia," Lucy said, standing, wrapping her coat around her, and walking to the door with dignity. "Your mother was worth two of you."

"Get out."

"And for your information, Rhodesia, it isn't rabbit. It's *faux lapin*."

"Aunt Lucy," Jane said, coming into the foyer as that estimable woman exited Rhodie's office with style and grace. "Did you bring your car?"

"I did."

"Would you mind running me over to Sondra Confrit's house? She's never missed a free meal in her life and I'm afraid whoever was assigned to pick her up forgot and Sondra is—I'm guessing—in high dudgeon. She's not answering her private line, which is ominous. Would you?"

"Certainly," Lucy said, feeling protective toward her niece, who, two years before, had left her parents in a New Jersey shore town to come and care for her. That Jane had been relieved of the directorship of a New Jersey county's municipal arts center and that her hopes of marriage to a particularly low personal-injury attorney had fallen through didn't negate one fact: Jane had come to Waggs Neck—instead of accepting a curatorship at a doll museum in Troy, New York—for Lucy.

In the beginning Jane had been bored: Lucy needed less caretaking than the family supposed; winter women activities were not stimulating enough; Manhattan cultural and social opportunities were near enough to be tantalizing, far enough away to make only occasional journeys possible.

But Wyn had befriended her and Jane began to develop her own presence in the village. Rhodie, learning of Jane's past experiences, seeing "possibilities," had hired Jane over her mother's objections to be the first salaried, professional executive director in ALAS's history.

Now Rhodie had turned, but Lucy hoped that the situation might be resolved to the benefit of all concerned. Peter could take over the ALAS directorship while Jane was admirably suited to head up the new Private Art in Public Places (PAPP) movement that a group of well-heeled winter women were organizing. They could marry and breed little fund-raisers, Auntie Lucy in the background giving help, cheer, and guidance.

Jane had arrived in the village soon after Wyn had made pots of money for Lucy by selling her Swamp Road acreage to developers who never developed. Lucy's officious youngest sister, Jane's mom, was afraid Lucy was going to blow it on home-shopping TV extravagances. Well, she hadn't blown it and, except for an occasional flurry (or furry; she petted her pink fun *lapin* appreciatively), the small fortune was not only intact but had quietly grown.

The funny thing was, Lucy noted, it was now Jane who needed taking care of, and Lucy, who had come to appreciate her niece's honesty and niceness, was glad to be on tap.

The old push button-controlled De Soto with the plaid plastic upholstery was parked on Bay Street facing east. Lucy, who was an excellent driver despite her reputation, didn't do U-turns. She thus followed Bay Street to Front and then took Front north to Water and then Water west to the site of Sondra's bay-front bungalow with the unfortunate southerly view of the village parking lot.

All the lights in the one-floor board-and-batten Cape Cod (circa 1949 and still in its original colors of white with red trim) were ablaze. This seemed unlike either Sondra's or Rupert's style, both infamous penny-pinchers.

There was a good deal of excited baritone coming from the living room, accompanied by the yipping of the Hales' Jack Russells when Jane rang the bell. She tried knocking after a few moments, and when there was still no answer—only more yipping and more baritone—she and Lucy went on in to find the CNN half-hourly sports update being broadcast at full volume.

Lucy found the clicker under the last edition but one of the *Waggs Neck Chronicle* and turned the television off while Jane shouted Sondra's name several times, quite loudly. Happily, the dogs, infamous ankle biters, were closeted in a small front storeroom.

There was a long silence and then a muffled, masculine response (either Rupert's or Sondra's)—"Be right with you" —came from the direction of the bedrooms-studios. Sondra had enticed Ginger away from his first wife (a jolly nonfeminist) with the promise of his own space. True to her word, she had added on a pair of small flat-roofed wings to the waterfront side of the property, one housing Rupert's bedroom-studio, the other, hers.

Moments later, Rupert Hale, bowing his head so as not to hit the overhang, came through the low-ceilinged corridor into the large all-purpose living room, wearing a belted sateen smoking jacket, a briar in his thin mouth. He seemed to be playing a rare role, that of the gracious host.

"What a good-looking coat that is," he said to Lucy with sincerity. "What can I do for you, ladies?"

144

"We were expecting you and Sondra at the Saturday buffet and when you didn't turn up . . ." Jane began.

"Shut up, Sweet Face and Marius." This to the dogs, who, surprisingly, did. "Sondra went along without me. I'm this close to finishing *Deuteronomy* and for once she took pity and gave me the night off."

"When did she leave?" Jane asked as Lucy studied a series of arty black-and-white photos of the beach displayed in the dark hall, losing interest when she found they were by Sondra. Lucy didn't care for Sondra, who had once pointed her out as "another victim of the revolution."

"Truth is, I haven't the foggiest. When her gal pals arrived for the poetry reading this afternoon, I took food and drink and holed up in my hideaway. Been there ever since. Actually, I did take a walk along the beach with the dogs about an hour ago, but I used my own door. It's really marvelous having one's own space. Almost like living alone."

"You didn't hear the TV?"

"Didn't you know? I've been soundproofed. If I hadn't stopped typing at that moment, I wouldn't have heard you shouting down the house. Lovely pipes you have, Lucy."

"Sondra hasn't turned up at the buffet," Jane said worriedly. "I wonder where she is."

"She may be cavorting on the beach in a newfound spirit of leather-bound freedom with a gaggle of feminist poets," Ginger said, puffing on his pipe. "Or she may have intended to walk and stopped in at the Eden Café. What difference does it make?"

"None," Jane said, irritated. "I only wanted to make certain you and Sondra got to the buffet if you wanted to. And since you don't . . ." She looked around for her aunt, who was standing at the end of the corridor in front of the hollow-core door that led to Sondra's suite.

"Or she may be in her room working," Lucy said, taking up where Rupert left off, uncannily imitating his uneven tenor. "Or, she may be merely taking a snooze." Whereupon Lucy opened Sondra's door, froze, and let out a hushed, "Dear Lord."

Jane and Rupert rushed over to her and would have entered the bedroom if Lucy hadn't thrown her thin fun-fur–upholstered arm across the entry. "No one is allowed in until the police arrive." At least she knew that much from years of watching Miss Marple.

Aunt and niece stood at the door looking at the unpretty sight of Sondra Confrit lying on her bed wearing only what appeared to be a pair of necklaces—one a thick ring of wire, the other an uneven choker of blood. A cameo pin, not nearly large enough, adorned her pudenda.

"Dear Lord," Lucy said again, fearing that if she took her eyes away from the bed, if she closed them even for a moment, she might fall down. "As awful as she was, Sondra didn't deserve this."

"Ginger," Jane asked, forgetting, calling Rupert by his *nom de village* in the heat of the moment, her mind a battlefield of conflicting impulses. "Are you calling the police?"

There was no answer, and Jane, putting her arms around her aunt, who felt frail, closed the bedroom door and led Lucy to one of the Lawson sofas in the living room. It was already occupied. Ginger Hale was on it, full length, having trouble breathing, large tears running down his face, the yappy Sweet Face in his arms, the moaning Marius at his feet.

Leaving Lucy curled up on the matching sofa, Jane—resisting the temptation to dim the lights and join her—found the telephone in the sad galley kitchen and dialed 911.

Chapter

18

⚡

SONDRA CONFRIT'S HOUSE, BEHIND ITS YELLOW POLICE BARRIER TAPES, looked bleaker than ever: a plastic cottage in a yard-sale toy set. Neither the underlandscaped lot nor the overcast light of the windy, chilling morning helped. Overhead, clouds were moving inland at a fast clip and the bay waters in the background were alive and angry, whitecaps speeding toward the pebble beach like marauders intent on serious damage.

The green crime scene van with its team of tweezer-wielding technologists was pulling out of the muddy driveway as Wyn, in her polo coat, Probity at her heels, walked up to the house. Homer had called her half an hour ago and told her to come on over. He had spent the night with the crime lab techs, carefully observing them taking hair samples from the bedroom carpet, depositing bloody bed linen in plastic bags. Homer, who once thought textbooks and instructors had taught him all there was to know, had become painfully aware that he had a lot to learn about murder.

His superiors, closing in on the politically volatile up-island rapist/murderer, called to tell him he had a couple of days to

147

"wrap it up before the shit hits the fan and we send in our people." Homer, who had licked a habit of grinding his teeth with autohypnosis, regressed now.

"You brought a damned dog to the scene of a murder?" he asked, opening the storm door for Wyn. He appeared as starched and alert as if he had enjoyed his usual eight hours of z's and a plateful of Eggo waffles and low-fat Canadian bacon.

"I wasn't exactly concentrating on murder scene etiquette when you invited me to join you." Wyn turned and told Probity to chill out. Then she entered Sondra's house, handing Homer a brown bag from Baby's that contained two extra-large coffees and two still warm chocolate croissants.

"Where's Sweet Face and Marius?" she asked, not missing the yipping and moaning.

"In with Ginger, writing the great American dog novel."

Like other houses Wyn knew in which violent deaths had taken place, Sondra Confrit's had a meat freezer atmosphere all its own. The inadequate, afterthought (it had originally been a summerhouse) baseboard heating system was giving its all but the chill in that long, crowded "great" room had nothing to do with a lack of electricity.

Homer, sensitive to his environment, walked quietly across the unraveling yellowish rag rug to the brown laminate counter that was supposed to visually separate the living/dining area from the kitchen. He placed the now dripping brown bag on it, gingerly removed the coffees and croissants, and handed Wyn hers. Biting into his croissant, he looked up sharply at Wyn. "What the hell's in this damn thing?"

"Chocolate."

"Jesus. Chocolates for breakfast?"

"That was the title of a silly novel my father liked. He thought it decadent and divine," Wyn said. She looked at Homer and found him looking expectantly at her. "All right. I brought Probity because I was feeling alone and spooked and wanted company."

"What am I, chopped liver?"

Wyn smiled for the first time in two days, Homer having used an expression her ex-husband might have, attempting to amuse. Am I beginning to really enjoy being with Captain Midnight? she asked herself, surprised. She turned away from the sight of Homer Price's concerned eyes and the cramped galley kitchen with its avocado-green Sears bottom-of-the-line appliances. The fridge was covered with magnet-attached notices, postcards, and stick-on reminder notes.

She looked at the living room with its matching sofas and earnest posters pushing Pro-Choice and the ERA. It all seemed as mean and unforgiving as a brand-new girdle.

"You okay, Wyn?" Homer asked, and Wyn thought one found sensitivity and maybe comfort in the strangest places.

"No," she said, sitting on the sofa, setting her coffee on a particularly ugly maple coffee table. "I am not okay. As you and every single Waggs Necker who might be interested is aware, I've been dumped by Handwerk in favor of the near-perfect Annie Vasquez."

"All you have to do," Homer said, joining her, "is crook your little finger and he'll come crawling back."

Homer's ladies' magazine imagery made her smile despite the tears that were beginning to form in her remarkable gray-white eyes. "Thank you, Ann Landers," she said, turning away, searching in her pockets, and finding the big blue-bordered man's handkerchief she sometimes remembered to carry. She had bought it in those early days after Nick had left her and she had found herself involuntarily crying in the downtown A train and over solitary coffee-shop-counter lunches. Tuna on rye toast still made her want to weep.

"How I hate feeling sorry for myself," she said. "It's so humiliating." It was then that Homer touched her for the first time. They had been careful to avoid contact. Wyn, because she wasn't a toucher to start with and she hadn't liked Homer all that much anyway. Homer, because big black men did not touch white women, affectionately or otherwise.

Still, he put his huge paw on her shoulder. "I'm sorry you're hurting," he said. Wyn, who was on the cusp of getting her tears under control, burst out into a long, relieving howl, holding on to Homer's big, scrupulously manicured hand as she cried it out.

A tap-tap-tapping from the rear of the house caught her attention as she mopped up the last of her tears and Homer retrieved his hand. "What's that?" Wyn asked, stuffing her handkerchief back into her pocket, welcoming the distraction. "Edgar Allan's raven haunting the bedrooms?"

"Rupert is finishing his masterpiece."

"Man of infinite delicacy," Wyn said, looking at Homer, thinking if she was going to cry in front of a man, it might as well be him.

"He says it's the least he can do, considering the fact that it's dedicated to Sondra."

"Her name will live on in infamy. Why am I here, Homer?" Wyn asked, resorting to her usual cut-and-dried delivery.

"I sent Ray home to catch some crib time—he should be back any minute—and I thought you might want to see the scene of the crime."

"Do I have to?"

"Yes." He led her to Sondra's suite. Her body, of course, was long gone and so were the bloodied pillows and sheets. But there was a deep red-brown scar on the mattress where her garroted neck had lain and the room reeked of body and chemical odors. Wyn wondered if she was going to bring up the chocolate croissant she had recently downed.

Homer, still munching on his, described for her the position and state of Sondra's body when Lucy Littlefield had found her. "A cameo pin?" Wyn asked as she led the way back to the davenport. "That seems a most unlikely send-off for Sondra. In fact, her death seems most unlikely. You'd think she'd choke on a roast beef sandwich or a chicken bone." She looked back down the hall. "Didn't Rupert hear anything?"

"You kidding? Man was deep in his opus. Only listens to his 'inner voice echoing around the wellspring of his being.'" He hesitated for a moment, uncharacteristically. "She wasn't all that beloved, was she?"

"Homer, son, allow me to let you in on a home truth: it's okay to speak ill of the dead. Sondra Confrit was a universally hated, bitter, bitter bitch. However, she'll go down in the history books, and not as Ginger's second wife but as one of the original architects of the sexual freedom movement. Though it's not easy to imagine her as a flower child, she set out the plan and the execution way back in the sixties. If it weren't for her, there probably wouldn't have been a Keny Blue.

"Sondra Confrit gave a great many women courage and advice and showed them the way to get more out of life. That she was a penurious, pretentious, frustrated, complaining harridan doesn't really signify."

They sat quietly for a moment, thinking one didn't have to be good to be an influence for the good. Finally Wyn said, "You don't suppose we have a serial garrote murderer preying on famous liberated bitches, do you?"

"No," Homer said, walking over to the thin front door, reinforced by the metal storm door, which was missing an important pane of glass. He let in a bleary-eyed but beautifully barbered Ray Cardinal, his maroon hair sticking straight up, his pink jaw suffering recently inflicted razor burn. "I think—emphasis on *think*—that whoever killed Keny Blue killed Sondra Confrit because she knew something. Ms. Confrit wouldn't be above using that something for her own advantage."

"No, she wouldn't," Wyn agreed, getting up, pulling her coat around her, saying hi to Raymond, looking at Homer for a long moment. "What are you going to do?"

"I'm going to have Robalinski brought in to help with inquiries." In the background, Ginger Hale could be heard typing away at his usual fifteen words per minute.

Wyn left while Homer was giving Raymond instructions to find Robalinski. He was supposed to be conducting one of the Symposium's several concurrent Sunday morning architectural walking tours, half of which began and ended at the library, the other half at Carlson House.

Wyn, wondering what the winter women and the other Symposium attendees would make of this latest development, gathered up Probity, who was investigating what was probably a dead bird on the bay shore. The wind at their backs, they walked across Water Street to School House Lane, Wyn wanting to avoid the Sunday morning *New York Times* enthusiasts at Washington and Main. Selma Eden, the only Sunday morning purveyor of the *Times* in the village, steadfastly refused to order more than twenty copies, fifteen of which were reserved for her "regulars." Long ago Wyn had decided not to have to court Selma's goodwill and had hers delivered.

Probity, anxious to explore the slim possibilities of the village park, led the way. Wyn gave her a few minutes to go after the squirrels, not wanting to think about what would happen if a squirrel ever turned on Miss Probity. They continued down School House Lane, ignoring the group of Symposium supporters standing on the steps of the library waiting for the next walking tour to take off. The women looked like winter birds in their sensible coats, chirping away excitedly at one another.

Wyn wondered if they knew of the latest murder and told herself to get real, what the hell did she think they were chirping about? She also wondered when the media would get hip to the possibilities of two celebrated sexual liberationists offed in as many days at a Symposium dedicated to feminist writings.

She continued on to her home. Probity, nose to the pavement looking for odd edibles, was nearly run over crossing Lower Main by a CNN van. The media had arrived.

The house was cold, Wyn having neglected to turn up the thermostat to its daytime reading when she left. That had been Tommy's job. She did so now, giving Probity her health food breakfast, sitting on Maggie Carlson's old green sofa in her comforting old coat. She looked at the uncanny Jackson Hall painting, refusing to think about the emptiness of her house (and life), concentrating on the murders.

Robalinski had a solid motive when it came to doing away

with Keny Blue. And if Sondra had found him leaving Keny's suite and was blackmailing him in some way (not beyond Sondra), then he had an equally strong motive for getting rid of the Mother of Sexual Liberation.

What's more, the modus operandi smacked of California and B movies, and it even seemed possible that Sondra had invited him into her boudoir.

It was all possible but was it likely? If a fabulous car had been involved, Wyn would have had no doubt. Peter just didn't seem fearless enough for the garrote. He would have shot his victims from a distance rather than gotten into a situation of intimacy, then quietly done them in with a picture wire. That took genuine guts or desperation, neither of which Peter appeared to possess.

The unwelcome thought came into her mind that Jane was fearless. A fortyish spinster who had allowed herself to get impregnated—Wyn had finally admitted to herself that Jane was with child—had to have plenty of guts.

Suppose Jane had arrived on Friday night, after the party, with the idea of asking Keny Blue to back off, to leave Peter alone, and to keep their undissolved marriage a secret until Peter might obtain a divorce. Suppose Keny had said are you out of your gourd and Jane had killed her. Suppose that Sondra had decided to confront Keny Blue again and had seen Jane leaving Keny's suite.

Stop, Wyn told herself. Unfortunately, she could imagine Jane, plodding and thorough, planning each detail right down to the sensational jewelry arrangement.

And Jane was a tasty suspect, a pregnant woman of a certain age in love for the first time in her life. She almost certainly believed Robalinski was going to marry her, and if she had found that he was already married to Keny Blue . . . well, Jane, with that pragmatic, deep, cold-blooded streak running through her, would be prepared to save her situation by dispatching La Blue. Of course, this would be pointless because Robalinski was also married to Rhodie, but then Jane wouldn't know that.

Wouldn't it be another one of life's cheap ironies if Jane had killed Keny and Sondra for naught? "This is ridiculous," Wyn said aloud, standing up, getting out of her coat, reaching for the telephone, deciding the best way to stop creating murder solutions around Jane was to ask her straight out if she was the murderer. If she did it, Wyn had no doubt that Jane would instantly and dryly own up.

But Jane was not at any of the places—library, Carlson House, Symposium office, New Federal Hotel lobby, Baby's— where Wyn had hoped she might be. She finally got through to Lucy, who said that Jane was probably leading the church walking tour and wasn't it exciting about Sondra Confrit? "This village is turning into a hotbed of crime," Lucy said with relish, and Wyn, only half listening, had another thought.

Lucy was definitely loopy. She was also fiercely attached to and protective of Jane. She read true crime exclusively and had the sort of capricious mind that would lend itself to picture wire and vaginal decoration. What's more, Lucy had arrived late for the Saturday night buffet and then had conveniently discovered Sondra's body.

Wyn didn't want Lucy, for whom she held an exasperated fondness, to be the murderer any more than she wanted Jane to be. But—in this instance her father's law-abiding child— she felt she had to alert Homer to the possibilities of Littlefield involvement. Which she did.

"Maybe the aunt and the niece worked together," Homer said, and Wyn could almost imagine that they did. "But my money's still on Robalinski. He had the best motive and he's ruthless enough. I asked Ginger Hale if he saw him yesterday afternoon and old Hale said there were people in and out of the house all day and evening but he kept himself locked in his room and only heard mumbles through the soundproofing.

"Clint over at the West Sea Hardware Emporium says he sold a bunch of wire of different widths to Robalinski when they were rehanging pictures after Rhodie had 'Little f 'redo the house.

"Anyway, that's enough circumstantial for me. I've got today and maybe tomorrow to try to produce a villain. Unless Robalinski has an airtight alibi, I'm going to charge. *If* Ray Cardinal can find him. He's checking out the walking tours now."

"Keep me posted," Wyn said, lying full length on Maggie's venerable old sofa, joined by Probity. She put her arm around the near-white dog and stared up at the ceiling, visualizing the rest of her gloomy Sunday. It wasn't pretty.

This won't do, she told herself, reaching for the telephone. Fitz's answering machine, in Key West, said he was away for the day, bone fishing. "That piece of information," Wyn told the answering machine, "is wasted, one hopes, on the local burglar."

Just when she thought she might as well go down to the office and work—her usual panacea for melancholy—she heard Tommy's truck pull into the rear driveway. A pale ray of sunshine just lit up my heart, she said to herself, hoping she didn't look as pathetic as she felt.

"Wyn," Tommy called, coming into the house through the rarely locked kitchen door, looking for her on the green sofa where he found her.

He was wearing a faded denim jacket that made his eyes seem more blue than ever. His double-layered yellow eyelashes belonged on a rich girl's doll. She recalled the words to a hymn she had especially disliked and her mother had sung with gusto: "An angel from on high."

"What's the matter, Tommy?" she asked, not moving. Clearly, from the way his cleft chin was set and his carpenter's hands were clutched, something was.

"My mom's in the hospital."

"What?" Wyn sat up.

"Rhodie Noble almost killed her."

Chapter
19

Irene Handwerk was doing so well with the morning Swap 'n' Shop that the WWAG management had given her the graveyard shift, two to four A.M. Despite the hours, this was a coveted time slot because Irene, as disc jockey, could have the engineer, who got off at six, set up whatever music she chose (Don Ho, Kay Kaiser, Emmy Lou Harris, the Loving Spoonful), then catnap on and off for two hours because this was billed as a call-in show but nobody ever did and the only commercials aired were prerecorded public service spots.

Irene, an enthusiastic woman in her fifties, vowed to change all that, but not many area listeners stayed up late, even on Saturday night. So she had to contend with the occasional drunk, calling from the Blue Buoy, asking for obscure oldies ("Too Pooped to Pop") not in the station library, the basic obscene phone call, and car phone call-ins from drivers lost in the back roads of West Sea, asking for directions. These were difficult to give when the callers didn't know where they were and couldn't identify any landmarks, though Irene, who had a middling sense of direction to begin with, tried.

156

That's my trouble, she thought, sitting in the isolated radio station, a redwood bunker located out on Swamp Road, just inside the village limits. I try everything.

Marriage (ending in divorce), motherhood (the irresistible Tommy), nursing (middle school), clerking (the bank, the five-and-dime, the health food emporium), and now disc jockeying. Her own mother, Ida, who lived contentedly in Robins' Way, one of the early town-house developments way west on Madison Street, wanted to know where it would all end. Irene said she'd just as soon not know. She was a woman who was rarely unhappy, taken, as her minister and secret lover said, by the wonder of it all, ever ready to celebrate life.

At five past four in the morning, Irene, after a particularly lonesome two hours, played her signature song (Gene Autry's lugubrious version of "Goodnight Irene"), set the alarm, donned her flame-colored army surplus parka, locked the door, stepped into the moonless night, and mounted her red and gold Honda motor scooter.

Humming her theme song ("Sometimes I live in the country, sometimes I live in the town . . ."), she two-stepped the scooter up the steep gravel drive and stopped for a moment while her eyeglasses (lollipop red frames) demisted. Donning gloves and helmet, looking up at the RKO-esque radio tower outlined in black against the navy blue night, Irene took another moment to inhale deeply, savoring the crisp, wet, clean air and the unspoiled solitude of the old asphalt road.

They're going to build a new development out here, sure as shooting, she told herself, taking one more cathartic deep breath. More imitations of a style that never was: acres of colonial white vinyl siding and Williamsburg-blue vinyl shutters. Might as well enjoy it while I can.

She found a stale, unwrapped stick of Juicy Fruit in her parka pocket—Tommy had borrowed it last, that bad boy—and stuck it in her mouth, chewing contemplatively. One of her fondest hopes was that Wyn would marry Tommy and they would produce a bundle (well, a pair) of platinum-haired children. Dear Jesus, they would be so beautiful.

Sighing—of course she knew of Tommy's defection—Irene revved up the Honda, put it in gear, and took the curve slowly. It was when she hit the top of the rise that she abruptly swallowed the wad of Juicy Fruit. For weaving its way up the center of Swamp Road was a behemoth of a car, its brights on, blinding Irene. Her sense of self-preservation warned her that she couldn't continue going down the hill if that car was coming up, because, sure as shit (Irene leaned toward the vernacular in times of stress), she would be goners.

She managed to steer the scooter off to the right as the out-of-control car sped up the road, going from side to side, hitting the rear tire of the scooter, propelling Irene and Honda into the air. The scooter was demolished as it hit one of the thicker pine trees. Irene, luckier, landed in the muck that made up much of the former Littlefield holdings.

Meanwhile, the big Mercedes careened off the other side of the road, bringing down half a dozen reedy, third-growth pine trees before it stopped, windshield cracking, horn ablast.

Luckily, Dax Fiori and Heidi Lum came along in Dax's Toyota truck a few moments later, having had a romantic, intensely physical hour at the end of Swamp Road where it met Waggs Neck Bay. Heidi, as competent as her mother, sent Dax to rouse whatever policeman was on duty and to call for an ambulance. "I knew I should have gotten a mobile phone," Dax said, himself immobile for the moment, while Heidi went and pulled the driver off the Mercedes horn.

"Would you please haul, Dax?" Heidi said, in that moment seeing—in the Toyota headlights—Irene and her twisted scooter on the far side of the road. She told Dax to toss her his flashlight. He did so as he sped away. Fearless Heidi stepped into the swamp, frightening a number of nocturnal creatures, and turned Irene over. Her cute red glasses were shattered, her helmet was dented, there was blood on her face, and her left arm looked like one branch of a swastika. But she was breathing.

"Heidi?" she asked tentatively, peering nearsightedly into her rescuer's flashlight-illuminated face.

"You okay, Mrs. Handwerk?"

"I don't know. I can't seem to move."

"You're not supposed to. Dax is on the way with an ambulance." Heidi hoped. Dax was easily distracted.

"Was the other driver hurt?"

"Probably, but she's alive."

"That's a blessing," Irene said, and Heidi rolled her eyes, knowing how she would feel in Irene's wet place about the driver who ran her off the road. "A tourist?"

"An accidental tourist. Rhodesia Comfort Noble. You ought to make big bucks out of this one, Mrs. H."

Irene passed out as the siren of the West Sea Hospital ambulance made itself known, waking a number of village households as it sped across Main Street, leaving alarm and curiosity in its path.

"They got Robalinski," Homer Price said, returning from the public phone, gulping the coffee he had purchased in the odoriferous (Wyn maintained it was the smell of the staff doctors burning excess money) West Sea Hospital cafeteria. He had picked her up a half hour before and driven her in his official car, siren ablaze, to the hospital, thus fulfilling one of Wyn's banal childhood dreams.

"I always wanted to ride in a patrol car with the siren going," she admitted.

"So did I," Homer said.

It was seven o'clock on Monday morning and they were sitting on Naugahyde chairs in a narrow, windowless third-floor anteroom, eyes half closed in defense against the strident fluorescents bouncing off all the reflective surfaces. "They stopped him at the Throggs Neck Bridge." Homer paused and Wyn looked up. "He was in your Jaguar."

"What?"

"Seems he traded his Miata for your Jag. The Miata's in your garage. Don't worry. Your car's fine."

"I don't need this, Homer."

"I know you don't, Wyn."

"When do I get it back?"

"You can pick it up in a couple of days. They got it in the police compound. The guy who runs it is a real motor head and he promised me, on his Irish mother's heart, that no one would touch it. He's already got the cover out of the trunk and put it over it . . ."

"Homer, would you please take me out to the beach, shoot me through what's left of my little dried stomped-on apricot of a heart, and then push my body out to sea?" Homer looked at her sympathetically as Wyn stared up into the fluorescence, wondering what heinous crime she had committed in a past life that would cause her to deserve this particular reincarnation.

"Has he confessed to anything besides car theft?" Wyn wanted to know, watching a pair of cheerful, chatting nurses guide a patient-laden gurney toward the operating theater.

"He wants a lawyer. He asked for you . . ."

"Can the victim represent the criminal in a court of law? That's an interest point to moot about."

". . . I said you didn't do criminal law and he said he didn't care, but then a faxed message arrived from a New York attorney announcing he was representing Robalinski and would arrive by noon. Ms. Noble's evidently not too messed up to use the phone."

"John Fenton won't let you see her?"

"He allows as how I may talk to her this afternoon, with *her* attorney present. A reckless-driving charge is topic A, but I have a few questions about Robalinski she might be able to clear up."

There was a shadow in the doorway and Wyn looked up to see Tommy. "Mom's okay," he said. "Doc Fenton wants her to stay in the hospital for a day or two and then she's going home." There was a moment's unhappy silence. Homer made noises about getting another cup of coffee but Wyn told him he didn't have to, that she was going to look in on Irene.

"I'm going to the city for a while," Tommy said.

"How nice for you, dear."

"I'll call."

Wyn stood up and, moving around Tommy, stepped out into the hall. "Don't bother. Ex-husbands' and ex-lovers' telephone communications are two delights I can easily live without."

"Wyn . . ." Tommy said, but she was already halfway down the corridor. He looked at an acutely embarrassed Homer Price, who had stood up, his handsome head grazing the fluorescent fixtures. "I guess I'm screwing up again," Tommy said to him.

"Tommy," Homer Price said, "if that's a question, I sure don't know the answer."

"A broken arm, multiple contusions—whatever they are—but the woman's indomitable, her spirit undaunted." Lucy Littlefield was saying this to Wyn from her perch on the edge of Irene Handwerk's hospital bed in the tiny private room Irene had lucked into. There was one window, which looked out over the brown pine woods that separated Waggs Neck from West Sea.

"Irene's high as a kite," Lucy was going on. "Whatever they gave her was a trip to the moon on gossamer wings. Look at her. Having the time of her life."

Irene Handwerk lay in the hospital bed, head slightly elevated, beatific smile on her appealing face, her faded blue eyes wide open, her hands grasping the hospital sheets. Wyn was reminded of Probity after a long day.

"Ruth and Camellia have come and gone"—Lucy pointed to a basket of somewhat bruised fruit—"and are busy arranging things. Providing Doc Fenton says it's cool, Reverend Bob's coming to fetch Irene tomorrow in the Methodist Lincoln and take her home. Ruth is renting a hospital bed from our mayoress's sick-room furniture department and Camellia says she's got Dehlia Bell to move in with Irene and look after her for a while. Though one can't help wondering who is going to look after Dehlia Bell—she has inherited her father's sad propensities—but that's not my problem.

"I am going to provide meals. I'm not going to cook, mind you, but I don't mind fetching tidbits from Baby's and the Eden and otherwise keeping Irene amused. We'll watch the shopping channel together. Now that she's going to be a rich woman, there's no reason why she can't sign up, and the great thing is, I get a ten-dollar credit when she does."

"How did Irene so suddenly become a rich woman?" Wyn wanted to know, taking a green ersatz leather and chrome chair and sitting next to Irene, who reached for her hand.

"Rhodie's going to have to buy her a car—don't you love that new midsized Lexus?—and pay for her hospital bills and give her some sort of settlement, don't you think? Otherwise we'll get you to sue the pants off her. And then there's bound to be insurance money and disability payments . . . I tell you, Wyn, it's an ill wind that blows . . ."

"Rhodie's generosity may not extend to a new Lexus."

"Well, you can't say anything bad about the Mazda 929 either . . ."

"As it was all my fault, I intend to be generous," Rhodie herself said. She was standing in the doorway, head held high, looking poised and agreeable. She wore her mother's old sable coat and a dark fur turban that hid her hair.

Annie Kitchen, who had brought along the turban and the coat, was downstairs in the labyrinthine parking lot, storing Rhodie's crocodile overnight case in the battered Kitchen station wagon. She had already decided to charge Rhodie mileage, but now she was in a quandary, wondering how much.

It was difficult for Wyn to believe that the poised woman who stood in the hospital corridor had been so out of control not so many hours before. "How is Mrs. Handwerk?" Rhodie asked.

Irene, hearing her name, mentally staggered back into the current time frame, staring up at Rhodie with wonder and delight. "You know," Irene said, "I thought you were dead."

"I'm not." Rhodie sailed into the room like a dowager attending a garden party. She took Irene's hand in her gloved one. "I am sorry and I intend to make amends."

"Imagine," Irene said, looking up at Rhodie. "Keny Blue wasn't murdered after all. Take it from me, you never looked better, Keny." Irene closed her eyes and sank back into whatever drugged dream she was enjoying, leaving the three women in a momentary tableau vivant.

"I told you," Lucy Littlefield said, getting off the bed, straightening the bedclothes and her own baby pink wool-like dress. "They've got her drugged to the tits."

Chapter

20

❧

WYN RODE HOME IN THE OVERHEATED COMFORT OF LUCY'S DE SOTO, fearing she would always remember Tommy standing in the mean hospital reception room, looking as lost as any fictive runaway boy. She knew if she had said something clever— like "Don't leave me"—he wouldn't have. But she didn't want him not to go because she asked him not to go. She wanted him not to go because *he* didn't want to go.

Oh, well, dumped again, she thought, working hard at not indulging herself in the guilty gratification that comes with self-pity, resisting the exquisite temptation to compile a laundry list of what-ifs.

Lucy was driving slowly and talking nonstop, as was her wont. Wyn only half listened, catching phrases here and there. "And you'd think," Lucy was going on, stopping to allow a black-and-white cat to dash across West Sea Road, earning the enmity of the truck driver behind her, "that Ruth would have something to report." The truck driver, fingers and epithets flying, maneuvered his enormous truck around Lucy's car.

"What with her father's German telescope and all the night action that's been going on . . ."

Despite her resolves, Wyn was visualizing Tommy and Annie and Caitlin, cozy in Tommy's vintage Chevy truck, merrily driving to Greenwich Village together. They're probably singing folk songs, she thought meanly.

At home there was nothing in the kitchen to eat or drink and she didn't have the desire to face May Potter at Baby's or Selma at the Eden or even Liz at the office. She plopped herself down on the green sofa and stared idly out through the French doors, willing her mind to go blank. The view didn't help, the winter garden looking like the setting for one of the less lively Russian plays, the Monday morning sky threatening snow, the ground as barren as a moonscape.

The garage doors were open and she could just see the tail of the Miata. Ray Cardinal, Homer Ray had told her, had found gloves and wire in the glove compartment. Good-bye, Peter.

Besides wanting her car back—why would they have to keep it for two days except for idiotic bureaucratic reasons?—she wondered if anyone could really feature a killer trading up before making his getaway.

Depressed further, she turned her gaze—as she invariably did when she was alone in the living room—on Jackson Hall's surreal study in alienation. Out of her unconscious came the thought that it was funny (odd, not ha-ha) that Irene had mistaken Rhodesia for, of all people, Keny Blue. Then, as microscopic red-hot wires in her mind connected, she experienced a small electric charge that got her out of the sofa and up the stairs to the room that had always been called the office.

Painted dark red with a pale ceiling and book-lined walls, the room had been furnished by Wyn's father with a worn Chinese carpet and an oversized rolltop desk. Its pair of windows still had the original late-nineteenth-century wavy glass, which provided a slightly distorted yet pleasing view of the eaved cottages of Madison Street.

David A. Kaufelt

Oblivious of this vista, Wyn went directly to the bookshelves containing her father's journals. He had painstakingly filled them with the photographs of village life he had taken from the time he was a boy keen on photography up to the end of his life. Also included in these albums were various news items clipped from the *Waggs Neck Chronicle* and sometimes, in Hap's own neat penmanship, personal explanations of the events pictured in his snapshots.

The collection, each volume bound in dark red leatherette and dedicated to one year, added up to a detailed if personal village history starting in 1943 (when he was eleven and had received his first hand-me-down Kodak camera) and progressing through 1970, the year of Hap's untimely death.

Wyn wondered what would have happened to Hap's hobby if he had lived past his thirty-eighth year and her own twelfth birthday; would Hap have been reduced to the portable video camera? As Wyn leafed through the pages of the volume entitled *1950,* she thought how intrusive those cameras were, allowing their owners to record everything, experience little.

In 1950, not a banner year for local news, Hap, a high school senior, had been engaged by the *Chronicle,* at two dollars a pop, to snap society news photos. Thrilled, Hap had saved every photo, rejected or accepted, including even the fuzzy ones in his collection.

An entire series had been snapped at the 1950 Symposium, then a much less elaborate event, meetings and readings all taking place on a Saturday in the library's Dome Room. The only instance of social refreshment had been one tea, held at the Noble mansion.

Wyn almost didn't recognize Sophie Comfort Noble, standing on the Dome Room stage, introducing the Symposium theme of that year, Literature of the Sea. She was about forty then, with a certain amount of embonpoint but still attractive and lively-looking in an inquisitive way.

She wore, Wyn noticed with a little shot of recognition, an

aquamarine barrette in her upswept hair. Even in the faded newspaper, Wyn knew it was *the* barrette.

Another photo showed Sophie greeting Maggie Carlson, looking like a bulldog on a tight rein, shepherding her senior high school English class up the library steps. The high school nurse, possibly because she had nothing else to do, was accompanying them on this field trip. The caption identified her as Mary LeBow, R.N.

After some rifling, Wyn found the news clipping from the society page she had been looking for. Dated February 1950, it was unsigned (Wyn suspected Maggie Carlson, pen-in-cheek), the writer evidently having to fill space and using old social comings and goings to do so.

> . . . Mrs. Noble, Waggs Neck Harbor's great patroness, returned from her second trip to Africa in time to attend the Annual Literary Arts Symposium (ALAS). Her first visit to Africa occurred during her honeymoon with her deceased husband, the war hero, General Arthur McBride Noble.
>
> On this latter trip Mrs. Noble was accompanied by several members of the Friends of the Annual Literary Arts Symposium (FALAS), including Dr. and Mrs. John Fenton, Jr. (pictured to the right of the column with their son, young John III); Mr. and Mrs. William H. Joseph (in the center of the group); and Messieurs Harry Bleuthorn, Hiram David, and Charles Wenn, three prominent village businessmen intent on engaging in a big-game expedition, which, due to extremes of weather, had to be canceled.
>
> There is some thought, Mrs. Noble reported, of using next year's Symposium as a medium for investigating African folk literature. In the meanwhile, Mrs. Noble, suffering from fatigue, will be spending the spring months in Southern California, accompanied by Mrs. Harry Bleuthorn (née Mary LeBow), taking a well-deserved leave of absence from her duties as Waggs Neck Harbor High nurse.

David A. Kaufelt

That was odd. Mary LeBow, only a few months before the unmarried school nurse, now married to Harry Bleuthorn and presumably pregnant with Keny, accompanying Sophie on a recuperative trip to California.

Wyn flipped back a few pages and found the photo of Keny's father as he was leaving for the trip to Africa. He was pictured with the other two "prominent businessmen" standing on the Noble mansion porch, smiling dutifully. Crew-cut hair and narrow lapels made them resemble contemporary CIA men. Harry was handsome in a meaty sort of way, coming off more the professional sportsman than the CPA that he was.

Coincidentally, in the same 1950 volume, Hap, as he sometimes did, had misfiled a photo and clipping from a 1952 *New York Herald Tribune* society page, picturing Rhodesia in her debut dress. She was handsome as an Edith Wharton heroine, her sad eyes reminding Wyn of Lily Bart and her bridge debts.

None of it quite made sense and Wyn's frisson of a quarter of an hour before seemed to have fizzled. Early menopausal symptoms, Wyn thought, moving Probity out of her way, replacing the volume, standing up, and finding herself at eye level with her mother's collection of Waggs Neck Harbor High School yearbooks.

Linda Lewis, as principal of Waggs Neck Harbor High, had rescued a number of early yearbooks from destruction by overzealous janitors (she refused to use the euphemistic "superintendents") cleaning out the old storeroom. When the high school librarian had the gall to insist that there was no room for the yearbooks unless Mrs. Lewis wanted to toss out the *Encyclopaedia Britannica* and several editions of the Holy Bible, Linda, knowing which side the hostile PTA would take, had the yearbooks transferred to the office bookcase in her then home, where they remained.

Wyn wondered how the retentive gene her parents had in common had skipped her. And then she thought about living in her parents' house with her mother's furniture, conducting her business from her father's old Main Street office, seriously obsessed with a coat she had bought while in college, residing in the town in which she had been born. Perhaps, she thought, the gene had simply taken a new turn, not necessarily for the better.

I should move, change my geography, change my life, she told herself, taking down the blue and white plastic-wrapped 1968 Waggs Neck Harbor High School yearbook, curious to see what Keny had looked like then. She thumbed through the glossy pages of cheerleaders and football players and big-bosomed homeroom teachers, some of whom she recognized, thinking that her mother had moved to New York and her uncle Fitz had moved (it looked like) to Key West. Maybe in twenty years or so she would hear Santa Fe or Buenos Aires calling her name.

That fantasy ended when she came upon a staged photo of Dickie ffrench directing the school production of *South Pacific*. His eyebrows, Wyn thought, looked as if they had had some work.

Off to his left was a profile of the student-actress playing Bloody Mary, wearing a peculiar beehive wig and a grass skirt and brassiere. For a moment Wyn thought, irrationally, that it was Rhodesia and then realized it was Keny. No wonder Irene mistook Rhodie for Keny. They shared the same fine bone structure, aristocratic nose, and serious eyes.

Wyn skipped the rest of the "School Activities" and went to the individual photos of the graduating class. There was Keny staring straight into the camera, pancake makeup laid on with a trowel, lips pursed knowingly, heavily shadowed eyes downcast in a parody of naughtiness. Wyn laughed, thinking of the reaction that photo must have gotten. She stopped laughing when she realized that the adornment in Keny's hair was the famous aquamarine barrette.

She put the yearbook back in its place and sat down at the notebook computer she had bought and not much used. Resorting to her father's histories and her own working knowledge of village events, Wyn produced a brief chronology that read:

1950	Dec.–Jan.:	Sojourn in Africa.
	Feb.:	Harry Bleuthorn marries Mary LeBow.
		Sophie and Mary spend six months in California.
	Aug.:	Sophie and Mary return to the village, Mary with a newborn babe.

She looked at it for some moments before folding it in threes and sticking it in the pocket of the dark gray flannel jumper that came in handy for village funerals. Poor Mary the Beard, Wyn thought.

"To hell with School House Lane," Wyn said as a beseeching Probity indicated she needed to evacuate. "I've got better things to do. Anyway, you're a vegan," Wyn rationalized, letting Probity out to do whatever she felt like in the winter garden. "Your poop is biodegradable."

It was all supposition and there were a couple of missing pieces, but Wyn felt she had to talk to Homer. The Man, Yolanda said, was up-island and wouldn't be back until the next day and there was absolutely no way to reach him. "You want to speak to Sergeant Cardinal?" Yolanda asked, taking time from cracking her bubble gum into the receiver for a full frontal yawn.

Wyn said she'd wait for the Man.

She spent the rest of Monday showing a self-described "neat" couple of attorneys from Patchogue a number of houses they enthused over. They had been in Waggs Neck looking for a client who had welshed on their fee. They hadn't found her but they had discovered the charm of Waggs Neck, they said. In the end the couple said, slyly, they were going to go home and think over what they had seen. In other words, they had had nothing else to do and wanted a free house tour. Wyn cursed them roundly.

She bought a pizza from the odious Pizza, went home, scarfed it up, drank a diet Coke, hugged her dog, and thought about her troubles. Maybe Homer would bring home the Jag. Maybe she should have talked to Ray Cardinal. But they weren't hanging Peter Robalinski on the morrow. She only hoped Homer would be home early on Wednesday.

With the extraordinary number of local and major catastrophes, the fact that life in Waggs Neck Harbor was going on as usual surprised Wyn. Peter Robalinski in jail for killing Keny Blue and Sondra Confrit; Irene Handwerk in the hospital, thanks to Rhodesia Noble; Tommy in Greenwich Village, thanks to Annie Vasquez. One would have thought that just this once the denizens of the village would have changed their Wednesday morning routines.

But nothing short of nuclear attack was enough to keep the hard-core members of Patty Batista's seven A.M. red-eye aerobics class from shaking their extremities for sixty tortured minutes and then repairing to Baby's for what was considered a well-earned caloric morning pick-me-up.

May Potter served heavily buttered cinnamon toast and thick homemade hot chocolate, with a gimlet eye on her customers, who today wore workout outfits that ran the gamut from suggestive to outrageously provocative. Lucy Littlefield's fluffy pink leotard was one thing, but a very pregnant Dicie Carlson's terry-cloth zebra-print thong was really "beyond beyond." Bishie, May's pathologically shy partner, always absented herself when Patty Batista's early-morning class came in for postexercise, preshower refreshment.

"I was thinking of Bull or Bully," Dicie was saying. This was after everything that could be said, given the group sitting around the table (the subject of Tommy Handwerk was obviously verboten), had been said about current events. She added blueberry preserves to the strawberry-preserve-laden cinnamon toast she was shoveling into her perfect mouth. "But David says definitely not and I suppose one can see his point."

"Decidedly," Ruth Cole said. She and Camellia had been forced into attending class by their doctor, John Fenton, who said it was just the thing for their arthritis. They wore billowy navy blue bloomer outfits left over from long-ago school days and three times a week grimly went through what Camellia described as "the worst medicine she had ever had to swallow."

Early on, before she gave up, Patty Batista had actually called Ruth a "lard ass." And once, to Camellia's dismay, Patty had stopped the class after five minutes to ask, "Do you want a bubble butt or not?" Camellia had said not and Patty had thrown up her hands and continued with the class. She referred to the sisters as "our charming Bay Street observers."

The Coles were immune to that sort of sarcasm, engaging (in the rear corner) in their own idiosyncratic, restrained version of Patty's low-impact exercises.

It was irritating, Ruth admitted, but the indignity had worked. For the first time in a decade she could move her toes without pain and Camellia could actually get Auntie's coral and pearl ring over her index finger knuckle.

"David," Dicie said, "wants to name him Paderewski. Or worse, Ginsberg. Although Ginsberg Kabot has a certain ring to it . . ."

Wyn, sipping at her chocolate, was not thinking about names for Dicie's child. If she was right, Homer was not going to be happy. Neither were the fellows busy making him the man of the hour. She didn't suppose a political career was right for Homer anyway. He was, she was realizing, too sensitive.

"How do we know it's going to be a boy?" Lettie was asking.

"We don't. David's against testing. If it were up to him, we'd birth the little bastard ourselves. As it is, David—threatening lawsuits—bullied West Sea Hospital into allowing a midwife to be part of our birthing team. Which is going to be the size of the New York Mets when he's finished. This morning, over and above John Fenton's objections, he added a placenta expert. I really don't know what's worse: having this baby or David orchestrating the having of this baby."

"What about Jasmine, if it's a girl?" Jane suggested, not caring to discuss David or placenta. Wyn would have guessed that Jane would totally collapse under the emotional weight of Peter's arrest. On the contrary, she seemed the acme of blissful serenity, unshakable in her conviction that "this was all a terrible mistake and will right itself in time." Overnight she seemed to have been transformed from a thin, spare WASP spinster into some undefinably ethnic Mother Earth. "I've always thought Jasmine was such a romantic name."

"I fancy it myself," Dickie ffrench, the token male aerobic student, said, smiling at Jane. "The scent itself is scrumptious."

"Jasmine sounds like a one-eyed, one-legged black slave of yore to me," Dicie said. "Besides, I know we're going to have a boy. I'd prefer a girl and I think, secretly, himself would like a girl, but trust me on this—it's a boy and he's going to be as disagreeable and closet-macho as his dad."

No one at the table felt like commiserating with Dicie but everyone had a point of view about names and a great many were bandied about.

Eventually Dolly, who had heretofore kept her mouth to the grindstone, as it were (she was always a dedicated eater) said that as long as Dicie didn't name him after a geographical area—one of John Fenton's patients had recently given birth to an Idaho—she would love any name her grandchild bore.

Mother and daughter looked at one another with genuine warmth. Wyn was envious. She and her mother looked at one another only rarely, and then with cool understanding.

"How touching, Dolly," Lettie said dismissively. "I don't suppose you'd consider Phineas, Dicie. My brother left no issue and it is an amusing and interesting name . . ."

Dicie was saved from having to answer because Camellia had launched into one of her instructional, reminiscing reveries set off by Dolly's geographical remark. "Now in my day there was a vogue for naming children after countries. China and India were exceedingly popular. Sophie, of course, used Rhodesia, where she spent what she described as an idyllic honeymoon. Rhodesia *does* sound nice, though I'm not so certain about Rhodie. We must ever be mindful of diminutives, Dicie.

"We had a cousin who died young named Britannia—

rather grand, I thought—and then there was the housekeeper's boy, Alsace. No good came of him, I understand. And of course there was Keny."

"Keny?" Wyn repeated.

"You didn't know," Camellia said happily.

"Darling, who cares?" Lettie, an old friend, permitted herself to say.

"I always did think it was odd that she only used one *n*," Dickie said. "But then I assumed it was a Keny affectation. Like the one earring and the one rouged nipple."

"Really, Dickie," Dolly said.

None of this sidetracked Camellia. "Let me see. Now Keny was born a year, give or take a couple of months, after a group of FALAS members went to Kenya. Nineteen fifty, if memory serves, and it usually does. Though one can't imagine Poor Mary having been included in that trip. There was a big to-do at the time; going to Africa was quite the journey. We all thought it high extravagance, though one did yearn to go. So glamorous. Sophie had, of course, organized it, and took along a bunch of attractive people. Perhaps Harry Bleuthorn, in memory of the great adventure, named the baby. I think it's rather a lovely name. I don't suppose, Dicie . . ."

"Kenya Kabot? Not a chance in hell, darling Camellia."

"I agree, but I do go all goose-bumpy over alliterative names," Lucy Littlefield confessed. "What about Kent Kabot? Or, if you're wrong and it's a girl, Katie Kabot? Christopher Kabot is not so terrible either. Then there's always made-up names. Like Kalie. Kalie Kabot?"

Jane put her hand on her aunt's mittened hand and, whispering in her ear, wanted to know if she had remembered to take her pill that morning.

Dolly offered Percy.

"Do you really want to have a grandson named Percy?" Dickie ffrench wanted to know. "In the 'Boy Named Sue' tradition? What about Marmaduke while you're at it?"

"Father's middle name was Percy," Camellia said, looking as if she might cry.

The conversation went on, but not for Wyn. She was beginning to feel like the bride of Frankenstein: another sudden electrical connection had occurred, confirming earlier conclusions.

She wanted to talk to Homer Price badly, but even his mobile phone (the number squeezed out of Yolanda) produced only a recording saying the mobility company customer couldn't be reached at this time. She knew she should wait for Homer before taking further action, but she didn't think she was going to.

Chapter

21

Hard cheese, Wyn decided, was the theme of this particular Wednesday.

After showering and changing, she went to the office and, just in case, tried Homer again. She was told by Yolanda—who today seemed to be playing the role of the perfect and cultured receptionist—that the Man still wasn't in. "No telling when the Man will be back, Ms. Lewis." Wyn asked her to put Ray on the phone.

"I will see if I can put my finger on Sergeant Cardinal, Ms. Lewis."

Wyn, losing it for a liberating moment, told Yolanda that she had better put her finger on him or she was going to come over to the Municipal Building and rip every spiked hair out of Yolanda's oblong head.

"Ms. Lewis, maybe you should give serious thought to seeing someone." Yolanda put her on hold. Wyn slammed the receiver down on the cradle.

Just when Wyn was about to make good on her threat, the phone rang and Ray's monosyllabic baritone indicated that the chief was still in Hauppauge, participating in Peter Robalinski's formal arraignment. "Lots of press."

So Homer was really being singled out for glory. The politicos Homer reported to must have figured it was time. A current drug scandal in their office needed a distraction. An oversized and strikingly handsome village police chief—of color, yet—who had solved a sensational crime involving celebrity, money, society, and sex was exactly what the spin doctor ordered. Not that Homer was loath to oblige; he had hopes, still, that the powers that were would eventually buy him as a natural for public office.

"Our first Afro-American President," Wyn had once said to him, catching him staring solemnly up at the picture of Ronald Reagan that graced his office wall.

"Yes," Homer had said without a trace of a smile.

Wyn sighed, despite the fact that she regarded sighing as a fatal flaw. Homer, she guessed, was going to wind up the scapegoat in this particular kaflooey, doomed to village service for the next decade or two.

Without thinking much about it, Wyn pitched the framed photograph of a grinning Tommy in his volunteer fireman costume into the wastepaper basket. The sound of thin glass breaking was not as satisfying as she might have wished. She supposed someday—not soon—she was going to have to make a conciliatory gesture toward Yolanda. She permitted herself another sigh.

The snow that was turning Main Street into a Currier and Ives facsimile didn't help. Wyn was immune to Christmas card charm and the thought of sloshing through a winter wonderland of filthy snow for the next few days made her want to call her travel agent. A visual of a New York policeman doing wheelies in her Jaguar gave her a headache. Ray had said her car would be returned by Friday at the latest, but that piece of information did not help.

She sat at her desk for a few more disconsolate moments, thanking the gods for small favors: Her appointments for showings had been canceled. All she wanted was to go home, make herself a cup of instant hot chocolate, lie down on the green sofa under a mothball-redolent counterpane afghan, and feel sorry for herself.

But that wasn't her style. She was her mother's daughter as well as her father's and she had too much knowledge now to let matters wait until Homer's return.

She called John Fenton and was, miraculously, put through immediately, the snow having canceled his patients as well. She told him her theory without mentioning names. Not that she had to. Dr. John was no dummy, despite his sexual enslavement to Dolly Carlson.

Yes, it was possible, he said. There were several possibilities: the victim might have otherwise survived the fall except for the severe contusions to the head; someone might have pushed the victim down the stairs and then taken the victim's head and bashed it against the molding, just to make sure; or someone might have come upon her after the accident and then bashed her head against the molding, to make sure.

Or it might have happened as stated. His colleague, the stunningly trite county medical examiner, had told him not to go fishing for worms in a barrel of rotten apples. There would surely be more worms than he could handle and these kinds of falls had been known to cause weird injuries. "After some consideration, the M.E. and I signed the certificate indicating accidental death."

"But maybe it wasn't?" Wyn pursued.

"Maybe it wasn't."

On the case now, feeling adrenaline mixing with the caffeine in her bloodstream, she dialed the Coles' cottage with something like enthusiasm. Camellia answered. No, she was *très désolé* but Wyn could not come over as she and Ruth each had one foot out the door, on their way to the Goodwill. Mrs. Morrell was going to give them tea in that small parlor next to the salesroom.

"Least she could do," Camellia went on, "considering we're on the board." Camellia and Carol Morrell had carried on a quarter-of-a-century enmity and they weren't about to stop

178

now. "Certainly, Wynsome, that Morrell person could find an extra cup for you among the cracked and filthy china she marks up so exorbitantly. Why not meet us there? I'll warn her that you're coming."

Wyn agreed and went to talk to a grim Liz Lum about her schedule for the rest of the day. Liz's recently home-permed hair resembled a nest of rusty miniature mattress coils; plum-pink blusher highlighted one pale cheek but was absent from the other; her clenched lips were adorned with the most bloodlike of lipsticks.

This personal disarray was explained by the arrival of Heidi's father and Liz's ex-spouse, the roving electrician, Michael Lum, in town visiting his mom. He had arrived laden with inappropriate gifts for his daughter purchased from the Frederick's of Hollywood catalog and a paltry check for Liz that put but a tiny dent in his long-outstanding child support payments.

Nothing, Wyn thought, was going to alleviate the black cloud in either Liz's or her own soul. "Bastards!" Liz said, furiously consigning a paragraph on her computer monitor to oblivion as if it were the opposite sex.

Before leaving for tea at the Goodwill, Wyn made the final and most difficult telephone call of the morning, arranging a meeting in an hour's time. Standing at the realty office door in her ancient galoshes, one arm in her ancient coat, staring out at the falling snow, she made a conscious decision to try to change the mood of the day.

Wyn's long-dead maternal grandmother had been a woman chock full of bad advice based on her own uneventful, heavily fictionalized life. "When you're older, Wynie, and know the meaning of the blues," she liked to say, "your best bet is to go out and buy yourself a brand-new hat. Something divine and silly and, oh, I don't know, extravagant. Makes you feel like a new person."

Wanting very much to feel like a new person, Wyn bid poor Liz good cheer and good-bye. Leaving her old polo coat in the office, she dashed across Main Street, managing not to slide on the ice under the snow. This is a mistake, she told herself as she entered Sizzle, discovering Dicie and Lucy Littlefield in front of the revolving Swatch display. They were discussing Peter Robalinski's arrest.

"Hard to believe he's a killer," Dicie was saying, already putting him in the past tense. "I thought he was sort of hot in an older stud-muffin kind of way."

"*Au contraire*," Lucy said. "He was a very cold man. I read his palm, you know. I saw spilled blood right there between his life and success lines. Jane maintains he's innocent, but if I ever saw a less innocent man . . ."

Wyn, asked for her opinion, declined to give one and crossed her own personal Rubicon by saying those fateful words, "I've come to look for a new winter coat." Ten minutes later Wyn emerged wearing the white made-in-Taiwan "fur" anorak Dicie and Lucie, between them, had talked her into. Dicie—radiant and ripe in pregnancy—genuinely wanted to bring her friend into the nineties. "You look fresh, Wyn."

Lucy, riffling through a bin of vastly reduced spangled tennis socks, chimed in. "The spitting image of Madonna."

"You can't have it both ways," Wyn had objected, reluctantly handing over her gold MasterCard.

She mourned her camel's hair polo coat, one she had owned since her freshman year at college, purchased under the direction of her mother in the better-coat department of Lord & Taylor's.

"Why don't you give that *schmatte* to the poor people?" her ex-husband, Nick, had asked on a number of occasions. "Get yourself a decent mink. Ma will be more than happy to take you to her furrier." Wyn had demurred. Shopping furs with Audrey Meyer on Seventh Avenue would not be, Wyn knew, a day in the country. At least not in any country Wyn wished to visit.

Even Natalie, who held on to panty hose long past their prime, had likened the polo coat to a blankie. Only Tommy appreciated it. "I can see you as a college girl, running around campus in that coat and a long red and white scarf. The kind of girl I always wanted to date and never got near." He certainly wasn't near now.

Wondering how Peter Robalinski, used to being coddled, was faring in jail, Wyn trudged up Washington Street in the old black galoshes and the new anorak. Its hairy hood covered more of her head than was safe or comfortable and Wyn pushed it up out of her eyes, catching sight of herself in the Goodwill's plate-glass window. I don't look fresh, she told herself. I don't look like Madonna. I look like a giant, hairy, sight-impaired two-footed Airedale.

Ruth and Camellia Cole were sitting just behind the Goodwill shop's side-parlor street windows, resembling mannequins in a Victorian display. They were drinking tea provided by the shop's longtime volunteer managing director, as she billed herself. They beckoned for her to come in.

"How amusing," Carol Morrell said with a shrill trill of a laugh. She was known as much for her poison tongue as for her imaginary ailments. "You don't suppose it molts in summer. I don't think my allergies could stand it."

Camellia missed "Wyn's new outer garment," as Ruth would refer to it for some weeks, fixated as she was on a pair of cocker spaniel-shaped andirons she had lusted after for years. "You'd think by this time she'd lower the price," Camellia complained, shooting a furious glance at Carol Morrell, who was providing a cup (Japanese Dresden) of tea and a chair (French "provisional") for Wyn.

Mrs. Morrell's long-suffering, hypochondriacal smile was sweet with vindictive retaliation as, chipped Russell Wright teapot in one hand, she deftly reached over the khaki hopsack curtains that divided the brightly lit window display from the dim interior and daintily removed an imaginary speck of dust from the nearest spaniel.

Camellia was distracted from this gratuitous provocation by a vision of dramatic black fur, topped by a huge white fur hat, speeding down Washington Street. "Isn't that Lettitia?"

"Must be," Mrs. Morrell said dryly. "Garbo's dead."

"It looks as if she just came out of the *Chronicle* and didn't want us to know about it. Now what on earth was Lettie doing in the *Chronicle*?" Camellia asked Wyn, focusing in on her new coat. "Wyn, you're so much like your father, bless your heart. You don't care what you look like as long as you're comfy and warm."

Ruth coughed delicately, the traditional signal alerting Camellia to put a sock in it. Wyn regretted accepting the secondhand invitation to tea; she felt she should have kept moving.

But she wanted just a little more ammo for her upcoming meeting. Outside the snow was turning Washington Street into a virginal white meadow while inside the steam-heated Goodwill the conversation went on. Mrs. Morrell agreed with Camellia: One look at Peter Robalinski and you knew he was a born murderer. Not that he hadn't done the world a favor, Lord knows. Neither Keny Blue nor Sondra Confrit had been favorites of Mrs. Morrell, who held to a strict Catholic line about the procreative process.

She went on to complain of arthritic complications and to wonder what Wyn had thought of Annie Vasquez. "Splendid, no? Turned out to be the real star turn of the Symposium."

Ruth, correctly interpreting the look on Wyn's angelic face, suggested that Camellia and Mrs. Morrell retire to the latter's office so they could discuss their commerce in private. They did so, engaging in a politely bitter conversation about the possibility of trading Camellia's reputed Meissen shepherd and shepherdess flower holders for the cockers. Wyn sighed (*If I sigh one more time today, I'm going out into Washington Street and lie there until the snow plow rides over me*) and got down to her own business.

Had Ruth, by any chance, been indulging in her nocturnal stargazing hobby of late? Ruth answered indirectly, saying she had suffered many sleepless nights in the past few weeks. "Pre-Symposium syndrome."

"I suppose the Symposium offices have been busy every night," Wyn said, throwing out the lure.

"Somewhat," Ruth said, playing with the dangling bait.

"Ruth . . ."

"All right," Ruth admitted, tired of the game. "For weeks that Robalinski person's green car has been parked by the rear entry until the wee small hours; Lucy's De Soto has been next to it. You could set your clock by the routine. Rhodie's bedroom lights switched off at eleven; at eleven fourteen the De Soto pulled into the Symposium space; sixty-five seconds later the sports car parked next to it in the disabled person's spot.

"Should have been towed, if you ask me; it's a twenty-four-hour violation. And I wish someone would explain why these people can't walk—it's all but a few blocks from their respective homesites—but there you are, the modern generation, restless and footless."

"On Friday night . . ." Wyn prompted.

"After the Meet the Authors I was ensconced in the attic quite early. I knew that after all that excitement I wouldn't sleep a wink. I saw Jane and Robalinski leave the New Federal through the back exit and repair to the Symposium office. And then, occasionally, I'd see their silhouettes on the shade. You'd think they'd be clever enough to turn off the lights and/or that there was money in the ALAS budget for curtains."

"Perhaps the Friends can donate them," Wyn said.

Ruth ignored this, not holding with spending FALAS money when the Noble fortune was well nigh bottomless. "Around midnight, Rhodie, looking, well, not intoxicated, but peculiar, appeared out of nowhere in the parking lot. One does appreciate the new halogen lighting they put in after the mayoress backed her Cadillac into Angela Fiori's van.

"Rhodie was all bundled up in Sophie's old sables, wearing inappropriate gloves. I might not have noticed but they were light-colored and looked like the pair she wears to trim those yellow roses Sophie used to cultivate. I never liked yellow roses. In the language of flowers, I believe, they represent treacherous love."

"Is there any other kind?"

183

"Facile cynicism isn't attractive in a woman of your background, Wynsome. At any rate, Rhodie went and sat in the green car. I supposed she wanted to get out of the cold and have a smoke.

"When she got out of the car some few moments later, she had ditched the gloves and was looking extremely purposeful. She flung open the rear door that leads to the Symposium offices as if she were Hitler marching into the Reichstag. It couldn't have been a worse moment from the evidence on the shades. I suspect she saw, or heard, what she didn't want to because she came bolting back out into the parking lot and was sick."

"Sick?"

"In simple English, she regurgitated. I thought I'd better go to her but in a moment she recovered, lighting another cigarette, walking with that insouciant air of hers across the parking lot, into the shadows, presumably toward home.

"It was only when I was preparing to descend to morning tea that Jane and Peter emerged, looking as if they had enjoyed a good night's sleep. Youth."

"Well, relative youth," Wyn amended. She pulled the anorak around her, searching for the sleeves, and then looked at her friend. "You know, Ruth, you probably should have said something before this."

"I probably should have, Wynsome. But I have known her since she was a child and I'm not sorry I didn't."

Before the Goodwill door closed behind her, Wyn heard Tommy's name uttered in Carol Morrell's influenza-afflicted whisper. As she prepared to shuffle up an icy Washington Street, she supposed she was doomed to hearing Tommy's name whispered for the rest of her life.

Dickie ffrench was just coming out of the *Chronicle* office, complaining about having to advertise yet again for a "suitable cleaning personage." "Just one thing after another," Dickie said. "Life's been absolute hell."

Wyn, trudging on, wondered if he had been advertising not so much for a cleaning personage as for a soul mate. And could that have been the reason Lettie had dashed by in such a soigné hurry? The new *Chronicle* Personal Column was a success, seekers of love and/or passion writing in from around the Greater Metropolitan Area, not to mention the 'burbs. "One does get a better class of correspondent in the *Chronicle, n'est pas?*" Lucy Littlefield, a personal column devotee, was credited with saying.

Trying to ignore the symptoms of progressive heartache—a tiny, icy fist gripping her innards—Wyn turned east on Bay Street. Bleak sun illuminated the icicles hanging from the old oak trees, turning Bay Street into a Harry Winston display of 40-karat diamonds. The snow-covered cupolas of the old whaling mansions evoked one-horse open sleighs, roasting chestnuts by an open fire, and all the other melodic wintertime clichés.

Only Poor Mary's sad and forsaken abode, dwarfed by Rhodie Noble's house, was out of place on this prosperous, fanciful street. Poor Mary LeBow, Wyn thought. She could have been a stock character in a gothic novel. Born in the old mansion, dying in the servants' quarters that stood in its shadow. Wyn shivered, and it wasn't only because of the wind and the snow and the inadequacy of her new anorak.

Chapter
22

ANNIE KITCHEN, ABBREVIATED WHITE RUBBER BOOTS EVOKING GO-GO GIRLS of another era, opened the black tombstone-shaped front doors with their frosted glass windows cautiously, as if she were the bouncer in a speakeasy.

"She's upstairs, waiting for you." Annie wrinkled her miniature nose as she struggled into her green nubby wool winter coat. With undeniable panache, she wrapped her black and gold gift-with-purchase Princess Borghese scarf—a Christmas present from Dolly Carlson—around her thin neck. Wyn wanted to tell Annie that she was too short for that gesture but held her counsel.

"Don't expect anything more than tea," Annie said with her usual grace. "If I don't go home now, Kitchen might have to get off his big fat rear end and microwave his own tamale pie."

Wyn was tempted to ask how Mr. Kitchen was getting along—he had undergone a much discussed, successful colon cancer operation in the fall—but she knew that would only be a long delaying tactic—that after she heard about Kitchen's plumbing problems (Annie's narrative style was nothing if not graphic), she'd still have to go up to the second floor and listen to a story she wasn't at all certain she wanted to hear.

Once Annie and her leviathan of a Buick station wagon had chugged away, the huge house seemed devoid of all noise. It was an unnatural silence. The snow was muffling what little Bay Street traffic there was, but even the usual refrigerator-furnace-creaking door noises of most houses were absent, the walls thick and sound-resistant, the double floors well carpeted.

Also absent was the identifying aroma houses accumulate over their lives. It smells like an efficient morgue, Wyn thought. Removing her galoshes per Annie's final request of the day, she regretted the shabby penny loafers she had put on that morning. Never having been upstairs in the Noble mansion before, she reached the second-story landing feeling like a child lost in one of Henry James's haunted houses. No casual ghosts here, she decided; real evil beset this place.

Rhodie's boarding-school drawl broke the eerie silence. "Wynsome, is that you?" She followed Rhodie's voice into the marbleized foyer off which were her rooms, each large enough to accommodate a welfare family of four. The suite, which took up most of the second floor, consisted of an obsessively organized dressing room/closet; a white-tiled bathroom reminiscent of a surgery; a womblike gray bedroom with a stark four-poster and a dolorous sixteenth-century Japanese watercolor of exquisite women killing time among cherry blossoms; and finally the sitting room, a twenty-five-foot-square Oriental-rug-covered and ornately furnished salon. It was made especially oppressive by double-thick gold-leafed braided crown moldings and a distorting, reflective silver-leafed ceiling. The crimson, yellow-tasseled curtains were pulled aside and the triple-paned windows revealed the ice-colored waters of Waggs Neck Cove in the near distance and, much closer, the insubstantial tar-shingled roof of Poor Mary's cottage.

"Dickie ffrench says it resembles a high-end bordello on the

Turkish–Iraqi border," Rhodie said. "Mother's possessions invariably evoke the sale table in the Souk. Dickie and I had planned to do the walls in white leather, donate the carpets to AIDS Help, and fill the space with avant-garde Milanese furniture. Well, I guess that's not to be. Maybe it's for the best; there's something very right in rooms that have been wrong from the start.

"Sit down," she commanded, pointing to a sinuous love seat with ormolu claw feet, fat arms ending in gilded Sphinx heads. An elaborately carved Burmese tea table stood in front of the love seat, holding translucent china cups and a steaming samovar. "Pour a cup for yourself, will you? I don't feel like playing mother today."

Propped up by intricate needlepoint pillows, perched on a huge, silk-upholstered chaise longue situated on the far side of the tea table, Rhodie appeared anachronistic in her mother's sitting room: a contemporary actress on a set for a pre-sound *Mata Hari.*

She was wearing the quintessential winter woman faded blue quilted robe and her mother's old worn slippers, black velvet with a fox head embroidered on the tip in gold. Smoking a mentholated cigarette, she stared out the windows into cold space. An unconvincing fire in the diminutive lady's fireplace, combined with central heat, still couldn't take the chill from that room.

Without makeup, her hair pulled back into its pre-California style and showing gray at the roots, Rhodie had not so much aged as matured in the past few days. Wyn, sipping at the syrupy black tea, thought she was less decorative but more handsome than ever.

Then she made a very un-Rhodie gesture: she extinguished her cigarette by dropping it into her nearly full teacup. There was a sharp hiss. The cigarette stood perfectly straight for a moment and then began to dissolve. Both women looked at it and then at one another.

Rhodie turned away first, studying herself in the oversized gilt-framed mirror that took up most of the eastern wall. "The picture of Doriana Grey," she said. *"Après."* She occupied herself with the business of lighting another cigarette. "I gather you're not here to talk real estate." Before Wyn could agree she asked, "What's the status on Peter?"

Wyn told her he was in Hauppauge and was being charged, this morning, with Keny's murder.

"He decamped on Saturday night, leaving me a charmingly ungrammatical note," Rhodie said, unmoved. Wyn thought she seemed too dispassionate, reminiscent of the days immediately after her hysterical reaction to Sophie's death, days when she appeared to be in a glass cocoon, no one able to reach her. "For a fellow who taught college-entry English for two decades, one has to wonder about the effect his lack of basic knowledge had on his students. The ones he didn't seduce, the ones he did. Peter's a sex machine.

"He's also a dope. And a gentleman. Intimated he was lighting out as a decoy. That he would lose himself in Canada, where he would acquire a new identity. As if he knew where to put his hands on forged drivers' licenses and convincing phony passports. Peter's read too many thrillers. But he was, is, not a bad person. His aim was to leave Keny's murder solved but the perpetrator uncaught."

"Fat chance," Wyn said, irritated by Rhodie's nonchalance. "Was it after you found the note that you took your midnight drive in the Mercedes?"

"I went berserk. Couldn't, can't, foresee life without Peter. Isn't that ridiculous? He's not all that bright and he's lifted his moral code from some southern California shaman. Worse, his real passion is cars; women seem to get in his way.

"But I love him anyway." She inhaled and blew a smoke ring Homer Price would have envied. "I read and reread the note until I had it committed to memory and then I gulped down a couple of Valium that seemed to have no effect, followed by a pony of brandy that did. Next thing I knew I was in Mother's Mercedes doing seventy up Swamp Road, believing that if I went fast enough, I might meet up with Peter at the highway.

"I was blitzed enough to believe he was going to drive out to Montauk and take the ferry to Rhode Island and then head north. Had I been sober, I might have taken into consideration Peter's confused California sense of geography. And the fact that the ferry doesn't run in winter."

Wyn was surprised. She felt no sympathy, no empathy, none of the emotions she might have experienced with another woman in a similar state. Of course, murder, Wyn thought, did get in the way of shared feelings. "Were you thinking of interring Keny in the family mausoleum?"

"Such a sly little Wynsome." Rhodesia lit yet another cigarette, drawing on it as if it were an oxygen mask and she were dying from lack of air. "How did you figure it out? No, really. I'm interested."

She looked about as interested as a carnivore before a vegetarian stew, but Wyn, wondering how this meeting was to end, decided to go with it. "It was the history of the cottage that made me suspicious. Your mother was not the sort of benefactor who made a secret of her largess. That she left the cottage to Poor Mary Bleuthorn and that Keny inherited it from her . . ."

"You want to hear something genuinely idiotic?" Rhodie interrupted, her attention engaged. "It wasn't so much the cottage that pushed me over the edge. Yes, I was furious with Sophie for giving it to Poor Mary. She was, after all, the woman who played surrogate mother—surrogate in the pre–test-tube sense of the word—to Sophie's bastard with Harry Bleuthorn.

"But it was the damn barrette. My father gave it to Sophie just before he left for the war. He had it made as a Valentine's Day present by Cartier, though you'd never know to look at it. He hadn't anything for me—his overseas posting was sudden—and he told us we'd have to share it. Then he went off and never came back.

"Do you remember how Sophie was about sharing? I don't think I've ever wanted anything so badly. I used to beg her for it and Sophie would say in that pity-me voice that drove one up the wall, 'Someday, Rhodesia, it will be yours; someday everything I own will be yours. Then you'll be satisfied.'

"You can imagine how I felt when, during my hell of a honeymoon, some well-meaning fool of a winter woman sent me the *Chronicle* edition devoted to that year's Symposium. It featured Baby Keny and her putative parents—Poor Mary and Harry Bleuthorn—all holding hands, standing on the library steps. Sophie was behind them, just in the frame, simply gloating.

"And can you guess what was sitting square on Keny's adorable head, nearly dwarfing it? The barrette. *My* barrette. The parting gift from my father that Sophie and I were to share."

"Was that when you found out Keny was your half-sister?"

"I had guessed before that. When Sophie came home from Africa she and Harry used to spend long afternoons in this very room and I don't suppose they were reading Chaucer. Then there was the trip—Poor Mary in tow—to the California cousins and Sophie returning looking haggard but happy and Poor Mary holding a baby named Kenya in her arms. It was all rather clumsy and a few of the more astute town bitches— Ruth Cole, Maggie Carlson—had a pretty good idea of what had gone on.

"Sophie finally told me later, in Los Angeles, while she was extricating me from my marriage. She wanted me to know I wasn't all alone in this world." Rhodesia sucked on her cigarette for a moment as if she were drawing poison from a snake bite. And then she looked at Wyn. "I underestimated you, Wynsome. When did you realize Keny Blue and I were— God, I choke on the word—sisters?"

"Two things set me off: Irene Handwerk thought you were Keny when she woke up in the hospital; Camellia Cole mentioned that Keny's real name was Kenya. I looked in my father's old files and found that Sophie had been to Africa in 1950 and that Harry Bleuthorn had been one of the party.

"Then there was a pre-Africa photo of Sophie wearing the barrette and later Keny appeared in a yearbook photo wearing it. Add to that the Sophie–Mary California sojourn and the odd Cadmus College scholarship . . .''

"Courtesy of the Sophie Noble Foundation . . .''

''. . . and throw in Sophie's inexplicable interest in Keny . . .''

"I think Keny only tumbled to the secret of her birth when Mother died and there was a substantial bequest to her. Perhaps the New York attorney told her. I only know that she was equipped with that piece of info when she arrived here.

"Mother loved her, you know. Really, really loved her. She was everything Sophie would have liked to have been and wasn't. Wild and vulgar and sexy and afraid of no one. I was only another Noble heiress, fated to be a well-connected attorney's wife, worried about urban blight and the proper schools for her children.

"My other option was to be what I became: a sex-starved old maid steeped in social work. My attempted escape via that ill-advised marriage was a slight aberration. My life had been mapped out for me from the day I was born. But Keny had no such constraints.''

"I suppose finding out she was married to Peter was the infamous last straw.''

"You know everything, don't you, Wyn?''

"Anyone who glanced at the title search for the cottage could have figured it out.''

"How charmingly modest. Anyway, I always hated and feared Keny. Nothing like sibling jealousy to create corrosive acid. But hate turned into something else last week when she came to see me, wearing the barrette, and told me—she was really tickled by the irony—that we were married to the same man. It wasn't Peter's fault; she had forgotten, silly Keny, to get a divorce.

"She rather thought the *National Inquirer* would pay big bucks for the story and there were all sorts of subsidiary rights we could 'glom onto.' 'Society Queen and Sex Pot Sister Married to Same Man' was one of her proposed headlines. She was going to have her agent call me and see what sort of a deal we could cut.

"What she wanted most, she said, was Peter back in her arms again. He was the best lover she had ever had and she wanted to bear his child." Rhodie folded her arms, hugging herself. "That simply could not be, Wyn."

"So you killed her."

"I hadn't planned to. After the scene she created at Carlson House, I went round to her suite at the New Federal. She was expecting someone or pretending to. Except for the barrette and the six-inch stiletto heels, she was nude. All that well-kept flesh. My stomach turned. She was so pleased with herself, posing and provocative and, I don't know, maybe taunting me.

"The place reeked of Keny's musky odor. I stood by the door clutching some leftover picture wire I had in my pocket, wire I had promised to get for Dickie to hang a portrait in the new library. I was still wearing the gardening gloves I had picked up without thinking when I left the house that evening. My mind, as you might imagine, was on other things.

" 'If there's nothing else, I have a date,' Keny told me. 'You wouldn't want to run into Peter on the stairs, would you?' " She was lying, but I wasn't to know until later that Peter was otherwise occupied.

"My inclination was to beg her, bribe her to leave us alone. I restrained myself. She was too like Sophie. She would've only gotten pleasure seeing me ooze and squirm.

"I started to leave, which was when she stood in front of the full-length mirror and began applying a strong gardenia scent to her breasts and other private parts. 'Peter loves gardenia,' she said, smiling into the mirror. 'You know, I'm serious about having a child, Rhodie. Wouldn't Peter be a dandy daddy?'

"She said the real laugh was that the baby would be legal, not a bastard like herself. What a giggle it would have been for Sophie, she said. 'You'll make a terrific auntie, won't you, Rhodie? Winter women usually do.' "

"That did it. I moved behind her and slipped the wire around her neck. I hesitated and Keny started to laugh. 'You don't have the balls, Rhodie,' she said. I closed my eyes and twisted it as tightly as I could. I felt an extraordinary release. I was tempted to take the barrette, but then it seemed there was a better use for it."

"And you put the wire and the gloves in Peter's car. Setting him up?"

"I meant to retrieve them, but discovering he and Jane Littlefield were lovers put any idea of saving his neck out of my mind. Especially when she came to see me early Saturday morning to tell me she had been impregnated by Peter and they had been married secretly two weeks before. Poor Peter, so aptly named. Just a boy who can't say no. I decided to leave the gloves and the wire in the car."

Rhodie stood up and walked to the window, pressing her forehead against the cold glass. "I really loathe the idea of going through the criminal justice system. I'll get off, don't you think? But it won't be pretty, will it?"

"I'm not so certain you're going to get off, Rhodie."

"Your compassion is overwhelming, Wyn."

"Your whiz-kid attorney is going to have to contend with Sophie's murder as well. Matricide always puts tears in the eyes of a jury."

Rhodie turned from the window to look at Wyn. "Now that's really clever."

"Her death seemed so convenient. And knowing Sophie, knowing how careful she was, especially with that new hip ... it's hard to imagine Sophie allowing herself to fall down the servants' stairs, which she claimed she hadn't trod on since she was a girl."

"If you knew what I had to put up with from Sophie. Months during the post–hip-replacement recovery, listening to her winter women sing her praises while she was driving me crazy with her unreasonable demands couched in baby talk.

"Luckily I had discovered—and it was as much a surprise to me as to everyone else—a new purpose in life. I was going to put our diminutive symposium—ALAS indeed—on the international literary map. I had experience with such events in Manhattan and it seemed feasible. I hired Jane and we were making headway, attracting the interest of some really first-rate people, when Sophie announced she was removing me as acting chair, firing Jane, resuming control.

"I was shocked. I honestly believed, dimwit that I am, that Mother was pleased that I was taking her 'child' into a new maturity. I learned late that Mother loved all of her children save me. 'The winter women are nervous,' Mother said. 'They don't want a professional as head of the Symposium. They don't want a world-class event. They want to keep ALAS pure and simple and local. They want their old Sophie back.'

"She was wrong, of course. The winter women were thrilled at the possibility of real writers coming to Waggs Neck in February. Mother, naturally, wasn't listening to any voice other than her own. She was calling a Friends meeting, she told me, to reinstate herself.

" 'You're free as the proverbial bird, Rhodesia. Mommy's recovered. Thank you so much for spending all these dreary months out here but now you can fly away, go back to New York to your settlement houses and the Fifth Avenue apartment. Mommy refuses to take up any more of your valuable time. *Vaya con Dios.*'

"I had packed and was literally out the front door when I realized I could not leave the field to Mother. It was too unjust. I had finally found something that would be mine alone and she was taking it away.

"I went back up the front stairs to find Mother at the head of the servants' stairway, shouting for Annie Kitchen. She looked back with that startled doe-in-the-headlights stare only after she started falling.

"I waited for her to hit bottom—there was that nice, satisfying thud—and then I went down to investigate. Only two sounds could be heard. Annie's televised soap opera and Mother's labored breathing. I took that frail skull and gave it a couple of good ones against the thick floor molding. The soap opera went on. The breathing stopped.

"I left the house and went immediately to the Symposium

offices, where Jane and I had an enjoyable hour talking about the form the new Symposium was going to take. I felt so free for those sixty minutes. And then they came and told me Mother was dead and I had to come back to the house and face that accusatory Betty Boop expression Mother wore in death.

"As you know, I had my breakdown then, providing conversational distraction for the winter women for months to come. I won't try to describe the sordid labyrinths my mind was wandering in and out of during the days and nights after I pushed Sophie down the back stairs. Suffice it to say that murdering one's mother, even one as unsatisfactory as mine, isn't all it's cracked up to be. Where are you going?"

"To the Municipal Building to try to get Ray Cardinal to call Hauppauge and stop a photo opportunity before Homer makes too big a fool of himself."

"What about me?"

"When Homer gets back, I guess he'll arrest you. Meanwhile, maybe you'd better get hold of that attorney you sent to represent Peter. Good thing you're rich, Rhodie. I'm not a criminal attorney, but it seems to me defending matricide and sororicide has got to cost a bundle. And then there was Sondra."

"Sondra? What on earth are you talking about? Why would I kill Sondra?"

"She saw you leaving Keny's suite."

"If she did, she didn't tell me. Sorry to disappoint, dear Wynsome, but the credit for dispatching Sondra belongs elsewhere. I didn't kill her."

"Then who did?"

Chapter
23

ONE BLEAK WEEK AFTER RHODESIA COMFORT NOBLE WAS ARRAIGNED AND remanded for the murders of her mother and sister, Wyn received a noon telephone call in her office from Yolanda. The Man wanted to know if Ms. Lewis could do him the courtesy of meeting with him in the next few minutes in the Municipal Building.

This was all put in such a formal, cordial way, Wyn supposed rightly that Homer had had one of his periodic chats with Yolanda. Wyn said sure, she'd love to meet with the Man. Cool, said the new Yolanda.

Yolanda, wearing a black shirtwaist dress to match her newly dyed and shorn tresses, escorted Wyn to the visitors' lounge with all the deference the Pope might expect from a new and dedicated convert. That must have been some talk, Wyn thought to herself.

"Anything I can get you to make you more comfy, Ms. Lewis?" Wyn caught a whiff of blasphemy creeping into Yolanda's holier-than-thou performance. Nothing could make anyone more (or less) comfortable in the Waggs Neck Harbor's Police Department visitors' lounge.

It was located next to the two-cell village jail in the rear of the Municipal Building and smelled like a drunk tank on a Saturday night. Wyn, after sitting on a stained plaid foam-rubber sofa for two minutes, decided she had had enough. She stood up to leave when Homer came in and closed the door from the corridor.

"Do you have to close that door?" Wyn asked.

"Yes."

"Why?"

"I got your favorite, the mayoress, plus the county D.A. and a hotshot criminal attorney in my office, trying to come up with a way to carve the promotional pie so that it suits each of their interests best."

"I gather you've made another arrest."

"You gather correctly."

"You don't look all that happy, Homer."

"It wasn't the result of my deductive powers. This was a confession."

"You'll get the credit."

"Not if the mayoress and the county D.A. have anything to say about it." Homer slumped down on the sofa next to Wyn, put his feet on an old desk chair, and took a White Owl from his uniform pocket. "You mind? They're not letting me smoke in my office." Wyn said that the way life had been treating her, she might as well die of someone else's smoke. Homer, taking this as a yes, lit his cigar, attempting a smoke ring à la Fitz, producing more of a triangle than a circle.

"You want to tell me about it, Chief?"

"No," Homer said, flicking ashes on the much-abused linoleum tile floor. "But I will."

At eight that morning, while Homer had been savoring a quiet moment and his coffee *con leche,* Ginger Hale arrived. He was carrying an old tan Samsonite suitcase and a raffish malacca cane and was being led by Ray Cardinal, who set Ginger's old Remington on the floor next to the visitor's chair. "Explain, Ray."

Ray, inarticulate to the point of muteness when the chief looked as he did, shook his head and opened his hands in a pleading gesture, guffawing and shuffling until Ginger came to his rescue.

"It's my fault, Chief Price. I absolutely insisted on barging right in. Mind if I sit? I'm exhausted. And might I have a glass of water? Throat feels like the Mojave at high noon."

Homer pointed to the water cooler. While Ginger Hale availed himself of this example of the taxpayers' generosity, Homer signaled for Ray to go back to whatever he was doing before this nut case wandered in. "What can I do for you, Mr. Hale?"

"Rupert, please. Anyway, it's what I can do for you, Chief Price." Ginger Hale smiled benignly, his big, fat harvest-moon face wearing such a peaceful and otherworldly expression that Homer suspected heavy medication.

"Yeah?"

"I am here to confess to the murder of my wife, Sondra Mercy Confrit."

This was melodramatic and rehearsed. This was not unlike the legendary behavior of the crazed ones Homer had been warned to beware of in police college, innocents who enjoyed confessing to hideous crimes.

But Homer believed Ginger Hale for four reasons: Ms. Noble continued to maintain her innocence of Sondra's murder; Ginger had had the opportunity; being married to Sondra Confrit, Ginger certainly had the motive; and Ginger looked as if he were telling the truth.

Homer told him to relax a minute—"Drink all the water you want"—while he got hold of Ray and had him set up the tape recorder and take notes.

Ray sat on the windowsill while Ginger noisily drank water as Homer read him his rights and offered him the opportunity to have an attorney present.

"Shall I begin from the beginning?" Ginger Hale asked, ignoring his rights.

"We only got a thirty-minute tape," Homer warned, knowing Ginger Hale's reputation for a lecturer's garrulousness.

"I'll make it brief, then. I didn't love my wife when I married her but I admired her greatly. She was, as you know—"

"Mr. Hale. The background material is important but . . ."

"All right. All right." He clapped his large, flat hands together and rested them in his lap. He was dressed for an occasion, wearing a banker's pinstripe suit, a club power tie, and tasseled loafers. Ginger looked, Homer thought, as if he were ready to take a meeting in some Wall Street office. "I know I can be as long-winded as Sondra but I'll try to cut right to the bone, as it were.

"As my affection for Sondra dwindled, my dislike grew in kind. She pestered me constantly. Talked at me rather than to me. I realized she had no other way of speaking but this didn't absolve her from one of the great sins, especially to someone of my literary distinction: patronization. Hammering at me, day in, day out, with that shrill voice with a single note and one song: herself.

"Our union was one of sheer desperation. I married her to get away from my first hausfrau of a wife and to find a little peace in which to pursue my writing. Sondra married me for public relations: I was to give her waning reputation credibility and profundity.

"I didn't mind her sleeping with members of any race, sex, or political persuasion. I didn't mind her slovenly ways (rings around the bathtub, coarse yellow hair clogging up the drains). And I surely didn't mind that the last time we engaged in marital relations was three years ago, New Year's Eve.

"I was sent over the precipice, Chief Price, only when I walked into her sleeping chamber and announced that after ten years' toil I was on the last chapter of my novel. Sondra, distressingly unclad, said in that inimitable voice of hers, 'Who gives a shit? No one will read it anyway.'

"She was insisting I attend the Saturday night Meet the Authors Buffet. Her devotees were going to be there as well as members of the press. I had to be in tow, a walking, talking validation of her significance.

"I don't know if you can imagine this, Chief Price, but do try: There I was, at the penultimate moment of my life, my fingers aching to hit the typewriter with the final words that would end the saga I had been working on for the past decade and put paid to what I immodestly believe is one of this century's most important literary careers. I know that anything I write from here on in is going to be a postscript, a nice little coda to my life in letters.

"And there was nude Sondra with unshaven legs applying deodorant to her equally unshaven underarms, jabbering away at me to escort her to some mundane, boring, depressing excuse for a social event.

"All I wanted to do was get back to my typewriter, but I knew she wouldn't stop—she was like a mean dog with a fatty bone—until I either agreed or killed her.

"So I killed her. It wasn't premeditated but I had been struck, I must admit, with the modus operandi of Keny Blue's murder. So aesthetically pleasing. And as luck would have it, there was a length of wire Sondra had bought to hang a recently framed Pro-Choice poster and, well, it seemed so simple. She hardly struggled. She watched herself dying in the mirror with disbelief written all over her bovine face. She couldn't believe that I, the little Pekingese she trotted out for assorted guests, had it in me. If she had struggled, I might have been brought back to my senses.

"And if she hadn't started to laugh—well, she did—I would have stopped, I'm certain of it. But even then, as she choked on her laughter, she didn't believe that Rupert Hale had the nerve to murder her. That did it. I had to continue. I suppose you might say Sondra died of incredulity.

"Remembering Keny Blue's departure, I lay Sophie on her overused bed and rifled through her drawers for an appropriate adornment. I thought, not unreasonably, that if you considered Sondra's murder to be committed by the same person as killed Ms. Blue, why then I'd be home free."

"I've spent the intervening time putting the finishing

touches on *Deuteronomy.* Not an hour ago I wrapped up the manuscript and popped a copy in the mail to my agent and another to my ancient mother down in Hobe Sound. She's fearfully fragile, but marvelous, alert as an infant. I knew, of course, exactly what I had to do next. And that was come right over here and confess to the murder of my spouse, Sondra Confrit.''

"Raymond," Homer Price said in his most noncommittal voice, "will you go type all that up yourself? Keep Yolanda's nose out of it. For once, let's have some rumor control. Then have Mr. Hale sign it."

"Where shall I be spending the night?" Ginger Hale asked expectantly, as if he were about to embark on a grand voyage and Homer was his travel agent.

The chief didn't answer, officially charging him with murder, reading him his rights again, having him sign a paper attesting to the fact that he had been read his rights and to the fact that he had been offered the presence of an attorney and had refused same. Homer then led him to one of the two boggy cells in the back of the Municipal Building to await Ray's transcript.

"Do you think they allow typewriters in real prison cells?" Ginger Hale asked, handing over his braces and other potential suicide weapons. Homer Price confessed he didn't know but he guessed the question was moot. Even with the most inept of court-appointed lawyers, Ginger Hale was likely to find himself not in a penitentiary, but in a hospital for the criminally insane.

"What did he have to say about Keny Blue's death?" Wyn wanted to know after Yolanda had announced that the mayoress and the district attorney had vacated his office. She and Homer sat on opposite sides of his desk, Wyn trying to avoid the cheery eyes of Ronald Reagan, one of the chief's heroes.

"Not much, only that he so admired the perpetrator. 'Genuinely poetic.' 'The art of mayhem.' Crap like that. Old Ginger only wished he could have been 'as deft with Sondra' as Mrs. Noble had been with Keny. Man's an old-fashioned lunatic.''

"You'll probably get all the publicity you want out of this one."

"Nope. The big boys are gun-shy after the Peter Robalinski fiasco."

"I thought the photo in the *Times* was flattering."

"How did you like the retraction they had to make in the next day's edition?"

"It was small and on page two and I don't suppose anyone saw it." She hesitated for a moment. "Why are you telling me all this? the naive girl asked."

"I thought you'd be interested. And I needed someone to talk to. Claire's back in Montclair, taking care of her darned mama, and you can only talk *at* Ray and Yolanda."

"Thank you, Homer."

"You're welcome. You want to have lunch?"

"Baby's?"

"Get real."

"I am not eating the Eden's homemade fake food."

"We'll go to Pizza's," Homer said, reaching for his hat. The two friends looked at one another and, for no particular reason, smiled. "Just do me a favor and try not to swallow the entire pizza two seconds after it comes out of the oven. I hate to see grown women cry."

"I bet that's not true," Wyn said, leading the way.

PART THREE

Memorial
Day
1994

Chapter
24

IT WAS A ZIP-A-DEE-DOO-DAH DAY. THE SUN WAS CRAYOLA YELLOW; the sky, Disney blue; the temperature, a delightful seventy-four; and, as an added bonus, the purple lilacs were in full bloom, bathing Waggs Neck Harbor in their soporific scent.

Given the above, the Waggs Neck Harbor Annual Memorial Day Parade was more than usually well attended. Villagers and Americana-lovers lined Main Street as the various school bands started at the pond and worked their way down Lower Main toward the bay, murdering "When the Saints Come Marching In." They were followed by the cheerleaders, led by Heidi Lum, wearing provocative short shorts. The shorts looked, Ruth Cole was sorry to note, as if they had been made from the Republic's flag. She was going to have to have a word with Liz.

The cheerleaders were in turn followed by representatives from the VFW, the Gold Star Mothers, and the various village religious and parochial organizations. Each gave their especial "all" as they passed in front of the shaky reviewing stand set up in front of the Municipal Building. The precarious stand held Mayoress Kunze, sporting newly crimped hair that caused her to resemble Margaret Thatcher (her idol), and a variety of village notables including a stone-faced Homer Price towering over everyone in his Chief of Police dress uniform and spit-shined boots. Attached to his huge hand was his four-year-old, Mack, sucking on a Tootsie Pop with orders to drool the other way.

No surprise, the whale float developed a leak and spritzed the Gold Star Mothers in their open Cadillac convertible. They took it in their usual good-natured stride, unlike the Lutheran ladies, who had complained bitterly (after the last Labor Day Parade) of ruined hairdos and damp clothes.

Wyn, wearing what she rightly feared was a fashion victim's white and blue and very nautical dress purchased, where else, at Sizzle, watched languidly from the top of the New Federal. Overcoming all obstacles—permit problems, Preservationist vs. Development acrimony, village council rancor, multi-threats of litigation—Lettie had inserted in the hotel's mansard roof a crenellated wall and a deck that housed her new Rooftop Café.

To mark the occasion of the café's launching, Lettie was giving the Friends of the Annual Literary Arts Symposium an elegant post-Memorial Day Parade luncheon.

The winter women were much present in their new late-spring finery, which unfortunately recalled, with the prevalence of baby blue and pale yellow, their Easter finery.

Jane Littlefield, who arrived on the custom-tailored arm of Dickie ffrench, was in a salmon-colored, gold-buttoned maternity suit that made her seem elegant and chic. Dickie had orchestrated the outfit as he seemed to be conducting every aspect of Jane's life. They had recently announced, to the village's pleasure and bemusement, the fact that they had been secretly married since February. Certain members of the community took joy in saying, "Yeah, yeah."

Camellia Cole, who maintained that Jane had been showing as early as February eighteenth, wondered if the child's actual father was a certain California gentleman. Ruth asked what difference it made and indicated that Camellia should keep her opinions to herself and her mouth shut.

"I still wonder," Lettitia Browne said, taking the chair next to Wyn's as the volunteer fire department rode by below in their antique engine and Wyn experienced a painful palpitation. Tommy, in Waggs Neck visiting his recovered disc jockey mother, Irene, was standing atop the engine, flashing that irresistible dimpled smile, looking as young and wholesome and American sexy as anyone short of Robert Redford (in his prime) could possibly look.

"I still wonder," Lettie Browne repeated a decibel or two louder, attempting to take Wyn's attention away from Tommy's vibrant visage, "about Dickie-Do. You could have knocked me over with an egret feather when Jane ran around showing off that nearly impressive emerald ring Dickie bought on layaway from Gold 'n' Jewel in West Sea. One just assumed he was as gay as a loon. All those darlings and dearies and that antique-y 'shoppe' and the socks with the little polo player and that gold chain bracelet and those wrists that need a good dose of spray starch . . .

"It all goes to show," Lettie said, standing up, straightening the dramatic Schiaparelli-pink Galanos sheath she was wearing.

"It all goes to show what?" Wyn asked, her gaze following the fire truck as it made a circle in front of Carlson House and cruised back down Main Street. The yellow fireman trousers outlined Tommy's dimpled butt in a familiar, heart-wrenching way.

"It all goes to show, as my late brother, Phineas, liked to say, 'the variety, the breadth, and the depth of the human experience contained in village life.' Oh, well, I can see you're not listening to a word I say. There are the Cole girls. I'm going to sic them on you and then you'll be sorry."

Wyn said she was already sorry. Jane and Dickie got to her first, bringing her a glass of flat-looking champagne. "You seem happy," Wyn said, not altogether kindly. Jane replied—with a wide smile and a discreet tap on her tummy that made one small mean part of Wyn want to smack her—that she'd never been happier in her life. "What do you think of the name Nick, providing it's a boy, of course?" Wyn told Jane what she thought of the name Nick.

"And this is to the grave," Dickie whispered in her ear, "but it looks very, very much, kitty cat, as if we've got the house. Peter's having his attorney fax you a signed contract *mañana*. Can you beat it?"

The dispersal of Rhodesia Comfort Noble's possessions was a continuing legal nightmare. It had taken months before it was judicially determined that her marriage to Peter Robalinski was invalidated by his earlier marriage to Kenya Blue. The California cousin, as the closest relative, was to be handsomely rewarded for her generosity and would, in the fullness of legal time, get everything.

Peter Robalinski, on the other hand, as Keny Blue's husband, had received the bulk of her estate, including the Poor Mary cottage, which he had agreed to sell to Jane for the sum of one dollar *américain*, as Dickie put it. Peter had said to Jane, on this last day in Waggs Neck, that he thought she was making the right choice in staying in the village, in not accompanying him back to Pasadena.

"Considering the fate of your previous wives," Lucy Littlefield, who had been present at that leave-taking, had added, "I would say, 'Amen, brothers and sisters.' "

Lucy was helping out on Monday mornings in the new shop—finally named ffrench Antiques—Jane and Dickie had established in the former Zero sports store premises. Lucy had offered to invest in the new venture but Dickie, evincing a remarkably sane business head, had firmly declined. "I can just see Lucy," he told Wyn, "ditzing around the shop in her pink bunny slippers, adding unwanted atmosphere, breaking Wedgwood."

Dickie and Jane excused themselves to engage in the choreographed dance known as "making the rounds." This required them to separate and take on opposite sides of the new terrace, smiling and laughing and chatting up various people in the hopes they would come and buy at the shop. Dickie was very good at this and Jane, while initially reluctant, had been a quick study and now enjoyed socializing as much as her spouse.

Lucy also liked to make the rounds, but not with the precision and forethought of her nephew-in-law. She sat next to Wyn and said, "Your ex and his ma and a whole bunch of people from Southampton were in on Monday—the only day I'm allowed to help—and Nick taught me the best word. *Chatchka.* Do you know what it means?" Wyn said she did but Lucy told her anyway. "I told Dickie that we should change the name of the shop to ffrench Chatchkas, but he wasn't amused. We're doing very well and the season hasn't even begun."

"How nice for you, dear," Dolly Carlson said, taking the chair next to Lucy. The antique shop she had opened in the keeping room of her bed and breakfast hadn't had many customers, mostly due to lack of visibility, inflated prices, and Dolly's disinclination to spend money on advertising.

"Where's your beau?" Lucy asked, referring to Dolly's lover, Dr. John Fenton. Lucy was wearing an ancient pale green tea dress, a straw hat with a big pink bow that tied under her increasingly sharp chin, and pink satin going-to-court shoes.

"Getting me a drink," Dolly answered shortly, and then looked at Wyn accusingly. "Are you aware that John had to go all the way up to New Hampton last Monday to the Mid-Hudson Psychiatric Center to give a deposition on Rupert Hale's sanity?"

Wyn said she was but that it was none of her doing.

"They're already thinking of moving him to an unsecured psychiatric center in Orange County."

"Ginger isn't really, really dangerous," Lucy said winningly, cocking her head to one side. "All he wants to do is sit in a little room and write his little heart out."

"Well," Dolly, a strict law-and-order gal, said, getting up and going to meet John Fenton halfway across the terrace, "you can pop him in a little room in your house, Lucy, and let him write his little heart out when he's released. Knowing our bleeding-heart jurists, that should be any day now, so you'd better plump up the featherbed and air out the curtains."

"She's pissed that ffrench Antiques is doing so well," Lucy said, allowing the Cole sisters to persuade her to join them in the glassed-in rooftop dining room. The parade was finally over and Camellia liked to be first in line at the buffet. The shrimp always went so quickly.

"Such a pity," Ruth said in her improving way, "that most people never do remember that Memorial Day is not meant to be a celebration but rather a remembrance of the Republic's dead heroes. Coming, Wyn?"

Wyn said she'd be along in a moment, that she wasn't all that hungry. Regretting the naval dress, thankful she had resisted the admiral's hat, Wyn sat on for a moment, looking over the newly crenellated roof garden walls down at the busy brick shops of Main Street.

Dicie and David, having declined attendance at Lettie's party, were scanning photographs of houses featured in the window of the Lewis Real Estate Company office. David's Water Street cottage was crowded, what with the baby, now casually strapped up against his manly chest.

Ringo Kabot had Dicie's black curls and David's strong nose and powerhouse lungs. He was going to have a personality to deal with. In the meantime he was bringing joy and contentment to Dicie and most especially to David, who did not come to joy and contentment naturally. His new novel, *Spare Parts*, had received a mixed review in the *Times* but had been chosen as a Dual Main Selection by the Book of the Month Club. Neither seemed to affect him; he was living for his child at the moment.

Children, Wyn thought, with malice. Infants. Babies. Lilliputian slave drivers. Yet pregnant women were abounding, many in their thirties and even forties. Keny Blue, of all people, had wanted to get herself impregnated—that would have been some baby. Jane, who had appeared to be the least ma-

212

ternal of women, was turning into Prenatal Mother of the Year. If Wyn heard one more word about how well Dickie was doing in Lamaze class, she was going to puke. "I do not want a baby," she said aloud. She wanted to be independent, unconnected (the thought of an umbilical cord was unthinkable), her own person and no one else's. Children only brought grief and bankruptcy and precipitate old age.

The wind came up and the sun, so strong a moment before, was obscured by a cloud, and Wyn realized she was alone on the terrace with a sextet of sere winter women, readying themselves to go into the café. She wondered if, down the line, she wouldn't become a winter woman: manless, childless, self-sufficient because she had to be, wringing what cheer she could out of sisterly affection and the Annual Literary Arts Symposium.

It was a destiny difficult for some to escape and Wyn wasn't even certain she wanted to. There was a great deal of comfort to be found among one's own kind in one's own place.

She thought of Rhodie, imprisoned for life in a maximum facility, reportedly starting a magazine devoted to the writings of women in prison. Poor Rhodie, Wyn thought, pushing herself away from the table, standing. She was about to follow her friends into the café when the new glass elevator doors opened and Tommy exploded out, as pale as a corpse.

"What is it?" she asked, alarmed.

"I'm scared," he said, coming to her, putting his arms around her, holding her tight. "I'm scared I'm going to go back to Greenwich Village and live the rest of my life without you. Marry me, Wyn. I'm begging you. Marry me. I don't want an open relationship. I want a wife and a partner and a mother-to-be. I want to stay here in my village, with you, and live our lives together. Marry me, Wyn. Let's have a cute baby that's going to drive us nuts and who we're going to love forever. Please, Wyn. Marry me."

She could feel his tears on her cheek. He smelled so healthy and good, like a baby himself. She said, when she could, "It's a possibility."

He pushed her away and looked at her through his dime-store-doll's lashes with his bluer-than-new-blue-Cheer eyes. "Not good enough, Wyn."

"All right. 'Barkus is willing.' "

She reached for him but he stopped her again. "No literary allusions. Or illusions. I want a definitive, no-crapping-around 'Yes, Tommy, I'd love to marry you, sweetheart, tomorrow if not sooner.' "

"Yes, you bastard, Tommy, goddamnit, I'd love to marry you, sweetheart. Tomorrow if not sooner."

He pulled her to him. Inside Lettie's chichi new café, Ruth and Camellia Cole, Lucy Littlefield, and the determined winter women who had managed to snag the front tables held their well-cared-for hands to their bosoms and sighed.